IMPULSE

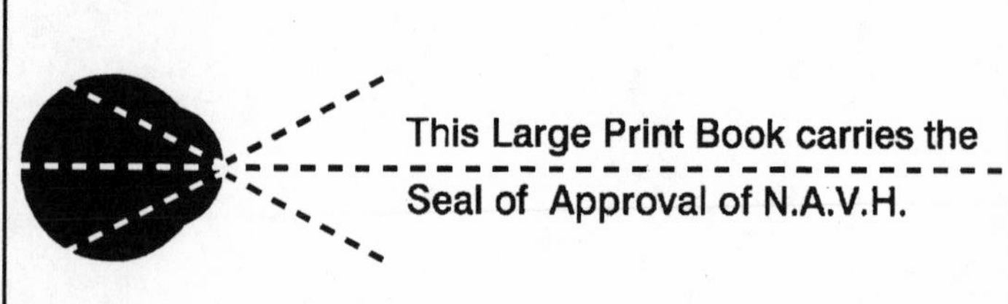
This Large Print Book carries the
Seal of Approval of N.A.V.H.

IMPULSE

JOANN ROSS

WHEELER PUBLISHING
An imprint of Thomson Gale, a part of The Thomson Corporation

THOMSON
GALE

Detroit • New York • San Francisco • New Haven, Conn. • Waterville, Maine • London • Munich

This book is a work of fiction. Names, characters, places, and incidents are products of the author's imagination or are used fictitiously. Any resemblance to actual events or locales or persons, living or dead, is entirely coincidental.

Wheeler Publishing Large Print Hardcover.
The text of this Large Print edition is unabridged.
Other aspects of the book may vary from the original edition.
Set in 16 pt. Plantin.

LIBRARY OF CONGRESS CATALOGING-IN-PUBLICATION DATA

Ross, JoAnn.
Impulse / by JoAnn Ross.
p. cm. — (Wheeler Publishing large print hardcover)
ISBN 1-59722-326-3 (alk. paper)
1. Serial murderers — Fiction. 2. Wyoming — Fiction. I. Title.
PS3568.O843485I46 2006
813'.54—dc22 2006019182

Published in 2006 by arrangement with Pocket Books,
a division of Simon & Schuster, Inc.

Printed in the United States of America on permanent paper
10 9 8 7 6 5 4 3 2 1

To the wonderfully supportive writers of PASIC,
who helped me stay reasonably sane
during the writing of *Impulse*,
and the members of my online writers' group —
who were there in the beginning
and stuck by me through all the post-Katrina changes,
right up to the end. I love you all.

And, as always, to the great love of my life
and my own special hero, Jay.

ACKNOWLEDGMENTS

With appreciation to Michelle Luther and the hugely helpful folks at Fremont Motor in Cody, Wyoming, and Melinda Brazzale, Public Information Officer, Wyoming Department of Corrections.

If night has a thousand eyes, it has as many fears.

— Marlo Blais

Go, stalk the red deer o'er the heather,
Ride, follow the fox if you can!
But, for the pleasure and profit together,
Allow me the hunting of Man —
The chase of the Human, the search for the Soul
To its ruin — the hunting of Man.

— Rudyard Kipling

PROLOGUE

It was the wind that woke him. Or, more precisely, a sudden hush as startling in its silence as the crack of a rifle shot shattering a dark and moonless night. When you lived on the rooftop of America, which Hazard, Wyoming, population 2,642 was — didn't the Chamber of Commerce even proclaim its status on the welcome sign at the city limits? — you lived with eternal wind.

Night and day it roared like a freight train, wailed like a banshee, screamed like a horde of insane berserkers. It hurled itself over the winter landscape, turning snowfields into a violent sea, creating churning swells that swiftly transformed vehicles, cattle, and the occasional foolhardy human into lumps of frozen white.

The same wind that ripped away tree limbs, fence lines, and peeled trailer roofs open like sardine cans also tore apart hope, love, and dreams, hurling them into the Big

Sky land of Montana, across the high plains to the Dakotas, and beyond. A geography professor at Wind River College had published a paper asserting dust from ancient buffalo bones had been found as far away as the Highland peaks of Scotland. Not a single person in northwestern Wyoming doubted the claim.

But every so often, just when even the most optimistic soul was ready to put a bullet into his skull to end his misery, the wind would stop.

Just like that.

As if God, or Fate, or whoever the hell controlled the weather in this wild, isolated part of the world had hit the pause button.

Unlike those lesser beings, who'd stumble out of their homes, confused and grumpy, snarling and snapping like feral animals being too early awakened from a deep winter's sleep, the man who'd once been the boy raised by wolves was not confused by the wind's sudden and silent cessation.

He'd been waiting for it.

Planning for it.

And now, with bloodthirst singing in his veins, he was ready.

1

Savannah, Georgia
September 26

Savannah may be the Hostess City of the South, but police detective Will Bridger would've bet a month's pay that The Rising, named after Ireland's Easter rebellion, and situated in a neighborhood so foreboding that even stray cats didn't wander the alleys at night, would never show up on any of the city's glossy tourism brochures.

It was a blue-collar, working-class bar down on the docks, where "Danny Boy," rather than Southern soul, played on the jukebox; Guinness, Harp, and Jameson were the drinks of choice; and patrons came, not to socialize, argue about sports, and chew the fat, but to get quickly, lethally drunk.

"Remember," Will instructed his partner as they walked across a parking lot packed with rusting pickups and motorcycles, "if you order one of those froufrou girly-man drinks in here, you could get us both killed."

From the Confederate flags flying in the back windows and the bumper stickers announcing don't blame us, we voted for jeff davis and yankee hunting permit, Will figured the faded kiss my redneck ass T-shirt he was wearing beneath his Harley-Davidson leather vest would fit right in.

Grayson Lowell snorted. "I'd like to see you tell Hemingway a daiquiri is a girly-man drink."

"That'd be a little difficult to do." Broken glass from beer bottles and discarded syringes crunched beneath Will's boots. "Since the guy's dead. Which is what we could be if you screw things up."

"Christ, we've been partners for the past ten years. Name one time I screwed anything up."

"How about the time Big Eddie Falcone came after us with half the wiseguys in town because you nailed his new stripper?"

"Danielle wasn't a stripper. She just happened to be working as an exotic dancer while studying for her master's in psychology. Tuition's not cheap, and dancing pays better than waiting tables."

It was Will's turn to snort his disbelief.

"Yeah, that's what they all say."

"She's currently a professor at The Citadel," Gray countered mildly. "And how the hell was I supposed to know that Big Eddie had his eye on her?"

"You should've detected it. That's what we detectives do." Will tapped his nose. "Detect stuff. Admit it, you let the little head do the thinkin' for the big head and it didn't give a flying fuck about consequences."

"Like you've never followed your dick into strange territory."

Will couldn't deny it. But it wasn't like he met all that many respectable women in his line of work. Hadn't he and Gray spent the past two days and nights talking to pimps, whores, meth dealers, crack addicts, carjackers, fences, gun dealers, and every other Lowcountry lowlife?

And, here's a surprise, they hadn't run across a single Sunday-school teacher in the bunch.

Though there had been one woman . . .

Don't go there. Best to keep the incident still known around the station house as Bridger's Major Fuckup in the past, where it belonged. Bygones.

Got any more snazzy platitudes, Bridger? a voice in the back of his mind taunted.

"Well, women shouldn't prove any problem tonight." He shook off the mocking voice, along with the unwanted memories, and pushed open the heavy door. "Not in this place." Any female who dared show up in The Rising without a Special Forces escort risked getting gang-raped on the pool table.

A thick, blue, acrid cloud lay heavily over the room that smelled of stale beer and bad blood. Bottles, mugs, and glasses lowered to tables and eyes turned in their direction as they walked into the bar. Two guys still wearing a paste-white prison pallor were shooting pool at the far end of the narrow room; the taller of the two, who'd shaved his head as smooth as the cue ball, made the simple act of rubbing talc into the end of his stick appear menacing.

The smoke-filled air was edgy with a nuclear, deep-seething violence. It wasn't so long ago that a good many of The Rising's patrons would have been wearing sheets, cone-shaped hats, and getting liquored up in the bar before a fun-filled night cross burning.

Since the damn Yankee government had taken away their recreation, there tended to be a lot of pent-up hostility simmering just below the surface.

Except for an Irish tenor extolling the rifles of the IRA from the jukebox, the room was suddenly so hushed you could've heard a pin hit the sawdust-covered floor sticky with spilled beer.

The bartender was watching television. NASCAR was running at the Brickyard and even with the sound muted it must've been one helluva exciting race because the guy didn't turn around to acknowledge them.

"Hey, buddy," Will said to the guy's broad back. "How about a couple whiskeys over here. Make 'em doubles. With Dixie chasers."

The bartender didn't turn around. "Ain't got no Dixie. Quit carryin' it when they started brewing that goddamn satanic Voodoo piss. This here's an Hibernian bar. We got Harp and Guinness on draft. You wanna drink with the devil, go hang out with the queers in one of them back-door fag joints."

"Gotta like a tavern with strong conservative, faith-based values," Will said agreeably.

He decided not to point out the dichotomy between the bartender's refusal to stock a brew that had been targeted by the religious right, and the leering devil, surrounded by flames, tattooed on the hulk's biceps.

He flashed his best good ole boy grin and

slapped a twenty onto the bar. “I’ll take a pint.”

“Pull one for me, too.” Gray reached into the pocket of his jeans, pulled out a thick roll of bills he made sure everyone could see, and took another twenty from beneath the rubber band.

For such a big man, the guy moved fast. A meaty hand with F.U.C.K. inked on the knuckles shot out; the money disappeared beneath the counter.

“So, where’s your sign?” Will asked as the bartender drew the pints.

“What the hell sign you talkin’ about?” White foam spilled down the side of the glass, sloshed onto a bar covered with white rings, and went ignored.

Generations of initials and suggestions, each more obscene than the last, had been gouged into the wood. Will traced the outline of one carved design with the index finger of his free hand; being the hotshot detective he was, he deduced the backward swastika hadn’t been carved by a Rhodes Scholar.

“The sign saying the customer is always wrong.”

The bartender’s eyes, close-set and glaring, narrowed. A vein the size of a night crawler pulsed dangerously at his temple.

"You don't like it here, why don't you get your fuckin' ass outta my bar?"

Will tossed back the whiskey. "'Cause, I'm lookin' for a guy. Thought you might've seen him." He took a long swallow of Guinness to get the taste of the rotgut out of his mouth.

"Haven't seen any guy."

Of course not. No one ever saw anything or anyone in places like The Rising.

"This guy's from out of town." Will placed another twenty next to the change the bartender had returned from the first one. "Name's Jose Montero. Kind of medium height, black hair, brown eyes, talks with a Latino accent."

"Beaners ain't welcome here," a guy two stools down from Will growled in a cigarette-roughened voice. He had a pack of Camel unfiltereds rolled up in a T-shirt that looked as if it'd last been washed sometime during the first Bush administration. "Especially greaser dopers."

Will lifted a brow. "Did I say anything about dope?"

Montero was a hit man for the Mexican Mafia — a gang heavily involved in drugs, extortion, and prostitution — who used murder as a means of discipline.

Last week Will and Gray had learned from

a Pagan motorcycle-gang informant that Montero was responsible for the recent disappearance of a fifteen-year-old runaway from Maryland who'd last been seen panhandling on the waterfront.

"The city's gettin' overrun with damn wetbacks lookin' to muscle in on the rackets." The bartender reached beneath the bar and pulled out a Louisville slugger. "So, either you're looking to do business with the guy" — the dark stain on the fat end of the bat looked suspiciously like old, dried blood — "or you're cops."

"Fuck that!" Gray was off the stool like a moon shot. "Do we look like fuckin' cops, hoss?" he demanded, sounding a lot more like a pissed-off Texan than the Back Bay Bostonian Will knew him to be.

"You'll have to excuse my friend," Will said smoothly when those thick F.U.C.K. fingers tightened around the bat's base. "He's got a bit of a short temper." That was an understatement.

"Short dick, too, I'll bet," a guy down the bar suggested with a gravelly laugh.

"At least I can find mine," Gray shot back. He raked a dangerous, stiletto-sharp look over the jokester, whose belly strained against a black Carolina Panthers T-shirt. "Without having to lift up five hundred pounds of lard."

Shit. Will heard chairs scraping away from tables. In some joints, the occupants of those chairs would be trying to stay out of trouble.

Not in The Rising.

Thing could turn real ugly real fast.

He wasn't the only one picking up those edgy vibes. "You'd best be gettin' your pal outta Dodge," the bartender snarled. "While you boys still got two good legs to walk out on."

"If you're not careful," Will drawled, "y'all are gonna lose your reputation for Southern hospitality. Let's go," he said to Gray without taking his eyes from the Hulk.

"Hell. Just when I was starting to have a good time."

Will knew Gray's heavy sigh was only partly feigned. Everyone on the squad knew that despite his patrician roots, Detective Grayson Lowell enjoyed a brawl as much as the next guy.

Will reached beneath his vest and pulled out the black Glock he'd tucked into the back of his jeans. He felt the stir of animosity ripple over the bar and knew that he was not the only man in the place carrying. Which was why he'd decided to show the pistol.

Since half the goons in the place were undoubtedly in violation of parole, he figured that now that he'd upped the stakes, just in case he and Gray were cops they'd wait for him to make the first move. Which he had no intention of doing.

Yet.

"I told you the guy wasn't going to be in there," Gray muttered as the heavy oak door slammed closed behind them. "The scum of the gene pool hang out in The Rising."

"The guy we're looking for kills people for a living," Will reminded his partner. "Besides, we gotta check them all. Drug dealing and prostitution are like politics in that they make for strange bedfellows." No one had followed them out. So far, so good. "And that Pagan did say the word on the street is that the Mexican Mafia's looking to hook up with Kerrigan."

Joseph Kerrigan, who owned the bar through one of a dozen of his companies, also ran a string of adult bookstores. He was connected, with fingers in organized crime pies — drugs, porn, money laundering, and bookmaking — all over the South.

"Like that's gonna happen."

Will didn't think so, either. But years of police work had taught him that anything, including Montero's snatching that girl as a donation to Kerrigan's rumored new sex-slave business, was possible.

They'd nearly reached the Mustang the SPD had actually sprung for when he spotted two guys standing beside a black SUV. One was making a rock fashion statement in a black, Metallica, burning-skull T-shirt; the other wore an olive green Che Guevara shirt cut off at the sleeves.

"Think that might be our guy?" Will asked quietly.

Gray followed his gaze. "Could be. He matches the description." Right down to the patch of the Mexican flag with the eagle-and-snake insignia on the shirt's sleeve. As they watched, a small package changed hands. "Bet you they're not trading baseball cards."

"Could be just some lowlife wantin' to get high."

"Could be. And if we bust 'em, we could end up spending the rest of the night doin' paperwork."

At that moment, the guy in the Metallica shirt looked up. Then cursed in Spanish, loud enough to be heard over the buzz of the neon sign. Then they both took off running like rabbits. In opposite directions.

"You go after Che. I'll take Metallica," Will said.

“Got it.” Gray pulled his own pistol from the calf holder beneath the flared jeans and took off, chest out, head back, just like when he’d been a near-world-class sprinter on the Harvard track team.

Metallica ran across the street and turned down an alley that ran behind The Rising.

Will followed, the heels of his boots hammering the cobblestones. Why the hell hadn’t he worn his Nikes?

Oh, yeah. Because it was hard to pull off a motherfucker rapist-biker act in squeaky new sneaks.

Fortunately, the alley was a dead end.

Unfortunately, Metallica wasn’t ready to throw in the towel. He vaulted a six-foot wooden fence without so much as missing a step.

Will followed.

“Police!” he shouted.

Which, big friggin’ surprise, only made the guy run faster, his arms pumping like pistons as he cut across a courtyard lit by a flickering orange gaslight, knocking over a wrought-iron table and chair to slow his pursuer down.

Will swerved around the table. Jumped the chair.

The guy turned halfway around; Will watched the automatic leap in his hand.

There was the sharp, nasty crack of a pistol. A tongue of fire shot from the barrel, an instant before the bullet hit the ivy-covered wall above his head, spraying bits of brick.

Will felt the sting at the back of his neck, as if he'd been hit with a handful of gravel.

"Shit!"

If he'd been an inch taller, he could've been a goner.

Another shot ricocheted off a metal security door in a shower of black splinters. His cheek burned. It didn't hurt much now. But it would. Once the rush wore off.

His shirt was torn, and from the dampness he realized he'd been shot. Shot?

Shit. This wasn't the way it was supposed to play out.

"Stop, goddammit. Police!"

It always worked in the movies.

Unfortunately this was real life and all that happened was that the guy kicked into overdrive.

Adrenaline screaming in his head, pounding in his chest, Will raised the Glock. Locked his right hand on his wrist to hold down the recoil, and pulled the trigger.

The shooter stumbled. Staggered. Then, wouldn't you know it, picked up the damn pace.

Jaw clenched hard enough to crack his teeth, his arm on fire, Will got off two quick shots.

The first went wide, clanging against a metal trash can.

The second hit home. He could've been shooting at the bull's-eye on a paper target at the police range.

Metallica stopped dead in his tracks. Will waited for him to drop.

But he twisted a half turn, a .45, Dirty Harry's gun of choice, in his hand.

And damned if the bastard wasn't smiling.

Okay. He wasn't going to go down easy.

Wishing he'd joined the fire department instead of the cops, Will pulled back on the hammer. His arm weighed a ton. His fingers were beginning to go numb.

"Police." His voice sounded raspy and winded to his own ears. "Drop. The. Fucking. Gun."

He sucked in a breath. His vision blurred, but not so badly that he couldn't see the .45 drop from his assailant's hand as Metallica crumbled to the cobblestone sidewalk.

Keeping his Glock trained on the supine form, Will crouched down beside him and had just placed the fingers of his right hand to the man's throat when Gray came running around the corner.

"I lost the son of a bitch," he said. "One minute he was there, the next he was gone. Like a freakin' ghost, or something. You okay?"

"Sure." Perspiration dripped from Will's forehead, stinging his eyes. "At least I'm doin' better than this jerkoff."

Blood was spreading across the front of the black, burning-skull T-shirt. A haze the same deadly red swam in front of Will's eyes.

Sirens shattered a night scented with smoke and cordite. Lights coming toward them.

"The guy's toast," Will managed.

He could hear Gray shouting something, but he couldn't make out the words through the buzzing in his brain.

He slumped against the wall.

Damn. He felt sick and his head was spinning like it'd gone off on its own and taken a ride on a Tilt-A-Whirl. A metallic, coppery taste was in his mouth.

More voices were shouting at him. Hands were tearing open his blood-soaked shirt. Lights from the cruisers flashed like strobes, reminding him of riding the Ferris wheel at the Coastal Empire Fair.

The gently swinging metal seat atop the double-decker, brightly lighted wheel had offered a dazzling, bird's-eye view of the midway, the city, and the lit-up bridge spanning the Savannah River.

But all of Will's attention had been riveted on the woman whose kisses were sweeter than the fluffy, pink cotton candy they'd shared earlier. The woman who'd actually had him considering settling down in a cozy little house with a white picket fence, two-point-five kids, and a big stupid dog.

It had been the closest thing to nirvana he'd experienced in his thirty-three years on the planet, and sitting atop the city, breathing in the fragrance of Faith Summers's perfume, conveniently overlooking that he'd been lying to her for weeks, Will had thought that if he were to die at that moment, he'd go a happy camper.

Riding on the soft, pleasant swells of memories, with calliope music floating through the shadows of his mind, he allowed his eyes to drift closed.

"Gardenias," he murmured.

A comforting sense of calm drifted over him as Savannah police detective Will Bridger checked out.

2

December 28

The arctic storm that had held Hazard, Wyoming, in its icy grip for days had left behind a midnight blue bowl of sky studded with stars. The mountains surrounding the town soared in rock and timber, and snow-fields were tinted Christmas-card silver and blue by the light of a full, white moon.

Erin Gallagher had driven by the lake earlier this evening, on the way from her job at the radio station, and noticed that the ice was remarkably free of snow. If that was still the case, it would be a perfect night for skating.

The sexy, satiated male in her bed rolled over, flung an arm over her pillow, then groggily lifted his sleep-tousled head.

"What's wrong?"

"Nothing."

She could not have said the same thing

only a few hours ago, when she'd escaped the lodge, feeling used and dirty.

When she'd picked him up in the parking lot of the mini-mart, she'd been looking for some quick, hard, anonymous sex. Punishment sex. The kind she didn't have to think about later. The kind that wouldn't leave her confused and hurt and feeling desperate and lonely.

But it hadn't worked out that way at all. His surprising tenderness had proven a balm, soothing her senses, easing her anxieties.

When he'd been inside her, he had, if only for those few stolen minutes, allowed her to almost forget her secret shame.

"The wind's stopped."

"'Bout freaking time." He patted the cooling sheets. "Come back to bed."

"I was thinking of going skating."

He squinted his eyes, peered at the bedside clock. "It's nearly midnight. And probably as cold as a well digger's ass out there."

"I'll bundle up."

"You're crazy," he muttered.

The depression that had been threatening all day lifted. Who'd have guessed that uncomplicated sex could be better than Prozac?

"That's what you love about me."

"Can't argue that," he responded on a broad yawn.

Erin knew he didn't love her. But there'd been a fleeting moment, just before he'd come, when he'd looked deep into her eyes, smiled, and brushed his lips against hers. The kiss, as light as the snowflakes falling like white feathers from the sky, was not meant to claim. Or even arouse.

Let's be friends, it had said.

She'd felt something in her heart turn over as she'd smiled back up at him. Friendly sex. And wasn't that a new concept?

Like everything else she'd been experiencing since moving to Hazard, the idea had her feeling reborn.

"We'll only go out for a little while," she coaxed.

"What's with this *we,* kemo sabe?"

"You're the man." She saucily tossed her blond head. "You're supposed to take care of me."

Proud of the independent woman she was becoming (despite this morning's painful backslide), Erin didn't really believe that. She suspected he didn't either, since she sensed his life was pretty much as screwed up as hers had been before she'd arrived here in Hazard.

But sometimes it was fun to pretend.

"Come back to bed and I'll take care of you."

The moon lit up the room, allowing her to see the tented flannel sheet. "What you want is for me to take care of that woodie you woke up with."

"I was dreaming of you." He flashed his dimples, the quick, boyish smile sending ribbons of golden light twining around her heart.

She hadn't known, until tonight, that he was even capable of smiling. But now, bathing in its warmth, she decided it had definitely been worth the wait.

"It was a really hot dream." Which she could certainly see for herself. He patted the mattress again. "Why don't you come over here and we'll take care of each other?"

She was tempted. Who wouldn't be?

Erin's gaze shifted from his muscled chest out the double-paned window toward the silvery blue landscape, then back to the bed.

Decisions, decisions.

One thing she'd discovered since moving to Hazard was that making choices about even the most mundane, everyday things was more difficult than she'd ever imagined. But wasn't that a good thing?

After having spent eighteen years with others deciding every single thing about her life — what she wore, what she ate, when she went to bed, and when she got up — every decision she made felt like a victory.

Most decisions, anyway. As her mind flashed back to another rumpled bed, another man, she could feel the dark gray wolf of depression lurking in the midnight shadows.

No! Don't think about that.

"Ten minutes," she agreed. "Then you come skating with me."

Sexy male dimples flashed again. "How about I give you fifteen minutes to convince me?"

3

"Wow."

Faith Prescott stood on the steps of the double-wide trailer that served as KWIND studios, staring up at the dazzling panorama of stars. You never saw stars like this in Las Vegas. The blinding, flashing neon of the Strip outshone them, not that any tourists cared, since she doubted anyone went to Sin City to commune with nature.

And speaking of lights . . . the aurora borealis shimmered emerald on the horizon, while ruby and sapphire danced across the sky in a light show Las Vegas could never hope to duplicate.

And, wonder of wonders, as if Mother Nature had decided to create one night of absolute perfection, the wind had actually stopped blowing.

Not that Faith minded the wind. She had, after all, certainly lived with it during those six months she'd somehow lost herself in the desert. Where she'd discovered that after a while, you sort of stopped hearing it. Like death and taxes, you knew it was there, but you just stopped thinking about it.

She'd lived in Hazard for a year now — which was a record for her — and was certain she could count on one hand the times when the wind had actually stopped.

Simon and Garfunkel had nailed it. Silence did, indeed, have a sound.

Or it would, if it weren't for the wasplike drone of the snowmobiles that had invaded the valley.

A shooting star streaked across the black velvet sky overhead, overcoming her faint annoyance. She drew in a breath of appreciation.

"You'd better be careful," a rough voice that sounded like a bald tire riding over river rock warned from the doorway behind her. "You keep that up and you'll get frostbite on your lungs."

She'd heard that countless times since moving to Wyoming. Enough that she'd actually asked a doctor, who'd assured her that the lungs' blood supply is so well developed it was virtually impossible to draw in enough cold air to cause any damage.

Because Mike Reed, the producer for *Talk-*

ing After Midnight, seemed to feel it was his duty to watch out for Hazard's newest city slicker, Faith didn't want to hurt his feelings by contradicting him.

"Wouldn't want to do that," she said truthfully.

She turned and came back up the three steps, then stomped her boots on the threshold mat so she wouldn't track snow all over the green-and-white-checkerboard vinyl floor. She glanced down at the stopwatch alarm she'd taken out with her.

"I've only got another forty seconds anyway."

The song her last caller had requested — ironically the bluesy country "Wild Wind" — lasted exactly five minutes and four seconds.

Midnight to six in the morning were often considered the throwaway hours by many station programmers, who preferred to concentrate on the "money" daytime shows. But, although Faith had hoped for a slot doing a more high-energy newscast, since coming to work at KWIND, she'd almost grown accustomed to working the night shift.

After years of waking up before dawn to report on morning drive-time traffic snarls, the hours after dark were proving a less frenetic and hurried time, which allowed the pace of programming after the rush of the day to be more relaxed. Listeners took the time to enjoy the music and, between cuts, engage in conversation, delving into topics they wouldn't have time to discuss while calling in from a cell phone while stuck in drive-time traffic.

Not that there was all that much traffic in Hazard. But the principle was the same, lending itself to long, uninterrupted sweeps of extended-play cuts, which not only allowed her to escape to look at the stars, but was exactly what the night owls who'd tune into KWIND during the midnight hours wanted.

She hung her parka on the hook by the door, returned to the studio, sat down, and put her earphones back on while Mike took his usual place on the other side of the window. She'd worked the board herself earlier in her career and, on those occasions when she'd worked nights, hadn't minded being alone.

But those stations had been in fair-sized cities: Fresno, Raleigh, Chattanooga, Savannah, Flagstaff. And they hadn't been in a metal box stuck out in the middle of nowhere. Somehow, tonight, the eeriness caused by the sudden cessation of wind made the trailer seem even more isolated.

Not helping her edginess had been the fact Mike had called her at home around nine to tell her that one of his mares was showing signs of colic, which could prove fatal.

Fortunately, the problem had been caught early, the horse was doing fine, and Faith had only been forced to work alone for the first hour of the show.

While she doubted that Mike, who was packing at least fifteen extra pounds beneath that Indian-print fleece shirt, could do much physically to protect either of them, the twelve-gauge shotgun he kept in the wall rack might prove a deterrent to anyone who might try to break in.

Not that anyone would, since crime in these parts consisted mostly of kids shooting up stop signs, drunken cowboys brawling in bars, and tourists who'd underestimated the combined effect of altitude and alcohol consumption driving into snowbanks.

Then again, wasn't Hazard exactly the type of small, isolated place depicted in all those B horror movies, where the dangerous and deranged showed up to slash babysitters and campers and generally commit murder and mayhem?

Although it was warm in the studio, Faith hugged herself to ward off the shiver that skimmed up her spine.

Dammit, she was letting her imagination get away from her! It'd been eighteen months since she'd felt so edgy and defenseless. She hadn't liked it back then. And she damn well didn't like it now.

Shaking off the chilly sense of unease, she focused her attention on Mike, who was signaling with his fingers through the glass window draped in flashing red, white, and green Christmas-tree lights. Three . . . two . . . one.

"And that was 'Wild Wind,' from Robert Earl Keen's *Live from Austin* album. You're talking with Faith, on 91.5 FM KWIND, Wyoming's best mix of classic and young country. Coming up we've got Miranda Lambert's 'Kerosene.' But first, here's a message from Joe Redbird's Used Auto Trader, where the Rocky Mountain High Country goes for a fair deal. If Redbird's doesn't have it, Joe'll get it."

Since coming to work at KWIND, Faith had found it hugely ironic that she'd ended up playing country music for a living. She also definitely identified with Lambert's line about life being "too long to live it like some country song."

Faith had been born into a country song. Her mama, a former Miss Teen Del Rio, had dreamed of escaping the Texas border town, moving to Nashville, and becoming a famous country-music star, just like Tanya Tucker or Reba McEntire.

She made it out of Del Rio by marrying an oil-rig worker she met while singing in a biker bar. He took her to Houston, where the marriage broke up five months later when she caught him in bed with a red-haired cocktail waitress from the roadhouse where she'd gotten a gig singing for tips.

Deciding that Diane didn't sound much like a country star, she changed her name to Tammy — after her idol, Tammy Wynette, who also hadn't had real good luck with men — and hooked up with a small-time hood who introduced her to drugs and supported their habit by boosting TVs and other electronics from the containers that came into the Houston port.

That marriage had ended when he was arrested in a sting operation after selling a case of video cameras to an undercover cop.

More men followed, including Faith's father, a Hells Angel who ended up in a maximum security prison for manslaughter before Faith had begun to walk.

Tammy had continued her downhill slide,

drifting around the Southwest, selling her body to pay for drugs as the singing jobs dried up. When she noticed her johns paying more attention to twelve-year-old Faith than they did to her, a lightbulb flashed on over her head. That's when she began selling her daughter.

Unsurprisingly, Tammy never made it to Nashville; she'd OD'd sometime in the night right after Faith's thirteenth birthday; at the time Faith had considered it the best — and only — gift her mother had ever given her. She still did.

As the brash, confrontational rock country lyrics began blasting out into the dark, spookily still night, Faith decided the idea of burning up your past made for a good song.

Unfortunately, as she'd learned the hard way, it wasn't all that easy in real life.

4

Salvatore Sasone hated three things: Democrats, spaghetti sauce from a jar, and cold weather.

Before being forced into making a living chasing down fugitives as a bounty hunter, he'd spent twenty years on the mean streets as a cop and had long ago concluded that laws passed by bleeding-heart Democratic politicians were responsible for the revolving door that was laughingly called the American judicial system.

Given that his great-grandfather had immigrated to America from Sicily, obviously an appreciation of spaghetti (which had, by the way, been invented in his ancestral city of Catania) had been woven into his DNA with his black hair and dark eyes. Right along with the need for sunshine and a warm climate.

There was no way in hell he would even be here in Bumfuck, Wyoming, if it weren't for a damn woman.

Sal had to give her credit. For an amateur, she'd done a damn good job of covering her tracks. The thing was, the woman was up against a pro.

Which, of course, meant that she had no freaking chance.

Oh, yeah, he thought, as he gulped down a bottle of foul-tasting Pepto-Bismol, one more thing . . . he also hated flying. His court-appointed anger-management therapist accused him of being a control freak.

Which, okay, so maybe he was. Especially now that he'd stopped drinking and didn't have booze to soften and numb the hard edges.

But what the hell was wrong with that?

If his ancestors had been laid-back, *que sera, sera,* whatever will be, will be, type individuals, the Roman Empire would've stopped at, well . . . Rome.

Even discounting that God couldn't have intended for people to defy gravity, Sal hated that he wasn't the one in the cockpit. He might not know how to fly a plane, but how did he know the pilot really did, either? With all the airline cutbacks these days, hell, they were probably hiring guys right off the street. And not just guys.

Christ on a crutch, he'd nearly shit a brick

when he'd walked onto the plane this morning and discovered he'd be handing over control of his life to a friggin' female.

That's when he should've folded his hand. But, reminding himself he was on a mission, he'd strapped himself into the seat of the flying tin can, which, a chatty elderly woman behind him informed her seatmate, was colloquially referred to as the Vomit Comet.

His own seatmate had been a Russian bear of a guy who was definitely taking up more than his share of space. The good news was that he proved no more interested in conversation than Sal himself was, choosing instead to spend the flight muttering curses when he wasn't taking hits from a silver flask he'd managed to sneak onto the plane in a red, white, and blue backpack.

As the turboprop jet bucked and dove over the Rockies, causing him to nearly lose the Egg McMuffin he'd wolfed down at Las Vegas' McCarran Airport, Sal discovered the flight was appropriately named.

By the time he'd managed to make it down the metal steps to the snow-dusted ground on rubbery legs, he'd seriously considered hitting his knees and kissing the tarmac.

It was all the damn woman's fault. If it

weren't for her, he wouldn't be going through all this freaking shit.

As he marched to the SUV parked outside the Red Wolf ski lodge, head hammering and stomach still churning as if he were coming off a two-week bender, Sal decided that if he could get the job done tonight, he could be on the first plane out of here in the morning. Back to the warmth and civilization of Vegas. Where he belonged.

5

It had only taken ten minutes, after all. And he'd fallen asleep right after he'd come. Erin thought about waking him, then decided that perhaps it would be better — easier — if he just woke up on his own and left the apartment while she was out at the lake. That way she could avoid any uncomfortable after-sex conversation until she had time to sort out her feelings about him. And about what they'd shared earlier.

As she drove past the bank — with its temperature sign announcing a minus ten degrees — and packed snow crunching beneath the tires of her six-month-old Subaru Legacy, Erin admitted that he probably wouldn't be the only one to call her crazy for coming out tonight.

She heard the distant whine of a snowmobile, glanced in the mirror, and viewed a black sled speeding across the snow, the driver probably practicing the trails for this week's Ride the Continental Divide sled race.

See, she wasn't the only one taking advantage of this still, moonlit night.

Before she'd escaped to Wyoming, skating had been a chore, a duty to be endured. It had, over the past months, become a joy again.

No. Not a joy. Something larger. Something almost . . . religious. Like a benediction.

Liking the sound of that, she parked beside the lake, then carried her white figure skates to a wide, flat boulder on the bank. She brushed the snow off with a white-gloved hand and sat down to lace up the skates.

Erin could not remember a life before skating. Her mother, a national-champion skater injured before the Sarajevo Olympics, had been forced to watch from a hospital bed as East Germany's Katarina Witt took home the gold medal.

Forced into retirement at the ripe old age of sixteen, Susan began planning the future. Not her own, which had shattered along with her knee when she'd landed that double axel so disastrously, but that of the child she intended to have. The child she'd groom into a champion.

Which was how Erin had ended up on double-bladed strap-on skates, being pulled around the rink by her mother before she could walk.

By five years old, she was taking lessons six days a week. Skating all seven. Perhaps God may have taken a day off to rest, but God hadn't had a mother determined to win Olympic gold.

She'd won her first competition a week before her seventh birthday and, at age ten, training twenty hours a week, became the youngest girl ever to compete in the senior ladies' level at the U.S. Nationals. That was the year her parents got divorced and her mother took her to Park City, Utah, to be trained by a former Russian figures coach at a skating center he'd established in the Rockies.

It was at thirteen when her fear of food set in as she struggled with the failure to control her body. A failure she carried in her budding breasts, the faintest curving of thigh.

By sixteen, her periods stopped, she'd given up her virginity to her coach, begun living on laxatives, and discovered she could ease the never-ending stress, just a bit, by cutting her arms with razor blades.

Blinded by their own agendas, both her

coach — who had, by then, begun using sex to control her, dishing it out as a reward for a good practice and withholding it as punishment for a less than stellar performance — and her mother, who had visions of high-paying commercial endorsements dancing in her head, refused to see that the teenager who'd never known a childhood was racing full tilt toward burnout.

It was on the eve of the World finals, after a disastrous practice, when all the medals, newspaper clippings, and national rankings couldn't overcome Erin's own certainty that she'd never be able to live up to what so many people expected of her. That was the night she took a pair of scissors her trainer used to cut athletic tape and stabbed herself in her wrist's vein.

Later, in the ER, Susan Gallagher demanded the doctor clear her daughter to skate the next morning.

Reading the shock and distaste on the doctor's face, at that moment Erin realized that if she really wanted a life — and she did — she'd have to create one on her own.

She walked out of the hospital, packed her bag, leaving all her beaded and spangled designer costumes behind, and never looked back.

She wasn't quite sure what she was going

to do, but she tackled this new challenge the same way she'd always approached her skating: by putting her entire heart and all her energy into it.

And it was paying off. Unlike the other girls who weighed themselves constantly, vigilant about falling prey to the dreaded "Freshman Fifteen," Erin not only accepted, she welcomed, every new ounce. Especially when she realized that her new curves attracted boys.

And speaking of boys . . .

She felt, rather than saw, his gaze. So, he'd come, after all. It was odd that she hadn't heard his truck. And it wasn't in the lot. He must have parked it back in the trees, wanting to surprise her.

She stood up, as comfortable on the slender steel blades as a girl who'd grown up on a tropical island would be barefoot.

The air was so dry and so cold, Erin could practically feel the ice crystals forming in her lungs.

Okay. If he wanted to watch from the shadows, she'd give him the show of his life.

"Then we can go back to bed and spend the rest of the night warming each other up again."

The memory of his hands roving over her body, his mouth swallowing her cries as she took him deep inside her, matching him power for power, sent streams of heat curling through her.

Maybe he'd become her boyfriend. She'd never had one before. Not really. Since her coach had been the closest thing she'd had to a father in years, going to bed with him had always felt like incest.

Unfortunately, the other boys she'd slept with — skaters, skiers, and once, the guy who operated the Zamboni, had always made her feel cheap. And ashamed.

And more alone than she'd been before she'd taken off her clothes.

But this time had felt different.

Because *he* was different.

Maybe, she considered with a smile as she stroked onto the frozen lake, the gliding movement as natural to her as walking, he really was boyfriend material.

The sound of the concave blades cutting into the ice was carried forever in the midnight chilled air as she picked up speed, crossing and uncrossing her feet, speeding through the turns, faster and faster.

She began her impromptu program with a triple-lutz, double-toe-loop combination, followed by a flying camel, arms outstretched like wings, her heart so light she wouldn't have been at all surprised if she suddenly became airborne.

With "Now We Are Free" from the *Gladiator* sound track soaring in her mind, clad in a snowy parka and matching ski pants, bathed in a spotlight of silvery moondust and the diffused red, green, and blue glow from the northern lights shimmering overhead, she flowed across the ice, flying through a series of double axels, a solid triple, a layback spin, finally finishing up with what had become known as "Erin's spiral."

The spiral consisted of a dizzying number of change-of-edge spins, not so different from a thousand other skater's spirals. What made the movement special was how her slender arms unfurled like a blossoming flower, the way she'd look up at her hands, her fingers fluttering, totally lost in what an ESPN commentator had first described as an otherworldly reverie.

The music in her head came to an end. For a long, frozen moment there was only the hushed sound of silence.

Erin knew she'd never skated so well. Never had she felt so free.

With exhilaration singing its pure sweet song in every cell of her body, she skated toward the copse of trees, where she'd sensed him standing.

"Okay," she said. "You can come out now."

There was no answer.

"Baby?" She narrowed her eyes, trying to see through the shadowed woods. "Where are you?"

Again, nothing.

Confused, she scanned the lake bank.

Touched by a growing sense of unease, she shivered, but not from the cold.

Ice cracked behind her.

She'd just started to spin around, to yell at him for practically scaring her to death, when a knife flashed evilly in the moonlight.

Before she could open her mouth to scream, the shiny blade slashed deep and wide.

A crimson river flowed from her throat, obscene against the snowy white of her fur-trimmed parka.

Eighteen-year-old Erin Gallagher never saw her attacker. She was dead before she crumpled to the ice.

Standing over her, the man who was once the boy raised by wolves tilted his head back and howled up at the huge, silver-dollar moon.

6

Seventeen hundred miles from the Savannah waterfront where he'd been shot three months earlier, Will was dragged from the nightmare, drenched in sweat, his out-of-control heart pounding so fast and so hard it could have been about to go into cardiac arrest.

The first time he'd felt this way, although he'd growled like a wounded grizzly, Gray had rushed him to Memorial Health University Medical Center, where an ER doctor who didn't look old enough to legally drive had stopped the wild heartbeat by massaging his carotid artery while a sadistic nurse slapped a wet towel onto his face.

"Have you experienced any stress lately?" the doctor had asked.

"Who hasn't these days?" he'd muttered from beneath the icy cloth. Working undercover Vice wasn't for sissies. Especially after you'd been dragged back from the jaws of death right here in MHUMC's trauma unit.

"Well, from your symptoms, and your positive response to treatment, my best guess would be you've got paroxysmal atrial tachycardia."

Will had ripped the rag away before he lost his nose to frostbite. "Any chance you could try saying that in English, Doc?"

"In layman's terms, the stress you've been under is causing your brain to send glitched electrical impulses to your heart. Which in turn, created an overload, which, in turn, caused it to lose its natural rhythm."

His encouraging smile was faked, as if he were auditioning for a role on *ER*. "It's really not that uncommon. And certainly not fatal."

He'd scribbled something onto Will's chart and handed it to the nurse. "I'm going to order an EEG, just in case. And I suggest you learn to be a little easier on yourself. Maybe take up yoga. Or meditation."

That'd be the day.

The wind, which had been battering the town ever since he'd arrived six weeks ago, had stopped. Moonlight was slipping between the slats of the blinds as he went into the kitchen, dumped a handful of ice cubes into a mixing bowl, and filled it nearly to the brim with water.

He took a deep breath.

Shut his eyes.

Then stuck his face into the bowl.

The icy water slammed into his system, instantly resetting his glitchy heart's rhythm. It might not be the most enjoyable way to start his day. But it was a helluva lot preferable to twisting his body into yoga pretzels.

Cursing himself for not being able to fight off the anxiety that had caused him to walk away from a job he'd loved and had been good at, and knowing from past experience that there'd be no more sleep tonight, he turned on the kitchen radio and spooned some Folgers (another thing that Doogie Howser clone had warned against) into the Mr. Coffee.

"Can you believe this night?" the all-too-familiar voice on the radio asked. "I've been here a year and this is probably only the third time the wind's stopped. Who knew Wyoming could be so silent?"

Who knew that the woman he'd shared those kisses with atop the Ferris wheel three years ago would show up in Hazard, Wyoming, of all places.

What the hell were the odds?

But, like Han Solo had said in *The Empire Strikes Back,* "Never tell me the odds!"

The woman currently calling herself Faith Prescott had the perfect voice for nighttime radio — dark and smooth, like rich cream over warm cognac. It slipped beneath your skin on lonely winter nights, encouraging hot midnight memories of her in his bed, those sultry, dulcet tones talking dirty in his ear.

"It's the kind of night you don't want to be alone." Her husky purr echoed his own thoughts.

Although she'd been in town a year, she continued to dominate breakfast conversation among ranchers who'd congregate every morning to clog their arteries with cholesterol-drenched eggs, hash browns, and country smoked ham and down gallons of coffee.

According to the scuttlebutt, the fact that she hadn't taken up with any of the locals had the members of the breakfast club wondering if she might be a lesbian.

Which would be, all agreed, if it was true, a crying shame.

She may not have given any of the males in town a tumble, but Will knew, firsthand, that Faith was no lesbian.

Despite Hazard's being a one stoplight town, so far they'd managed to avoid each other since he'd returned. Which was just as well, given that his life, which had always been exactly how he liked it before that damn shooting, had become impossibly complicated. He had no time for a woman with tiger eyes and a sinfully alluring mouth.

But that didn't stop him from fantasizing lying with her on that bearskin rug at the Red Wolf Lodge.

The night-chilled air thickened with the scent of musk. In his fantasy, they were both naked, her fragrant body gleaming in the flickering orange glow from a fireplace large enough to stand in.

He'd just run his fingertips up the silken skin of her inner thigh and was planning to follow the path with his tongue, when the wall phone had the image shattering like splintered ice.

He scooped it up. "Yeah?" His unusually harsh voice was roughened with pent-up sexual need.

"Sheriff?"

Inner alarms began blaring. "What's happened?"

Sam Charbonneaux, Hazard's chief deputy, was one of the most capable cops Will had ever worked with. He never would've risked waking his boss up in the middle of the night for anything minor.

"It's bad, Sheriff." The deputy's voice

sounded clogged. "Real bad." There was the sound of a ragged intake of breath. "It's that skater."

"Skater?"

"You know, the kid from those soup commercials. Erin Gallagher." He paused to drag in another deep breath. "She's dead."

Damn. Erin Gallagher had been America's best hope for a gold medal in this year's Winter Olympics before she'd turned her back and walked away from figure skating. While Will wasn't up on celebrity news, Josh subscribed to *Sports Illustrated* and he remembered the teenage skater appearing on the cover.

He was vaguely aware that she'd moved to Hazard in September to attend college, but since she hadn't gotten into any trouble, their paths hadn't crossed.

Until now.

After a brief conversation, he determined that Sam wasn't exaggerating. Instructing the deputy to secure the crime scene, Will hung up and immediately called the coroner, who sounded less than thrilled at getting dragged out of bed in the middle of a freezing winter's night.

After pouring the now brewed coffee into a stainless steel thermos, Will trudged back to the bedroom to throw on some clothes.

Five minutes later, he'd written a note, letting his father — with whom he'd moved in with after returning to Wyoming — know that he'd been called out and had no idea when he'd be back.

He was at the door of the mudroom, about to head out to Silver Lake, when he turned back. After all that had happened, he didn't want to leave without saying goodbye to Josh. Because you just never knew when you might not be coming back.

The room was typical teenage messy, clothes thrown over the chair, strewn over the floor; skis, a Christmas gift still unused, propped up against the wall; a set of dumbbells beneath the window; a can of Coke sitting abandoned on the night table.

The screen saver on the laptop computer showed a sun-drenched beach fringed by palm trees; Will knew his sixteen-year-old son missed the freedom of his former unsupervised days in L.A., resented all the changes in his life since his mother's death, one of which was being handed over to a cop father who had a shitload of problems of his own.

Josh was also not adjusting well to life in this isolated high-range town where the wind blew nearly nonstop, snow stayed on the ground from October to June, and nothing much ever happened.

Remembering his own rocky teenage years, which, if it hadn't been for his father's influence, would've landed him in juvie more than once, and feeling a surge of fatherly fondness for this son he'd never known existed until that attorney had shown up in his hospital room in Savannah, Will stepped over the flotsam of teenage life to the side of his son's bed.

He wouldn't wake him. Just touch him. A hand to his hair, as Will had been denied the ability to do back when Josh was a baby and probably wouldn't have shied away from every paternal touch.

When his fingertips skimmed the empty pillow, Will belatedly realized he hadn't heard any breathing.

He turned on the bedside lamp, blinking against the sudden glare of the light flooding the room.

Shit. The bed was empty. Since Josh wasn't real good about making it each morning, Will couldn't tell if it had been slept in.

Frustration, mixed with ice-cold fear, threatened to trigger another attack.

With his damn glitchy heart hammering against his ribs, Will hissed out a breath and yanked up the shade. Dark eyes, a legacy from his Arapaho grandmother, scanned the vast, endless white landscape outside the window.

Where the hell was his son?

7

KWIND's phone had three lines, one for station business, two for callers. The way the programming worked, Mike would answer the caller lines, then type the caller's name into his computer, which would then show up on Faith's monitor.

With both lines blinking, she chose the call from Mothertrucker, a female long-haul truck driver, one of her core group of loyal listeners.

"You're talking after midnight on 91.5 FM KWIND with Faith."

"You hear anything about what's goin' on over at Silver Lake?"

"Not a thing," Faith responded, suspecting all those snowmobilers who'd invaded the town for the upcoming race must've gotten together for an impromptu party that had gotten out of hand.

Faith had never given much thought to snowmobiles, but after the past few days, she feared she'd hear the wasplike drone of the engines long after they'd left Hazard.

"Sounds like Tso'appittse's been doin' his thing again."

"Tso'appittse?" She had difficulty getting her tongue around the unfamiliar syllables.

"The Shoshone Bigfoot." Mothertrucker huffed out a breath. "Reckon you ain't heard of him?"

"No, I haven't."

"He's big. Giant-size. And rocky, with pitchy hands. And he feeds on human flesh."

"Yikes," Faith said lightly. She grinned at Mike, who, oddly, did not smile back. "I wouldn't want to run into him in a dark alley."

It was probably some sort of teenage prank, kids out of school for the holidays, trying to liven things up by scaring the lowland city slickers who'd ventured up into the mountains to ski the Wind River ski resort's deep-powder slopes.

"You don't want a believe in him, that's your choice," the caller said. "But if you'd been listening to your police scanner, you would a heard the sheriff's calling for the coroner."

On the other side of the glass, Mike was vigorously nodding and pointing to the scanner he kept on just in case some fool movie star — his words, not hers — got a toot on and skied off White Owl Mountain.

"Well, that's certainly intriguing," Faith said. And a bit unnerving, given that her house just happened to be on the shore of that very lake. "And since we here at KWIND like to think of ourselves as the voice of the community, we'll check it out right away. Stay tuned for updates. Meanwhile, we've got Alan Jackson, Toby Keith, and Martina McBride on tap."

Faith put the prerecorded song mix into the rack. But not wanting to leave the other caller — named B. Hunter — holding, before starting the mix she hit the blinking button.

"You're talking with Faith after midnight on KWIND."

Radio work often required being able to think on two levels at once, which is what she was doing now, talking with a caller while her mind scrambled to figure out how, if something newsworthy had really happened at the lake, she could cover it without risking several minutes of dead air.

"If this is about whatever might be happening out at Silver Lake . . ."

"Don't know anything about any lake." The deep male voice was roughened with the twang of the desert Southwest. "Just thought I'd call and chat with you for a while, Faith, baby."

Her mouth went dry as the Nevada desert she'd believed she'd managed to escape. The glibness that radio work required deserted her.

"This is a talk show, right?" the man she'd desperately hoped never to see again prompted. "Talk and music?"

"It certainly is," she said over the roar of rushing blood in her ears. "But we seem to have a slight . . . event . . . to cover."

Faith would willingly venture into the lowest circle of hell to avoid any further contact with Salvatore Sasone.

"We'll be back live as soon as we can. Meanwhile, we've got a lot of good music still on tap for your listening enjoyment."

Fighting off a wave of light-headedness, Faith cut off the man she'd come here to escape before he could respond. Then put her elbows on the table and dropped her head in her hands.

Oh, God. Disbelief and fear pounded in her heart. Wyoming in winter was the last place she'd ever expect the man to turn up. He and cold weather went together like Budweiser and caviar.

How the hell had he found her? She'd done her homework. Read pages of articles online about how to create a new identity, had spent hours plotting logistics with a friend who ran an underground railroad for women hiding their children from abusive spouses, and had even risked getting arrested when she'd paid $500 for a phony driver's license and Social Security card.

She'd thought for sure she'd covered her tracks, working at below-minimum-wage waitress jobs across three states for six months before she'd finally felt safe enough to try getting back into radio.

She'd believed that short of leaving the lower forty-eight states to hide out in Alaska, this would be the last place Sal would ever think to look for her.

She'd been wrong. Dead wrong.

"What's the problem?" Mike said into her headphones.

She lifted her head, which felt as if some maniac were swinging away with an ice pick inside it.

"Nothing," she lied.

Was he out there now? Watching her? Waiting for her?

"What did you hear on your scanner?" she asked, struggling to beat back the sharp, mouth-drying panic Sal's call had instilled.

"Nothing that Mothertrucker didn't tell you. The sheriff's out at the lake with the medical examiner. Could just be someone decided to go for a midnight stroll across a frozen lake and keeled over from natural causes. Or maybe we got lucky and one of those blasted sledders who are keeping everyone from getting a good night's sleep fell through the ice."

"Wouldn't it be pretty to think so."

Faith pushed herself to her feet, hoping her wobbly legs would hold her as she made her way to the control room — which, although only a few feet away — felt like a mile.

"But we won't know," she said, "unless we go out to the lake." She didn't add that they could both well be killed if they stayed here.

"Aw, Christ, Faith."

He glanced out the window at the fluffy white flakes illuminated by a bank of outdoor lights. Beyond the warm yellow glow, the woods looked cold and black and deep. And dangerous.

"It's starting to snow again out there." His frowning face was reflected back at them in the glass. "Why the hell would you want to go freeze your butt off playing Lois Lane?"

"Because if something has happened, this is our chance to scoop all the Jackson press."

That much was the truth. Being at the

center of things in this remote corner of the state, reporters in Jackson typically got all the action.

"And I should care about that why?"

"Because we'd get people talking about us, which would make more tune in, which would boost us on the Arbitrons, which in turn would relate to more advertising dollars, which could earn us all a raise in the new year. There's always a chance the brass might even throw in an extra bonus to go with those Christmas turkeys they gave us all."

She glanced up at the oversize wall clock. How long ago had Sal called? Was he on his way? If so, how much time did they have before he showed up?

Mike was a nice guy. But even with that twelve-gauge, he was no match for Sal Sasone.

"I wouldn't turn down a bonus. What with the spike in the cost of fuel and feed this winter." He'd been building up a horse-breeding business with the hopes of leaving the station to work it full-time. "But Kendall's KWIND's go-to guy for news."

"Brian's in Idaho, spending the holidays with his family."

What Mike didn't know, and Faith wasn't about to tell him, was that Brian Kendall had confided he was auditioning for a drive-time news slot on Boise's KIZN.

"Shit. That leaves Leon."

Leon Ducett was a senior at Wind River College. He was also only an intern — though possessing testicles, he'd probably be more appealing to Fred Handley, the chauvinistic Cheyenne dinosaur who owned a string of rural radio stations stretching from western Idaho into the Dakotas.

Apparently having never heard of laws against workplace discrimination, he'd made it all too clear that he didn't believe women's voices had the depth of authority to give listeners the news.

More than a little desperate when she'd interviewed, Faith had hoped she'd be able to change Handley's mind. But so far that hadn't happened.

"Doesn't matter, since Leon's got a hot date," Mike divulged. "He was leaving just as I got here and warned me that if I called him for anything less than an invasion of body snatchers, I could kiss my scalp good-bye."

"Well, that sounds pretty definitive. I wouldn't want to risk your scalp." She reached over and rubbed his shaggy blond hair. "A coroner means a body. If we leave now, we'll be the first ones on the scene," she coaxed.

He rubbed his jaw. “With all those entertainment-magazine and TV folks up there in Jackson covering those movie stars, it could turn into a media three-ring circus. Like O.J.” His grin suggested he liked that possibility. “Next thing you know, your pretty face could be all over TV and you’ll be sitting on the couch next to Matt Lauer.”

“If I’d wanted to be on television, I wouldn’t have gone into radio.”

TV was much more regimented. More dependent on looks. Flash over substance.

There was also the fact that if she’d been on TV, she wouldn’t have been able to hide from Sal for as long as she had.

The caller line rang again; her nerves tangled into tight, cold knots.

“Okay.” Mike blew out a long breath and stood up. “Let’s see if we can find you a newscast.”

Saved by the bell. And the pretaped mix that would, if necessary, continue to play for ninety minutes. “Have I ever told you that I love you?”

“Yeah, yeah.” He shot a resigned look out at the falling snow. “That’s the same thing all the drop-dead gorgeous women in my life say.”

Dearly hoping she wouldn’t encounter an

armed bounty hunter parked outside the trailer, Faith yanked her snow-white, hooded parka from the hook and together they walked out the door, leaving Toby Keith calling for whiskey for his men and beer for the horses.

8

There was blood.

So damn much blood.

Erin Gallagher lay on her back in a grove of trees near the bank of the lake, arms outstretched as if she'd been crucified, the shiny silver blades of her white figure skates pointed outward at forty-five-degree angles.

The front of her white parka and ski pants were soaked with blood; more blood surrounded the fur-trimmed hood like a crimson corona. It had, unsurprisingly, already frozen to the consistency of a raspberry Sno-Kone.

The 2 million candlepower halogen lamp Sam had fastened onto the roof rack of his SUV was like looking into the sun. Will felt as if he ought to be wearing a welder's helmet.

But while the harsh white light combined with the flashing red, white, and blue police beacon to create a flat, surrealistic look to the landscape that reminded him of a bad Salvador Dalí painting, it managed to light up the area well enough for the deputy to photograph the scene.

"Her throat was cut." The gash was deep, but narrow, as if it had been done with a razor. Or scalpel.

"Exsanguinated," the coroner confirmed. "Both jugulars sliced by someone who knew what he was doing. Another few centimeters deeper and it would've taken her head off."

Dr. Jack Dawson's complexion usually wore a year-round tan from summer sailing and winter skiing. In the glow of the halogen light, it looked a little green. Which made sense, since, as Hazard's orthopedic surgeon, he was more accustomed to dealing with skiers' broken legs and shoulders. Having so little crime, the county didn't need a full-time coroner, so local physicians rotated monthly.

The last murder anyone could remember was back in 1992, when Earl Monroe had gotten sick and tired of Lyle Pollard playing "Achy Breaky Heart" over and over again and shot the jukebox down at The Watering Hole Saloon.

Unfortunately, Earl — who'd just learned his wife had been stepping out on him with a used-car dealer from Jackson — was hammered, causing his aim to go high. The bullet hit the metal frame of the Coors light hanging over the pool table, ricocheted, and struck Tom Wheatly, who was minding his own business, nursing a beer at the bar, smack in the middle of his forehead.

After Earl sobered up, on the advice of his attorney (given that the bar had been filled with witnesses at the time), he'd pleaded guilty to involuntary manslaughter and was sentenced to three to eight years, landing himself in the state penitentiary in Rawlins.

Six months later, his exemplary behavior got him moved to the Wyoming Honor Farm, where he was put to work in the farm's wild-horse adoption program and demonstrated such a natural gift with horses that when he won parole after five years, the warden actually said he was sorry to see Earl go.

But this death was much, much worse than any drunken juke shooting.

"Who called it in?" Will asked.

"A couple sledders." Sam, looking sicker than Will felt, nodded toward a pair of men standing beside pricey, green racing Arctic Cats. "One of them had to take a piss, pulled into the trees, and tripped over the body. I've already taken their statement, but Desiree's keeping them occupied in case you wanted to talk with them."

Will decided that the deputy had made the perfect call, assigning Desiree Douchet the job of keeping the witnesses at the scene. Desiree was what Josh would call a hot chick, though any male who dared call her that to her face was risking getting slapped in the slammer.

"Convenient that out of all the miles of woods, the guy just happened to feel the urge to pee in the only spot where there's a dead body." Will had never trusted convenient. Nor coincidence. "Did either one of them see anything? Another snowmobile? A cross-country skier, or SUV in the vicinity?"

"A black Yamaha sled passed them, going toward town about a quarter of a mile up the road, but they didn't think much about it, since the damn things are all over the valley this week. There's no telling if it had anything to do with this. Maybe Desiree can get something else out of them."

"I strongly doubt that, given the fact that most males' brains turn to mush when talking with Deputy Douchet," Jack said.

"Helps that it's winter," Will said. "She's more covered up in that parka."

Will's gaze shifted to Trace Honeycutt, who was busily roping off the crime scene.

Having graduated this past June with an associate arts degree in criminal justice from Wind River College, the deputy was as young and green as spring meadow grass. Watching the enthusiasm with which he was stringing the tape made Will feel about as old as the mountains surrounding the town.

Sighing, he returned his attention to the victim. His stomach slid north, into his throat. He swallowed, forcing it south again as he crouched to study footprints in the frozen blood.

"What's this?" Pulling a pen out of an inside pocket, he used the point to lift up the blue-and-white woven lanyard around her bloodied neck.

Laminated between two sheets of plastic was what appeared to be a poem.

"Not your typical ski pass," Sam observed.

"Not by a long shot," Will agreed.

He stood up and rubbed the back of his neck as he scanned the frozen, white landscape.

Although he'd always found being a murder cop too staid for his blood, given that detectives always came in after the fact, when all the shooting and stabbing had been done, the two years he'd spent on the homicide squad had taught him to put himself in a victim's place.

So, now, as his dark eyes scanned the frozen lake and forest of dark trees, he tried to see what this dead girl would have seen. To experience what she would have felt in those last moments of her life.

The lack of defense cuts on her gloves suggested she hadn't fought back. Had she known her attacker? Had the person who'd wielded the blade that had nearly decapitated the victim come out here with her?

It was unlikely that she'd come out to such an isolated location all by herself. Then again, she could've been drunk. Or high. Or maybe just fucking foolhardy.

Whatever her reason for being here at the lake, a young woman who'd undoubtedly had dreams and goals, and friends and family who cared about her, was now dead in his town, on his watch. It was up to him to find her killer. And make goddamn sure he paid.

"I don't suppose you can give me an approximate on the time of death?" he asked Jack.

"Not from examining her body. Being frozen invalidates the usual death indicators, like rigor mortis, lividity, and changes in body temperature.

"The most valid way to determine death is by stomach contents. When her body froze, whatever was in her stomach froze, as well, and didn't get any further digested."

"So if we can find out where she had her last meal," Will said, "you'll be able to tell by the state of digestion how long she lived after eating it."

"Theoretically." Dawson's frown deepened. "But I gotta tell you, Will, while I'm comfortable enough handling the coroner's job for run-of-the-mill car wrecks, drownings, and the occasional skier ramming his head into a tree, this could end up being way beyond my forensic skills. Especially when it's obvious that we're talking a capital crime.

"The DA's going to want all the details nailed down tighter than a tick when he goes to trial. Since Evergreen High's science department probably has more equipment than I do, I think we ought to send the body to the coroner in Jackson."

Will couldn't argue with that suggestion. Nor did he allow himself to consider that there might not be a trial. That would mean someone would get away with murder in his town. Which damn well wasn't an option.

"That's probably not a bad call."

He wondered if he should also call in the state DCI guys, then decided that while he might have burned out after the shooting, he hadn't gotten stupid since leaving Savannah. If he couldn't handle a single murder in a town of less than three thousand full-time citizens, then he may as well turn in his badge.

He glanced over at the dark green Legacy Outback parked in the gravel lot. "You check that vehicle out yet?"

"Didn't want to leave the body," Sam said. "What with all the company we're getting, I figured since she wasn't going anywhere, it could wait until you got here."

Another good call. "You done taking photographs?"

"Yep."

Will found the keys in her outer parka pocket. As he crunched his way across the snow, he wondered, as he often did, if Sam had resented not being promoted to sheriff when Don Bohannon had retired to Galveston.

Sam was, after all, more than qualified. But he was also full-blooded Shoshone, born and raised on the Wind River Reservation, and while local prejudice might not be as bad as it had been when they were both kids, once Will had decided to return to Hazard, Sam's chances had probably been about equivalent to those of a tropical hurricane hitting Wyoming in January.

The door of the Subaru chirped as he hit the button on the key fob. A bright red, white, and blue backpack lay on the front passenger seat. Will opened the front flap and found a slender nylon wallet.

There were two credit cards, a photo ID card from Wind River College, a Colorado driver's license, and $60 in cash. That the three twenties were crisply new suggested she'd recently visited an automatic teller.

Her driver's license listed her height as five feet two inches, weight a whopping ninety-eight pounds. With her blond hair and blue eyes, she'd been a pretty, all-American girl.

Bad enough that Hazard had just experienced its first murder in over a decade. That the victim was the girl the press had dubbed America's Ice Princess was going to create one helluva lot of press attention.

Especially during this week between Christmas and New Year's when neighboring Jackson was ass-deep in celebrities. Following those celebrities were a horde of reporters who followed them around like flies buzzing around a herd of bison.

Speak of the damn devil . . .

Headlights flashed across the ice. As if conjured up by his dark thoughts, a red-and-black van with kwind painted on the side in blinding yellow letters pulled into the far side of the parking lot.

9

"If it is a hoax, it's certainly drawn a crowd," Faith said as Mike pulled off the road into the parking lot, which appeared to have recently been plowed.

The lot was across the lake from her house, but close enough that if it hadn't been snowing, she could probably have seen the glow of the lights she always left on so she wouldn't have to return to a dark house.

"Looks like the real thing." Mike cut the engine. "And I think we've got the scoop all to ourselves."

He didn't exactly rub his gloved hands together with glee, but Faith could tell he was pleased about that. He may not have wanted to come out into the middle of a freezing night, but the prospect of a bonus seemed to have changed his mind.

Faith noticed the green SUV parked at the other end of the lot. "We may not be the first." The cold invaded the van the moment the heat stopped blasting through the dashboard vents. "Isn't that Erin's Legacy?"

Erin Gallagher had been giddy as a schoolgirl on laughing gas when the station manager had hired her on as an intern. She thought she might go into sports broadcasting, and Dan Morgan, producer of a Saturday-morning show highlighting Friday-night high school games, had promised to give her a shot interviewing local athletes.

"Looks like hers," Mike agreed. "Christ, the little gal may be no bigger than a peanut, but she sure does hustle."

"I wonder how she found out about this."

"Probably heard it on the radio."

The cold hit like a slap in the face as Faith left the van. She sucked in a breath that actually burned, pulled up the hood of her white parka, and tightened the cord around her neck in a futile attempt to hold out the night air that felt like icy fingers at her throat.

As the sheriff approached on a long-legged, predatory stride, his grim gaze held not an inkling of the sensual memory that continued to haunt her dreams at least once a week. His mouth was a tight, compressed line, and the stubble of unshaven beard gave him a rough and dangerous look.

He was wearing a black, fur-lined trooper's hat instead of the Stetson he usually wore, but the man had cowboy written all over him. He was tall and rangy, with broad shoulders, a rugged face that could have been chiseled out of the granite mountain behind them, and a jaw wide enough to park his big, black, macho Jeep Cherokee on.

Last time she'd gotten a trim down at The Wild Hair salon, she'd heard a woman mention that his maternal grandmother had been an Arapaho, which, Faith imagined, explained the reason his deeply set eyes were so dark it was hard to distinguish between iris and pupil, and the straight, jet-black hair he didn't wear as closely cropped as most cops.

Despite the icy nighttime temperatures, he was wearing a pair of jeans, but in deference to the deep snow had exchanged the pointy-toed, hand-tooled Tony Lamas he'd worn in Savannah for black pac-boots.

"The scene's closed off," he announced, as if she were too blind or stupid to notice all that yellow-and-black plastic tape.

His brusque, authoritative tone was worlds away from how he'd once talked to her.

"That means no civilians." His scowl darkened as he flicked a glance over her shoulder toward the KWIND van. "Especially no press."

Faith had never been a real big fan of authority. And after all the lies he'd told her, she was even less a fan of Will Bridger's.

"In case you haven't noticed, Sheriff, this isn't Dodge. And you're definitely no Matt Dillon."

His eyes were hard as jet beneath the ledge of his brow. "Thank you for pointing that out to me, Ms. Prescott."

Although they were now standing toe-to-toe, they were on opposite sides of a deep divide, two equally stubborn combatants engaged in a turf war.

"I'm here in a news reporting capacity, Sheriff. You calling for the coroner in the middle of the night just happens to be news."

A line, stretched taut across his forehead like barbed wire, deepened when he narrowed his eyes.

"And you know I called for the coroner how? Maybe you heard it from one of those whacked-out listeners who called in to warn people that Martians had landed on White Owl Mountain?"

"A listener called it in," she admitted. "But Mike also heard it on the scanner."

"Sure as hell did," Mike said, finally diving into the dueling conversation.

From Will's muttered curse, Faith had the feeling he'd love to confiscate every police scanner in the valley.

"What are we talking, Sheriff?" she pressed on. "An accident? Or murder?"

He folded his arms across the front of his brown sheriff's department parka. His ruthless mouth twisted in what appeared more sneer than smile.

"Perhaps you've gotten a bit rusty on newscasting, Ms. *Prescott.* Otherwise you'd remember that the cause of death isn't my call to make."

The sarcasm stung. As did the scorn he'd heaped on the new last name she'd taken when she'd gone into hiding.

"I understand the coroner determines the cause of death," she said between set teeth, hating the way he was making her feel defensive. When, after what had happened, he should be the one uncomfortable. "But still, you must have an opinion."

"None I'm willin' to go on the record with. So, you two may as well just get back in that van and go back to the station."

"Come on, Will," Mike said. "When did you, of all people, get to be so damn rigid?"

"When I swore an oath to protect and to serve the people of this county. I'll probably be calling a press conference in the morning. You're both welcome to attend."

And wasn't that big of him? "Thank you for the invitation." Faith's smile was bright and utterly false. "I'll definitely be there."

Along with a gazillion other reporters from Jackson. Faith didn't know what Will was sitting on, but she doubted he'd be calling a press conference if some snowmobiler had died in an accident preparing for this week's race.

"Meanwhile, since we're already on the scene, why don't you share what you can with us? In case it's slipped your mind, you happen to be a public servant. KWIND listeners are the public. Therefore you work for them."

"Is that a fact?"

He rubbed a thumb against his forehead in a way that suggested if he'd been wearing the Stetson, he would have tipped it back.

"Absolutely. Besides, you've already let one reporter past your precious yellow tape, so —"

"What are you talking about?" His sudden harsh glare could've blistered paint off the side of the KWIND van.

"Obviously I'm talking about Erin Gallagher."

He went as eerily still as the night air.

"What do you know about the Gallagher girl?"

"That's her Subaru." Faith gestured toward the compact SUV.

The *abandoned* SUV.

No! Please, God. Don't let it be . . .

"I didn't let the girl past anything."

His words were a nearly incomprehensible buzz in Faith's ears. Her lungs seized; her heart beat faster.

Please, please, please.

Faith squeezed her eyes shut tight, as if somehow it would prevent her from hearing the worst. It didn't.

"Erin Gallagher's dead."

10

The color drained from a complexion the hue of freshly whipped cream, and her brandy-hued eyes widened with shock. Watching her struggle with her emotions, Will felt an unbidden twinge of guilt for not couching the news more gently.

"Christ," Mike muttered.

"That's impossible." Her hood slipped back as she dragged a trembling hand through the slide of dark hair. "Are you sure?"

"Yeah." Denial was a typical response to any death. And murder was something most civilians had trouble grasping. "I'm sure."

"But I just saw her this evening." Faith looked across the snow at the circle of blinding lights, as if expecting to see the dead girl suddenly appear and start doing triple lutzes across the frozen lake. "Talked with her."

"About what?"

She was picturing it. Trying to imagine the scene. Struggling to envision the vital young woman with the life force drained out of her. Will thought it was just as well she couldn't.

Death by murder wasn't anything like it was portrayed on *CSI* or *Law & Order*.

It was real.

Real ugly.

"You said you'd seen her." He struggled for patience, despite his concern that the killer might be somewhere nearby. "When? What did you talk about?"

"She dropped by the station about six."

"Your show doesn't start until midnight."

"Maybe that's why we decided to call it *Talking After Midnight.*" Faith dragged her hand through her hair again, then pulled the hood back up. "I'm sorry. I didn't mean to be sarcastic. It's just that . . ."

Her gaze drifted back to where Erin Gallagher's body lay waiting for the ambulance to take her to the Jackson morgue.

"It's hard," she murmured.

"Yeah." When she finally looked up at him, seeming surprised by the empathy in his tone, Will suppressed the urge to assure her he wasn't the bastard he'd behaved like three years ago down in Savannah. This wasn't about him. Or her. "It is."

"Was she raped?"

"That's not —"

"Your call. I know." She briefly shut her eyes. Took a deep breath, then tried again.

"I was working on tonight's song list. I've never worked a talk/music format before coming here, so when I first started, I just went along with what the guy before me had played. I decided when I got up this morning that it was time to start making the show more mine. To reflect my own tastes, without losing the listeners, who've become accustomed to a certain sound . . .

"But that's not what you asked."

She drew in another deep breath. Let it out to hover like a ghost in the frosty air between them.

"Erin and I only exchanged a couple words. I asked how school was, she said fine. I said good." Faith shrugged. "She said she was thinking of going skating if the wind ever stopped."

"Which it did."

"Yes. Talk about a case of bad timing. If she hadn't come out here tonight, she'd still be alive."

Possibly. Possibly not. It all depended on whether she was the intended victim, or just in the wrong place at the wrong time.

"Why was she at the station in the first place?"

"She's an intern. She answers the phone, files logs, that sort of thing. She usually comes in about three evenings a week to work with Drew. That's Drew Hayworth. He has a call-in show."

"The shrink."

The first time Will had heard the program, he'd thought the guy sounded like a Frasier wannabe. Of course he was admittedly prejudiced, given his experience with shrinks.

"Psychological anthropologist," she corrected mildly.

"So she worked for this shrink — this Dr. Hayworth tonight?"

"I suppose. Though she didn't stay very long, so she might have just wanted to talk with him."

"About what?"

Faith shot him a level look. "You'd have to ask him."

"I plan to do that. Is that normal?"

"What?"

"Her coming in to talk to the doctor?"

"I'm not privy to their conversations, Sheriff. But I do know Drew's very popular at the college. It's tough being a teenager these days," she said, telling him nothing he hadn't already figured out for himself. "A lot of kids seem to enjoy having someone impartial to talk to about school, the opposite sex, family problems."

"Did Erin Gallagher have problems? With school? The opposite sex? Family?"

"I really wouldn't know. You'd have to ask —"

"The shrink."

"Psychologist," she corrected again.

"Yeah."

Will turned to Mike. "You ever talk with her?"

"Sure."

"What about?"

"Jesus, Will, I don't remember. Stuff. Weather, the Broncos — she was a fan, which makes sense since she spent all those years at the Olympic Center in Colorado Springs. Whether men or women tipped better."

"How did that come up?"

"She waits — waited — tables at the lodge part-time. Last Monday she came in complaining about a bunch of women who'd had their office Christmas party there, took up three tables for two hours, and only left behind two bucks. I agreed that sucked. End of conversation."

"She ever mention getting into hassles

with anyone there?"

"No. But you gotta understand, we didn't have that kind of relationship. Teenage girls don't tend to spill their guts to middle-aged men just because they happen to work in the same place.

"Maybe you've spent so many years interrogating suspects, you've forgotten what it is to have a casual conversation. To simply talk with a person without giving them the third degree."

Mike shook his head, which was covered down to his bushy blond brows in a black woolen watch cap. "Of all the people in this town, you're the last one I ever would've expected to become such a hard-ass."

This was the bitch about becoming the law in a town where you'd grown up. Last time Will had seen Mike Reed, the two of them had been drinking beer and shooting rats down at the reservoir. By the time they'd polished off the second six-pack, they were drunk enough that rats were pretty much guaranteed a stay of execution.

"I'm just trying to do my job, Mike. Best I can."

"There was something," Faith volunteered hesitantly.

Will didn't ask. Just waited.

"It may not mean anything."

He continued to wait.

"She had scars."

"What kind? Where?"

"Thin slash marks. On her wrists."

"Self-inflicted?"

"She never said. So, I never brought them up."

"Think she talked to Hayworth about them?"

"You'll have to ask him."

"I plan to."

Will knew that after joining the school radio club, which Faith coincidentally mentored, Josh had started hanging out at the station. He wondered if his son had found the shrink easy to talk to.

He was thinking maybe Josh had shared stuff that might give Will a handle on how the hell to reach his messed-up, angry-as-hell kid when a pickup came roaring into the lot and an already lousy situation looked as if it was about to get a helluva lot worse.

11

"What the hell? Josh?"

Will watched his missing son leap out of the truck, leaving the driver's door open as he raced toward where Erin Gallagher lay.

"That's a sealed-off crime scene," Will yelled.

Ignoring the warning, as he had everything else his father had said to him, Josh vaulted the barrier of yellow tape.

All the way out here to the lake, Will had tried to think of where in the hell his rebellious teenage son might have taken off to. Any friends he might have been out with.

Not that the kid seemed to have that many friends, which wasn't surprising if he was even half as surly at school as he was at home.

Back in Savannah, Will had busted a teenage prostitution ring. The surprising thing was that the kids had operated out of one of the city's toniest neighborhoods. They drove

Beemers, wore designer duds, and got their kicks selling their bodies to traveling salesmen and perverts from the burbs. When he'd busted the ring, they'd been clearing ten thousand bucks a month.

At the time he'd had nothing but scorn for their yuppie parents, who'd been too wrapped up in their own versions of the American dream to look around and notice their kids were in serious trouble.

But now, watching his son drop to his knees and puke his guts out, Will was forced to wonder if some of those parents had known something was going terribly wrong in their family, but hadn't a clue how to deal with it.

And couldn't he freaking identify with that?

Because the idea hit too close to home, Will dragged his mind back to the icy crime scene and his distraught son, who'd wrapped his arms around himself as he rocked back and forth.

Had Whitney ever rocked their child? Will sincerely doubted it. Although their brief time together, when he'd been stationed at Parris Island marine base, had been spent mostly in bed, his son's mother had certainly never appeared to be the Madonna type.

"Oh, God," Josh moaned. "It's all my fault."

Which could mean a lot of things.

Will felt like a damn cop standing over his kid, who was now dry-heaving.

He was a damn cop. But he was also a dad.

He crouched down. "You okay?"

"How the fuck can I be okay?"

Red-rimmed eyes looked up at him. It was the first time his son had looked at him with anything other than, at the best, disdain. At the worst, naked scorn tilting dangerously toward hatred.

"After I killed Erin?"

Everything in Will went still.

Everything but his damn glitchy heart.

Shit, that's what they all needed right now: the sheriff in charge of the town's only murder investigation in over a decade destroying crime-scene evidence by passing out facedown in all that frozen blood.

He took a deep breath in an attempt to clear his spinning head.

"Get up."

"I'm sick," his son moaned.

"Tough." Will reached down and curled his fingers around Josh's upper arm, even as nerves tangled sickly in his own gut. "We have a saying you might not have heard down in la-la land." He jerked his teenage son to his feet, where he swayed like an aspen in a hurricane. "Cowboy up."

He began half-marching, half-dragging him away from the scene. "You have, unfortunately, just become a person of interest. Which in cop speak means we're both up shit creek if you talk to me any more about this situation. So, I'm turning you over to my deputy, who'll take you down to the station."

"I'm going to jail?" Blue eyes looked the size of Frisbees in a complexion as white as new fallen snow.

"You're going in for questioning," Will corrected. "But here's the tricky part."

His fingers dug into Josh's arm, hard enough to make his eyes go even wider. But he did not, Will noticed with a tinge of parental pride, flinch.

"You will also not say a goddamn thing until your lawyer gets there."

"I don't have a lawyer."

"Lucky for you, your father does."

Paula Marshall was an old high school girlfriend. Widowed, with two kids of her own, she was engaged to Lonny Harper, former Evergreen High shortstop who'd returned to town after college and opened up an equine veterinary practice.

"It seems my son may have some information about Erin Gallagher's death," he informed Sam, who'd surreptitiously been watching them while putting away his camera.

"That so?" Will had always prided himself on being damn good at concealing his thoughts; Sam was even better.

"Apparently." Will released Josh's arm. "He's agreed to go down to the station for questioning. But has requested an attorney."

Sam rocked back on his heels. "That so?" he repeated, this time directing the question to Josh.

The father in Will wanted to slug Sam for making that end run around him, for seeing if, just maybe, the kid was naive enough to talk without lawyering up.

Unfortunately, the cop who'd busted that teenage prostitution ring knew he'd do exactly the same thing under similar circumstances.

Josh shot a desperate, what-do-I-do-now? look up at Will. Gone was the pierced, punk rebel who'd been driving him up a wall. In his place was a terrified sixteen-year-old kid. And rightfully so.

"He needs to hear it from you, Son," Will advised.

"Yessir." His Adam's apple bobbed violently as he swallowed. "I want" — his voice cracked — "uh, a lawyer."

"That's your right," Sam agreed mildly.

Although they'd had their problems these past months, Will was good at reading people. Any cop was, since all too often your life depended on it.

Every instinct he possessed told him that Josh would be more likely to sprout wings and go soaring off over the top of White Owl Mountain than kill anyone in cold blood. But by coming here tonight, and making that goddamn statement about having killed the girl, he'd landed himself smack in the middle of a murder investigation, and Will wouldn't be doing his job if he just let his son walk away.

As he watched Sam and Josh head off across the lake toward Sam's rig, Will's heart took another unruly leap and began to wildly clatter against his rib cage.

Making a mental note to have someone bag whatever his son had thrown up — in case they'd have to match it with the contents of the dead girl's stomach — he turned toward the parking lot.

No surprise, the KWIND van hadn't moved.

Having spent so many years undercover, when having his face land on the news could've gotten him killed, Will had never liked reporters. Having to make any kind of deal with them grated even worse.

At least, being from the radio, they didn't have a video camera. Fortunately, Hazard was too small for its own television station, and by the time those vultures from Cheyenne, Casper, and Laramie showed up, he should have the crime scene cleared so Erin Gallagher's parents wouldn't be seeing shots of their murdered daughter's body on their TVs.

Which was, he told himself as he reluctantly headed toward the van, something to be grateful for.

12

What were the odds of the first murder in decades taking place just when Sal Sasone happened to arrive in Hazard?

It had to be a coincidence, Faith assured herself. There was no reason for Sal to have murdered Erin. *She* was the one he'd threatened to kill. She was the one he'd tracked to Hazard.

The ironic thing was if the sheriff had been anyone else, she might have gone to him about Sal being in town. But what could she say, really? That a bounty hunter she'd been hiding from for eighteen months had called the station? Where was the crime in that?

There was also the undeniable fact that she'd broken the law. Several laws, actually. Oh, she may have had a valid reason, but did she really want to get into all that with Will Bridger? Especially right now when the most important thing he should be concentrating on was finding Erin Gallagher's murderer?

He may have lived all those years in the South, but Mr. Tall, Dark, and Arrogant still had the purposeful, long-legged cowboy stride down pat. All he needed to complete the gunslinger image was a pair of pearl-handled Colt revolvers hanging low on his hips.

"If you're waiting around for some live-at-five sound bite, you might as well pack it in," he said.

"What about Josh?" Faith asked, putting thoughts of Sal aside for now. With most of the law enforcement officers in town at the lake, it wasn't as if he'd be able to get away with anything if he did show up. "What's he got to do with all this?"

"I'm not going to comment on an ongoing investigation."

"Is your deputy taking him home?" She paused a beat when Will's brows dove down to a strong blade of a nose she remembered him telling her had been broken during a high school football game. "Or to jail?"

His stony face gave nothing away. But because she was watching him so carefully, and because, like it or not, she seemed to still be tuned into him emotionally, Faith saw the shadow move across his inscrutable eyes.

"It appears Josh may have been the last person, other than the killer, to see the victim alive. Deputy Charbonneaux is going to take his statement."

"Are you saying the boy's a suspect?" Mike asked.

"I'm saying that Deputy Charbonneaux will be taking his statement." From the way Will kept rubbing his chest, Faith suspected he was clearly uncomfortable. "Because of the ongoing investigation, I'd also appreciate you keeping that under your hats until he completes his interview —"

"Interview?" Faith switched into news mode. "Or interrogation?"

The discomfort was instantly replaced with overt irritation. As she'd discovered the hard way, Will Bridger was a man used to calling the shots. Well, wasn't that just too damn bad?

"Interview." He looked annoyed enough to chew nails and spit out staples. "As you may or may not know, the first forty-eight hours is critical in a case like this. I'm sure you wouldn't want to impede the investigation."

"Of course not," Faith agreed quickly. "People need to know if there's a killer on the loose in Hazard, but we can hold back reporting on the interview for the next few hours."

"I appreciate that."

She could tell that admission cost him. Actually, this conversation was costing her, as well.

"I also don't want the victim's name released until we can notify her parents," he said.

"I'm more than willing to give you time to do that. But given that there's nothing in the law that prevents me from going on the air with what I know, it only seems fair that I receive something in return." After all, he owed her.

"Let me guess. You're angling for an exclusive."

"Let's just call it a head start. A bit of lead time that'll allow me to break the story before your press briefing."

He cursed beneath his breath. Rubbed his unshaven chin.

"I'd like to point out that you appear to have a body but no suspect," she said when he didn't immediately respond. "Unless your son fits that category?"

"No." He'd begun rubbing his chest again. "He doesn't."

She glanced over at the two men with Desiree Douchet. "Are those witnesses? Could you share their names?"

"I don't know how it worked in the last place you worked, Ms. Prescott, but here in Hazard, the sheriff's office isn't an information-gathering agency for the press. You're the newshound. Seems you should be able to ferret that information out."

Faith struggled for patience. Blew out a breath.

"When will you be willing to talk with me?"

"Be at my office at eight o'clock. Sharp."

Good move, Faith acknowledged. He undoubtedly knew her show ran from midnight to 4 a.m. For Mike and her to make that interview, they'd either have to stay up all night or get by on less than four hours' sleep.

Well, she'd wanted to get back into news. And, unfortunately, criminals didn't exactly work bankers' hours.

But, as much as she hated to give him credit for anything, Will was right about the forty-eight-hour rule. If the police couldn't crack a case within the first two days after the crime, there was a good chance it would go unsolved.

And Erin deserved better than that.

Her emotions under control again, she

nodded. "Eight o'clock."

He gave her a long, measured look.

Then, without another word, he turned and strode back toward the brightly lit crime scene.

The man watched the events unfold amidst the beehive of activity with interest.

He hadn't expected Sheriff Bridger to be so competent. So totally in charge of both himself and the situation. Gossip around town had him a burned-out head case who'd run back to his hometown like a cowardly dog with his tail between his legs after a cop shooting had gone wrong down in Savannah.

Apparently those rumors were, if not wrong, at least exaggerated.

And wasn't that just interesting?

He'd learned at a young age that the world was divided into two types of individuals. There were predators. And prey.

He'd been born a predator. Surprisingly, it appeared that just perhaps Will Bridger had, as well.

Which, following that line of thought, would make *him* the sheriff's quarry.

Hmm.

That certainly changed the game.

Hunter/quarry.

Predator/prey.

The two were intrinsically entwined. Yin and yang. One couldn't exist without the other.

But, in the end, one of them would die. The other would live.

As he watched the teen vomiting just feet from the lifeless body of the slain girl, the man who'd been raised by wolves smiled.

He'd always loved the hunt.

13

The sheriff's office was located on the second floor of the hundred-year-old courthouse, next door to the fire station. The acrid scent of burning coffee and stale cigarette smoke hit Josh's nostrils and set his gut to churning again the moment he walked in the door.

Earlene Spoonhunter, the night dispatcher, who Josh figured had to be at least as old as the building, glanced up from the afghan she was crocheting. Her eyes, as black and bright as a raven's, gave nothing away.

"The sheriff called," she informed Sam in a flat Western tone as expressionless as her gaze. "Seems a tourist swerved to miss a fool sledder crossing the road, hit some black ice, and ran his rental SUV into a tree. He ended up with a broken arm and some burns from the air bag; Will's taking the guy to the hospital and figured he should be here in about thirty minutes."

"Well, we're sure as hell not going anywhere," Sam said. He opened a side door, gesturing Josh into a small room. "Have a seat, kid. Can I get you something? Maybe some coffee to warm up? Or a can of pop?"

Josh had seen enough cop movies to know the drill. The trick was to bond with the suspect by offering him something to eat or drink. Get him off guard, so he'd spill the beans. The thing was, Josh didn't have any beans to spill.

"I wouldn't turn down a 7UP."

"Don't have any 7UP. How about a Mountain Dew?"

Josh shrugged. "Sure."

"I'll be right back."

The deputy, who made the old lady in front seem outright chatty, shut the door behind him, leaving Josh alone in a room with a brown metal table and four battered wooden chairs that looked as if they'd been retrieved from the Dumpster behind the Salvation Army.

There was a mirror on the wall. Suspecting he was being watched from the other side, Josh slumped down into a chair and, resisting the urge to rub his clammy, cold hands together to warm them, folded his arms across his chest.

He felt the aloneness come crashing down like a huge stone onto his shoulders. Felt the dark weight of it inside him.

He'd always felt alone. Most of the time he'd managed to convince himself he'd gotten used to it. Preferred it. He was also a world-class liar; especially when he was lying to himself.

This wasn't his first time in police custody. He'd been "detained" once for shoplifting a leather L.A. Lakers jacket by the security guard at the Nordstrom South Bay Galleria in Redondo Beach.

A call to that year's stepfather, who was conveniently the managing partner in a Century City law firm, had made the problem disappear, and after receiving an apology from the store manager for the "misunderstanding," Josh had been on his way.

He'd also been picked up a few times in roundups of kids at an after-hours club in Westwood, but none of those times had been anything like this.

This was serious shit. If he didn't manage to convince that stone-faced Indian deputy that he didn't know anything about what had happened to Erin, he could end up in a cell.

Not just a cell. He could go to prison, where motherfucker, baby-raper gang members were just waiting for a shiny new ass to ream.

Fuck. Sweat began to roll down Josh's back.

At the same time he began to shiver, and although he fought against it, trying to clench his jaw, his teeth began to chatter like castanets.

His head was spinning, and although there couldn't be anything left in his stomach, he was hit with a greasy nausea that made him feel on the verge of hurling again.

The last time he'd felt this rotten was after he'd gotten some bad ecstasy at a rave. When he'd started imagining that the other dancers were sharks trying to eat him, the girl he'd been with had gotten scared enough to take him to the hospital, where the ER doctor had stuck a saline drip in his arm. By the next morning the hallucinations were gone and he was feeling okay again.

Josh had the scary feeling that it would take a lot more than fluids and a night's sleep to rid his mind of the images of Erin, covered in her own dark red blood, her pretty white throat cut all the way to the bone.

14

The streets were dark, the storefronts shuttered, as Will drove to the jail after delivering that tourist who'd been injured in the accident to the ER.

Hazard had garnered a bit of fame back during the early seventies, after the movie *Butch Cassidy and the Sundance Kid* had come out. According to legend, Butch and Sundance had enjoyed the pleasures of the working girls at The Shady Lady, one of several Hazard brothels in the booming red-light district.

The outlaws had long gone, as had the gold prospectors and mountain men, but the cowboys and the Indians — the majority of whom lived on the joint-use Shoshone/Arapaho Wind River Reservation — had stayed.

Hazard was surrounded by mountains: the stunningly beautiful Tetons, soaring a mile high of the town; the Wind River Range, which presented some of the most rugged territory in the state; Heartbreak Ridge, curving around the southeast edge of the valley; and towering over everything, its lofty peak often sheathed in clouds, White Owl Mountain, named for the mythical Arapaho bird of winter.

Growing up here, Will had taken the mountains for granted. In fact, there'd been a time he'd thought of them as a prison. Coming home, after years in the Lowcountry, he could appreciate their wonder.

Back when he'd been as young and stupid as Josh, he couldn't wait to escape what he saw as a world of grinding boredom broken up by periods of backbreaking-hard ranch work. Which was why, when that judge had worked out the deal with his father to allow him to avoid going off to juvie, he'd joined the marines.

The irony was that the Corps, in their wisdom, had, for some reason he'd never be able to figure out, decided to make him an MP.

Surprisingly, he'd been good at his job. Good enough to get promoted into criminal investigations as soon as he reached the required age of twenty-one. Although he enjoyed the work, he'd chafed under the rigid military rules and regulations and hadn't reenlisted.

But his talent for chasing down bad guys had gotten him hired by the Savannah police department, where he quickly discovered civilian law enforcement agencies had their own set-in-stone rules and bureaucratic bullshit. After things went south, and Josh landed in his lap, Will had believed that after all these years, and having achieved a small measure of respectability, it wouldn't be that difficult returning to his hometown.

He'd been wrong.

From the moment he'd accepted the job as sheriff, he could feel the weight of the town's expectations, like giant boulders pressing down on his shoulders. He doubted many of the people who'd known him back in the bad old days would've ever expected him to grow up to be the guy in charge of Hazard's laws. He had, after all, been the wild kid, the rebel without a clue who'd gotten drunk, stolen cars, and brawled on Saturday nights.

But never had he landed in any trouble anywhere near like the mess his son might be in.

His son.

Even now the idea seemed almost beyond belief. Weird enough he'd ended up being a cop. But a father? A father was supposed to be the grown-up, the guy in charge, the dad who always knew best and who protected his children against all those dangers lurking outside the safety of their home.

The road to hell was definitely paved with good intentions. Will's reasons for having come back to Hazard were complex, but the bottom line was that Josh's unexpected arrival in Savannah had changed both their lives. He hoped for the better, but unfortunately, that remained to be seen.

If he'd stayed in Savannah, his son wouldn't have met Erin Gallagher. And the kid sure as hell wouldn't have landed himself in the middle of a murder investigation.

Will's fingers tightened on the leather-padded steering wheel. He flexed them. Drew in a deep breath. Let it out again. Drew in another. Inhale. Exhale. Find the center.

Yeah. Right. Like meditation was going to solve this problem.

Josh admittedly had some issues. The kid was angry, confused, and every bit as rebellious as Will himself had once been. And although from what he'd been able to glean from the lawyer, Whitney sounded as if she'd been about as far from June Cleaver as a mom could get, and although Josh refused to discuss it, Will suspected Josh was also grieving for his dead mother. The mother who'd not only neglected to inform Will she'd gotten pregnant, but had, for sixteen years of his life, lied to their son about his real father's identity.

Any kid would have to be majorly pissed. Will sure as hell would've been. But even with all he had going against him, there was no way Josh could harm anyone.

Will knew that. Unfortunately, people tended to believe the worst. Which meant he had to find Erin Gallagher's murderer fast. Before runaway rumors put a scarlet bull's-eye on his kid's back.

Recalling all too well a time when he'd been perceived as Hazard's bad boy, he vowed not to let that happen.

15

"Well? Will you come?"

Staring into the orange and red flames blazing away in the fireplace, the man raised by wolves could see the scene so clearly, it was like watching a movie. One in which he'd played the starring role.

The girl standing in front of him smelled like a tropical garden. Not that he'd ever been to the tropics, but he had not a single doubt that Hawaii would smell exactly like nine-year-old Mandy Longworth.

"Does your mother know you're inviting me?"

"Of course."

Her cheeks, already a deep pink from the bite of the Rocky Mountain winter wind, blushed even deeper. "She said I could ask whoever I wanted."

He'd never been invited to a birthday party. Partly because he'd never fit in with the kind of popular kids who went in for that sort of thing. But mostly because he knew that no parents would want a boy from Muddy Hole — a ramshackle neighborhood of rusting trailers on the wrong side of the tracks, guarded by residents' snarling junkyard dogs — inside their magazine-perfect homes.

"Bet you invited everyone."

"I always invite the entire class."

"Back in Texas." Her father, a big shot at Odessa Oil, had transferred his family here from Dallas. "Where you went to some fancy private school."

She tossed her blond head. "If you're calling me a snob, you're just stupid and you don't have to come to my party if you don't want to."

"I didn't say that." He wasn't used to girls talking back to him. He wasn't used to girls talking to him, period.

"Then you'll come?" She held out the invitation again. When she touched his sleeve with a fluffy white mitten that matched the trim on her hood, he felt a fist gripping inside his chest.

"Sure." He shrugged. "Unless something comes up."

The dimple in her cheek flashed and her cornflower blue eyes brightened, as if someone had turned a lightbulb on inside her.

"That's great."

A woman across the parking lot began calling her name. Shit. If he'd had his stepfather's pistol, he would have shot the bitch.

"That's my mama." She waved. The woman waved back, her smile a twin of her daughter's. "I'd better go. I have a ballet lesson this afternoon."

Halfway to the black Suburban, she turned back. "You don't have to bring a present. Like Mama always says, having a birthday at Christmas just means I get too many gifts all at once, anyway. It's the company that's important."

"If I come, I'm going to bring a damn present."

Her eyes widened a bit at the cuss word. But she didn't argue.

"Whatever you want." She flashed him another smile, then raced off toward the car.

He'd filched a charm bracelet from the Mountain Mercantile. Her mother's blond brows had lifted suspiciously at the gift, which she'd probably figured he hadn't been able to afford. And she'd been right. But he was glad he'd taken the risk because everyone else had brought birthday presents.

She'd thanked him and held out her thin,

white arm, like a princess inviting a serf to put it on her wrist. But the minute his fingers had brushed against that silky, white flesh, they'd turned as thick and useless as sausage. While the other kids laughed as he fumbled with the clasp, he'd imagined pouring gasoline on them, setting them on fire, imagined their flesh burning and those stuck-up expressions melting off their faces.

Their scorn infuriated. But not as badly as the pity on Mandy Longworth's face.

Don't think about that! He drew in a deep breath. Let it out. Closed his eyes and focused on a more appealing memory of the day.

Desire stirred deep in his groin as he recalled Mandy's joy when her parents handed her a fluffy, white kitten. Its slanted eyes had been bright blue, its button nose pink, and it was wearing a silver bell on a red ribbon around its neck. The cat, which she named Snowball, spent the rest of the party curled up in Mandy's lap, blissfully purring like a small motor.

It hadn't been purring two weeks later, when he'd taken a razor and shaved off its soft white fur.

Or when he'd pelted it with a steaming-hot shower.

The kitten's mewling cries had been like

electric wires running beneath his skin, creating a surge of energy like nothing he'd ever before experienced.

With power singing in his blood, he'd taken the wet and blistered animal out into the woods behind Muddy Hole, where he'd tied it to a tree with brown twine.

Although hunting season was over, there was always a chance some cross-country skier or poacher might hear the animal's shrieks, so he'd stuffed a sock down its throat. Then taken his stepfather's bow from its black leather case.

He hadn't been a very good archer, but the fifth shot had proven the charm.

All it took was the memory of that feather-tipped arrow pinning the cat's body to the trunk of the towering Douglas fir tree to make him hard.

He unzipped his jeans. Took out his cock and began stroking himself as he remembered pretty little Mandy Longworth's red-rimmed eyes when she'd come to school after finding the kitten's skeleton strewn over her backyard. They'd known it was Snowball because of the filthy red ribbon and bell still tied around its neck.

Coyotes had been the general consensus.

Packs of wild dogs another popular choice.

But from the way Mrs. Longworth had

stared hard at him the next time she'd picked up Mandy at school, he'd had the feeling the rich bitch suspected the truth.

But suspecting wasn't knowing. And knowing wasn't proving.

Still, it wasn't long after that holiday birthday party that the Longworths' house was put back up for sale and the family moved back to Texas.

Mandy Longworth's Christmas kitten was the first life he'd taken. A great many animals and humans had died by his hand since that memorable day. The lovely young skater, who'd reminded him in so many ways of Mandy, was only the most recent.

But not the last. As he ejaculated on a surge of hot pleasure, the man who was once the boy raised by wolves was already imagining his next kill.

16

Although he'd been in what deputy Trace Honeycutt insisted on calling The Box countless times, watching Sam question his son turned out to be the worst experience of Will's life. Even worse than getting shot.

And it damn well hadn't been easy on Josh.

It was nearly four in the morning by the time they left the station. The ashen green had faded from Josh's face, leaving his complexion as white as bone. His eyes were swollen and red-rimmed and he stank of fear, sweat, vomit, and beer.

At any other time, Will would want to know where in town two underage kids had gotten their hands on booze. But right now, that was the least of his concerns.

If Josh was to be believed, and Will did, Erin Gallagher had been at the mini-mart when he'd stopped to get gas around nine thirty. She'd invited him back to her apartment, and like any other sixteen-year-old boy on the planet would've done, Josh had accepted. They'd had sex, ordered out for pizza, watched a video, drunk some beer. Had another round of sex. After which, Josh had proven himself to be a typical male by falling asleep.

When he'd awakened, she'd already left the apartment for the lake.

"You doing all right?" Will asked as they drove the darkened road leading out of town to the ranch he'd grown up on.

"Oh, yeah. I'm just fuckin' fantastic."

Will decided this wasn't the time for a lecture about language.

"It's not your fault."

"Yeah. Shit happens, right?"

"Sometimes clichés are true." Hadn't he told himself that time and time again after the shooting?

"Well, that one's fucking goddamn original. Maybe you oughtta put it on a bumper sticker. You'd probably sell millions. Maybe even enough to buy a house somewhere in California, or Hawaii. Get out of this shit-hole."

"Sarcasm's good. At least it's better than wallowing in guilt."

Josh folded his arms across his chest. "I don't want to talk about it, okay?"

"Actually, I don't want to talk about it, either. Since we're in a really weird father/son/law-enforcement place. I'm not sure of the legalities, having never been in this situation before, but if you were to tell me something that might help me solve Erin Gallagher's murder, even if it might complicate our relationship, I wouldn't be able to ignore it."

Josh was staring out the passenger window, at the mountains looming over the valley. "Like we have any relationship."

"Sure we do."

That drew a sharp look.

"It may be a fucked-up, shitty one. But you gotta admit it's a helluva lot more of a father-son relationship than we had this time last year."

"You didn't even know I existed this time last year."

"My point exactly. And it's something you might want to keep in mind next time you find yourself getting pissed off at me for not having been around to go to your soccer games."

"I don't play soccer."

"Neither do I. Which, I suppose means, as distasteful as the idea is, that you've got something in common with your old man after all."

Josh didn't respond. But Will had been a cop long enough to know that his son was thinking about that.

He'd shut his eyes tight, as if trying to block out the sight of Erin Gallagher's mutilated body.

Unfortunately, Will knew all too well that the horrific images had been scorched onto the teen's brain and would probably haunt him for the rest of his life, popping up when he'd least expect them, bringing back this night he'd undoubtedly give anything to forget.

"If you'd gone out to the lake earlier, you could've been killed as well."

"Like anyone would give a shit."

Why didn't the kid just take Will's Glock and shoot him through the heart. Christ, hadn't he changed his entire life for his son? What the hell else could he do to prove he was trying his damnedest to be a good father?

"I'd care. So would your grandfather."

Again, nothing.

"I didn't kill Erin," Josh said after they'd gone another quarter mile. "I know I said I did, when I saw her body, but I didn't mean I'm the one who cut her throat."

"I never, for a single second, thought you were."

"You going to catch the bastard who did it?"

Will nodded. Firmly. Resolutely. "You bet."

It was Josh's turn to nod. "Good. Then you can shoot him. Beginning with his balls, then working out from there."

"Unfortunately, it doesn't work that way," Will said. "But believe me, Son, we're in perfect agreement about wishing it did."

17

Going right back on the air, knowing that Erin was zipped into some ugly black police body bag, undoubtedly on her way to Jackson, since Faith guessed Hazard wouldn't have the forensics necessary for a serious autopsy, had been one of the most difficult things she'd ever done.

Each time she'd dodged a caller's question, she'd wanted to break down and weep.

If that wasn't bad enough for her nerves, she kept waiting for Sal to call again. Or worse yet, to show up at the station, armed to the teeth, prepared to shoot anyone who got in his way.

But he did neither, and the only calls were from listeners wanting to know what had happened out at the lake. Keeping to her agreement with Will, Faith merely revealed that a body had been discovered by two sledders, that the sheriff was conducting an investigation and would be holding a press conference in the morning.

Fortunately, the audience tended to drop off in the last hour of the show, allowing her to mostly play music and watch out the window for headlights.

Which, thank God, never appeared.

Having hated the way she'd allowed Sal to control not just her life, but her emotions, Faith had been determined never to let anyone frighten her again. Nevertheless, she wasn't about to protest when Mike insisted on following her home, as he had every night since she'd begun working at KWIND.

He waited in front of her rented house while she pulled her Explorer into the garage and unlocked the kitchen door. She was probably the only person in Hazard to bother to lock her doors, but she'd lived too long in cities to be able to just walk out the door and leave her home open to anyone passing by who might decide to wander in and steal her stuff.

Not that she had anything worth stealing. In fact, the only pieces of furniture in the house were a sofa, a bed, a chest of drawers, a kitchen table, and four wooden chairs she'd found at Grannie's Attic Antiques down on Main Street. But for her they signified a major lifestyle change since they were the first she'd ever owned.

The diesel engine on Mike's old pickup truck clattered as he continued to idle, giving her time to get inside her house, waiting until the garage door rumbled back down again.

Then, with a little toot of his horn, he was gone.

Normally, when she arrived home from work, she'd make a cup of tea and settle down with a book for an hour or so to unwind before going to sleep.

Unfortunately, the past few hours had been anything but normal. Going from room to room, she closed the draperies and made sure all the windows were locked.

From her early years with her mother, to another two years spent in the revolving door of Texas's foster care system — which she'd escaped by merely walking away one day when she was fifteen, only to end up living on the streets — Faith had been a gypsy all her life.

But, dammit, from the time she'd first arrived in Wyoming, she'd felt a little internal click, as if she might just possibly belong in Hazard. That the town was a place she could belong. A place she'd fit in. A place she could call home.

Although this three-bedroom house was much more than she needed, she'd actually been considering taking her landlord up on his offer of a buy/lease deal. The problem, of course, was that Faith *Prescott* didn't have any credit record, which made applying for a loan impossible. And she'd been afraid that using her real name could create a paperwork trail for Sal to follow.

Perhaps he'd changed.

That'd be the day.

"Better tell Bridger to be on the lookout for four horsemen riding down the streets of Hazard," she muttered. "Because if Sal Sasone has decided to stop trying to control his world and everyone in it, it's a sure sign of the Apocalypse."

It was nearly five o'clock. In the summer a pale predawn light would be shimmering on the horizon. This time of year, and thanks to the heavy cloud that had drifted across the moon, the hour was the darkest time of the morning when she pulled aside the curtain just enough to look out the bedroom window.

In the distance, she could see the glow of the lights across Silver Lake, revealing that someone was still working the crime scene. On this side of the lake, it was like trying to see into the depths of a deep, black well.

Was he out there? Watching? Waiting?

No. Lurking outside a house in the dark,

especially in the cold — which everyone knew Sal hated almost as badly as liberal Democrats — was not his style.

Or at least it hadn't been. He'd always been much more up-front, more in-your-face. The last time she'd seen him, he'd been angry, drunk, and dangerous.

Beyond dangerous. He'd been deadly.

Eighteen months was a long time. If he'd continued his downhill slide into alcoholism, no telling how worse his paranoia and possessiveness might have gotten.

Fear skimmed its cold, bony fingers up her spine and wrapped around her heart as she retrieved a suitcase and a large red leather bag from the back of the closet.

The bag held a heavy Colt revolver that, ironically, she'd received from the very same man who'd tracked her to Wyoming.

She put the ugly gun on the mattress, within reach. After making sure her boots, parka, gloves, and keys were close by, Faith began yanking clothes from the chest, which just yesterday she'd allowed herself to have the foolishly optimistic idea of refinishing.

18

Josh had decided things couldn't get much worse. Until he walked into the sprawling, old log house and saw his grandfather sitting at the table, steam rising from a thick mug.

"'Bout time you boys got home," he said. "I fixed some steak and eggs. They're in the oven."

"I'm not hungry." The thought of food roiled Josh's empty stomach.

"You're gonna want some food in your belly," Jim Bridger said. "A body needs fuel to work."

Josh just wanted to go to bed. And sleep until spring. Or at least until he turned eighteen and could escape this dead-end town.

Star Trek had it wrong. Wyoming was the final frontier.

"I'll eat later." Maybe by March he'd be able to choke something down.

"You'll eat now." Josh's grandfather pushed himself out of the chair and grabbed a dish towel from the wooden counter and took a platter from the oven. "We've got to get going."

"Going?" Josh looked over at his father, who was hanging his jacket on the peg by the door. "Where?"

"With the wind having stopped, this snow's just gonna keep on falling, instead of moving east. So, we'd best make sure we've got lots of feed out for the stock, before the roads close down." Jim put the plate in front of Josh. "We'll be gone a couple a days," he told Will.

The look the two men exchanged told Josh they'd already discussed this. Without — no surprise here — giving him any choice.

"You just want to get me out of town so I can't talk to reporters."

"I'm sorry." Will poured a cup of the thick, black sludge that bore no resemblance to the Starbucks Josh was used to in L.A. "Did you want to talk to reporters?"

"Hell, no."

"Well, then," Jim drawled, "there you go."

"But I don't want to run away, either."

That was a lie. He did want to run. As fast and as far as he could. All the way back to California. Better yet, down to Mexico.

"You're not gonna be runnin' anywhere," his grandfather agreed brusquely. "You'll be doing ranch work that needs to be done. I figure after we get the hay tossed out, we'll ride the fence line a ways, checking for breaks. A cow fall into a gulley this time a year, we won't find her till spring. Which'll be too damn late."

"I don't know anything about fixing fences." Josh had, however, been surprised to discover he actually had a knack for riding horses.

"'Bout time you learned. Like I always used to tell your father, boys are like dogs and horses. Ain't worth a damn if they're not being used."

"I haven't been to bed yet."

The old man arched a silver brow. "That's not what I heard."

Josh shot a look at Will. "You had no right telling my private stuff."

"Nothing's private when you're talking about a murder. Besides, it's not like I wrote it up on a press release and gave it to Faith Prescott to read on the radio. Whether you like it or not, whether you'll even admit it or not, you, your grandfather, and I are a family. And family doesn't keep secrets."

Josh snorted. "Like you don't have secrets."

"None that involve you."

"Oh, no?" Josh welcomed the temper he felt beginning to heat up in his gut. It beat the hell out of the sick, greasy cold he'd been feeling. "What about whatever the hell happened down in Savannah? Whatever it was that had you dragging me up here to Sticksville?"

"Eat," the older man said firmly, cutting off any further discussion. "You can sleep in the truck."

To his son he said, "Sam called from over at the Gallagher girl's apartment. Said he found an address book, but he couldn't find any listing of her parents."

"That's because she doesn't talk to them," Josh volunteered grumpily. *"Didn't* talk to them," he corrected.

It was still hard to think of Erin in the past tense. How could that be? He'd been warm and mindless inside her, just a few hours ago. He wondered if he'd ever get used to the idea of her being gone. His father might know. As a cop, he undoubtedly knew a lot about people dying. But Josh was damned if he'd ask.

"Why not?" Will asked.

"Because she hated them."

And I know just how she felt. He didn't say the words, but they hung in the air just the same.

"They should be on her school admission records," Will said. He started to leave the room, then turned. "That was a damn good interview you gave to Deputy Charbonneaux. Straightforward, and you stuck to the facts. He cowboyed up real good," Will informed his father.

Jim Bridger nodded. "Doesn't surprise me in the least. He might not have been raised up in the West —"

"California's as far west as you can get," Josh broke in.

"California's the coast," Jim corrected. "The *Left* Coast. I wouldn't let it into the West with a search warrant. . . . But, like I was saying before I was interrupted," he continued, turning back to his son, "our boy comes from good stock."

Our boy. Made him sound like a colt he was considering buying. Or a yearling he was planning to auction off.

Josh was still thinking about that idea twenty minutes later, as he and his grandfather drove down the mountain.

"People aren't cattle," he said.

"Now there's a newsflash," Jim said drily. "Maybe we ought to pull over so I can get out a pen and paper and write it down."

"I just meant that just because a guy fucks a woman and accidentally makes a kid, it doesn't mean that kid will grow up to be anything like him."

"The old nature-versus-nurture argument." Jim nodded. "As a father, I like to think that I had some influence over my son. And I've got a strong enough ego to be damn proud of how he turned out. Though I've gotta admit, back when he was your age, trying to have any kind of conversation with him was a lot like bull riding."

Josh didn't want to bite. But, after a lengthy pause stretched between them, he couldn't resist asking.

"Why?"

"Because I was damn lucky if it lasted eight seconds. Shoot, that boy had a flash-fire temper."

"My father?"

"The very same. Of course, at the time, I was younger and a lot more hotheaded, too. I'm mellowed some since then. And we were both having trouble dealing with the loss of Will's brother right on top of his mother dying of cancer."

"I had an uncle?"

Josh had been given sketchy information about his grandmother's death when he'd asked about a framed photograph on the wall in the den. But no mention had been made of another son.

"He died before you were born. Rolled the truck he was driving over when he was fourteen."

"He wouldn't have been old enough to have a license."

"Like you never drove illegally before you got your license?"

"Maybe." Josh decided there was no need to mention running his mother's Jag off the Coast Highway when he'd been fourteen.

Jim reached into his shirt pocket, pulled out a pack of cigarettes, lipped one out of the red-and-white hard pack, and punched the lighter on the dash.

"He and your dad were coming back from the feedstore. Matt, that was his name, was about a week out from getting his permit. Like most kids in this part of the country, he'd driven off road around the ranch before, but he'd never been on the public road.

"From day one, he was always trying to keep up with his big brother, had to try to do every damn thing Will did. That day he had himself a yen to try real drivin'. It was a dry road without a lot of bends, so Will — who would've been sixteen at the time —

let him take the wheel."

The lighter popped out. Josh had never claimed to be the most sensitive guy on the planet, but he suspected, from the way the old man was taking his time lighting that cigarette, that the subject of his younger son's death was still painful.

"Things were going along okay for a while," Jim said on a stream of exhaled smoke. "Then he took a curve too tight, overcorrected, and rolled the rig. Your dad got thrown clear."

He drew in on the cigarette again. "Matt wasn't that lucky. Got himself stuck in the cab with the roof smashed down on him and the engine block clean into the front seat on top of his lap.

"Will broke his shoulder and two ribs, but he managed to hike the five miles back to town to get help for his brother. Took the rescue guys another hour with the Jaws of Life to cut Matt out. Doc said he probably died instantly."

"Jesus." All Josh had done was smash a fender and break an axle. "That blows."

"Wouldn't argue that," Jim Bridger agreed around the burning cigarette clamped tightly between his teeth.

"Your dad wouldn't talk about it, still doesn't that I know of, but I figure he took it pretty hard, especially comin' on top of having lost his mother, because it was right about then he got wild. Started getting into all kinds of fool trouble."

"Mr. Law and Order wasn't always a Boy Scout?" That was as much a revelation as that he'd had an uncle who'd died. Especially given the fight they'd had yesterday after his father had found the roach clip he'd forgotten to take out of his jeans pocket before throwing them in the hamper.

Jim snorted. "Not by a long shot. I probably wasn't the best father back then, what with all that had happened, and my generation didn't believe in talkin' stuff to death the way folks seem to these days. Plus, we'd been having a drought, which led to some real lean times with the ranch, but even if none of that had happened, it might not have made all that much of a difference.

"Like Paul Newman said in that movie, *Road to Perdition,* it's a natural law. Sons are put on this earth to trouble their fathers."

He slanted Josh a look. "Seems you're doing a bang-up job of that, Son."

"My mother got married six times."

Even to his own ears, that sounded like a whiny-kid excuse. Though it was fact. Whitney of the half dozen last names had clawed her way up L.A.'s social ladder, discarding husbands the way she'd kick off her shoes when she walked in the door.

"I never paid any attention to her husbands, since I knew they'd be gone. But I sure as hell never thought I'd end up with a cowboy cop for a father."

"When you were a little kid, you might not've thought you'd grow hair on your crotch, either," Jim drawled. "But there you are."

Since Josh could think of no response to that typical Jim Bridger comment, he fell silent, watching the white snow drifting down from the sky illuminated by the beam of the truck's headlights.

By dying in that plane crash in the Andes on a flight back to the States from Rio, his mother had left her lawyer to clean up the mess, the same way the maids had been forced to pick up her Manolos.

Josh rubbed the pad of his thumb along the crease etching its way across his forehead. The same one that had been the first thing he'd noticed about his father.

For the first time since he'd been dragged to Savannah and dumped on Will Bridger, he thought about him having lost both a mother and a brother when he was about the same age Josh was now.

And wondered if, just maybe, he and his

father might have more in common than their physical resemblance.

19

The sound of someone pounding on the door jolted Faith from a light sleep.

Damn. She'd drifted off. And now it looked as if Sal had finally caught up with her. Unfortunately, the landlord still hadn't made it out to the house to put the peephole in the door.

"Faith?" the deep voice called out. "Open the damn door!"

Not Sal at all. Relief was short-lived by the idea that it was Will Bridger standing on her porch. What the hell was he doing here?

From the way he was pounding, she knew he had no plans of going away, so she opened the door.

He was standing in the spreading yellow glow of the porch light, arm upraised as if to hit the door again, his deep scowl carving those horizontal lines in his forehead. "Are you okay?"

"Of course." Or as good as a woman could

be who'd just been at a murder scene and had an armed and vengeful bounty hunter after her.

"You always answer the door holding a cannon?"

"It's not a cannon. It's a Colt .45."

"Yeah, I noticed that right off. If you're looking to run off the Fuller Brush man, that should fit the bill."

"Given that I'm out in the woods, less than a quarter mile from a murder scene, and there's a killer on the loose, I'll admit to being a bit nervous."

"So you went out and bought yourself a revolver in the middle of the night?"

"Actually, I already had it. It was a gift."

"Yeah, why get a woman chocolates or flowers when you can buy her a weapon?"

She shrugged, refusing to get into specifics with him. "Is there a reason you were attempting to break my door down?"

"I rang the bell. Several times, as a matter of fact."

"It doesn't work. The landlord has promised to take care of it but hasn't made it out here yet. But surely you've more important things to do than go around to people's houses and test doorbells."

"You're right. I do." He folded his arms across his chest in a way that was far more cop than the gazillionaire international businessman she'd once believed him to be. "And we're wasting time here. Are you going to invite me in?"

He glanced past her into the living room, pricking some small bit of feminine pride that had her wishing she'd at least managed to get more of those damn moving boxes unpacked. "Or does KWIND pay you so much you can afford to heat the great outdoors?"

"My heat is my business." Could she sound any more petulant? What was it about this man that always had her behaving so damn uncharacteristically? "And I'd rather you just go away."

"Sorry. That's not going to happen. I happen to be sheriff. And this is, after all, my hometown."

"How can I even be sure you are a real sheriff?" Of course he was, but as stressed-out and exhausted as she was, Faith couldn't resist the dig.

"Dammit, Faith." He plowed a hand through his dark hair.

"And it may be your hometown, but I was here first." She suddenly had a mental image of two toddlers, glaring at each other across a sandbox.

"Oh, hell." She moved aside. "You may as

well come on in." She had, after all, had three years to get over him. She could handle being alone in her house with the man.

"Since you asked so nicely, I believe I will." He stamped the snow off his boots. Glanced around the room. "You moving in? Or out?"

"I haven't gotten around to unpacking yet," she hedged. That much was true. There was no point in telling him she was about to leave not only this house, but Hazard. "What are you doing here?"

"Something occurred to me. About your parka."

She glanced over at the white, hooded jacket hanging on the hook by the door. "What about it?"

"It's the same as the one Erin Gallagher was wearing."

"That's not surprising. The store was having a sale and had marked the rack of these down to sixty percent off. Apparently white doesn't sell very well here. Why?"

"What if she was mistaken for the actual target?"

"What do you mean? If it wasn't her, then who else . . ." Faith could feel the blood drain from her face. "You can't be suggesting that whoever killed Erin might have actually been after me?"

"It's just a hypothesis. But you *are* the closest house to the lake. You do own a jacket identical to the murder victim's. If someone had come out here to harm you, he could've confused her for you. Is there anyone you can think of who might want to harm you?"

"No," she said quickly. Too quickly, she realized when those familiar deep lines creased his brow again.

"You sure about that?"

"Absolutely positive."

"No stalker types or deep breathers who get off on you talking dirty on the radio?"

That hit too close to home.

Tell him, both her conscience and her common sense advised.

Assuring herself that Sal wasn't a danger to anyone but her, and not wanting to share her private life with a man who'd already proven himself untrustworthy, Faith decided to bluff and arched a brow.

"You must have me confused with someone else, Sheriff. I'd never talk dirty on the air. Even if it wasn't a personal choice, the FCC doesn't allow it."

"Maybe you don't say the actual words. But your smoky voice drifting out of the radio in the dark, inviting listeners to spend the night with you, undoubtedly has a lot of men around here conjuring up some pretty down and dirty thoughts."

Of all the things he might have said to her, Faith certainly hadn't expected that! Could he actually have been sitting alone in the dark (in bed?) listening to *Talking After Midnight* and thinking dirty thoughts?

An image of Will sitting up in bed after making love flashed through her mind. They were both naked, and he was feeding her an impossibly sweet, ripe Georgia peach, and afterward, he'd licked the juice off her breasts, which had led to . . .

No, dammit! Faith ruthlessly cut off the low, unbidden, and definitely unwanted sexual awareness the memory instilled.

"Well, if you're here hoping to turn those dirty thoughts into a reality, you're flat out of luck, Sheriff. Because it so isn't going to happen."

He tilted his head back and looked up at the ceiling, as if seeking strength from some higher power. Or perhaps he was just checking out the water stain from when some previous tenant had apparently allowed the tub in the second-floor bathtub to overflow.

"You're not going to make this easy on me, are you?"

It was her turn to fold her arms. "Why should I?"

"How about because I care about you."

"And I should believe that why?"

His muttered curse was cruder than any she'd ever heard, even during those teenage years she'd been living on the streets. And far worse than she'd ever heard from him.

Then again, when she'd made the huge mistake of falling in love with this man, he'd been William Prescott Wyatt, a man who could outsuave Pierce Brosnan or even Cary Grant.

"Look." His dark hand, which had once been intimately familiar with every erogenous spot on her body — including several she hadn't even realized she'd possessed — swiped through his hair again. While it wasn't a typical cop buzz cut, it was still shorter than it had been back when it had felt like black silk against her heated flesh. "Why don't you make some coffee? If we're both going to be living here in Hazard, we have to settle this once and for all."

He had a point. But she wasn't feeling the least bit reasonable.

"I'm not a short-order cook. If you want coffee, either go home and make it yourself or see if you can sweet-talk Hannah Long into opening up The Branding Iron café and making you some. And it only needs settling if one of us has a problem. I certainly don't. And if you do, I suggest you get over it."

His black brows came together in a rough, almost menacing way. *Almost* because she'd been intimidated by much more dangerous individuals. "You didn't used to be this hard."

The irony was that she'd been far tougher than he could ever imagine and had, for the first time in her life, allowed herself to be soft with him. "Maybe you weren't the only one pretending to be someone you weren't," she said with blatantly mock sweetness.

Instead of coming back with some smart-ass answer, he merely shook his head. His shoulders slumped as if he had the weight of the world crushing down on them.

Maybe not the world. But he was definitely carrying the entire town on those wide, manly shoulders. Although she hadn't wanted to so much as acknowledge his existence, it had not escaped her notice that small-town lawmen were expected to handle everything from barking dogs to barroom disputes to citizens angry about parking violations to the more serious issues such as domestic abuse and drunk drivers.

Yet here he was, trying to find a cold-blooded murderer, and she was stuck in a feminine-pique mode.

"I'm sorry." She meant it. "You have a great deal more to be concerned about than something that happened so long ago. I'd honestly forgotten all about it."

"Now who's the liar?"

There was both humor and what appeared to be sadness in his heavily lidded eyes, making her wonder if just possibly he regretted what had happened as much as she did. Well, probably not as much. But at least somewhat.

It would certainly be more than she'd been giving him credit for these past three years. Not that she ever thought about him all that much.

Okay. So they were both liars. And wasn't she even worse, for lying to herself?

"I made some coffee to warm up when I got home," she said. The truth was she'd made it to keep awake on the drive out of town. "Since you won't go away, you may as well have a cup."

20

Will hung his heavy jacket on the hook next to hers, then followed her, weaving the narrow path between the boxes, to the kitchen and sat down at the table while she poured the hazelnut-flavored coffee into two thick earthenware mugs.

"Thanks," he said as she placed one of the mugs in front of him.

She had no idea if he was thanking her for the coffee, or for agreeing to talk with him about their rocky past. Which wasn't going to happen if she could help it.

"You're welcome."

"There's something I don't understand," he said with a dogged cop's persistence. "If you'd forgotten all about me, why did you move to my hometown?"

She remained standing, keeping the kitchen island between them. "I don't suppose you'd believe I threw a dart at a map and it just coincidentally hit this spot in

Wyoming?"

"Of all the towns on all the maps in all the world, you just happen to settle down in mine?" He took a drink, then shook his head. "Sorry, sweetheart, I don't think so."

"Don't call me *sweetheart.*" He'd lost that right on a steamy night three years ago when the joint FBI and Savannah police force had come bursting into her town house with guns drawn. "And how was I suppose to know this actually was your hometown? Given everything else you lied about?"

"Okay, I'll give you that point. But it's interesting you chose my middle name as your last name."

"Prescott wasn't your real middle name. Your name, which I belatedly discovered when I was subpoenaed to testify against my employer, just happens to be William James Bridger."

"Well, that makes one of us who knows who the other person really is. You were," he reminded her needlessly, "Faith Summers when you were in Savannah."

"Radio personalities often use on-air names." That was the truth. "Sometimes a station will even require it." Another true statement. She was on a roll here.

"So that's the reason for the phony name

in Savannah?"

"Yes." Okay, that was a huge hedge. Faith Summers hadn't had a police record.

"Still, it seems to me I wasn't the only one holding back information," he argued. "At least in my case, I had a good reason. I was trying to bring down a guy trafficking in women being brought into the port of Savannah, then sold to prostitution rings up and down the Eastern seaboard."

"And you actually thought I was involved in that sex slavery ring?"

"Never." He said it firmly enough that she believed him. "Not even in the beginning. But you'd left broadcasting to work as a press spokesperson on a congressional campaign for the guy who happened to be the one clearing the way for those women's work permits to be approved.

"The Feds had two dead Ukrainian girls who'd floated up onto the coast. All the evidence pointed to them having been killed, then thrown off a ship coming into the port of Savannah. We were talking life or death, dammit, and when the trail led to your boss, I was willing to do whatever the hell it took to link the bastard to that ship."

"Whatever it took, including sleeping with me for information." That idea still grated. No, not *grated,* hurt.

"Hell, no." He was on his feet, towering over her. "Dammit, Faith, if you'd only let me explain —"

"That would've been difficult, since, as a witness, I was under court order not to speak with you."

"You also left town right after your testimony."

"It's hard to report the news after becoming the lead story for weeks. The station management agreed that it'd be best if I didn't return to work."

"They weren't the only station in the city."

No way was she prepared to admit staying in the same city as the man who'd broken her heart would've been too painful. Not to mention humiliating.

"Although we both know I didn't give you any information, thanks to having slept with you, I'd lost my credibility."

"Okay. I can buy that. And I'm damn sorry for costing you your job." He took another drink. "Great coffee, by the way."

"Thank you." Faith did not trust that easygoing tone. Actually, she wasn't sure she could trust anything about Will Bridger.

"I suppose you know that you can locate just about anyone on the internet these days."

Her stomach pitched. "So I've heard."

He locked his arms behind his head, causing the muscles of his upper arms to swell against the sleeves of his khaki uniform shirt.

"I did some Googling a couple weeks ago and guess what?"

"What?" She could see it coming. Like a bullet straight at her.

"Faith Prescott didn't exist until she hit Hazard and began working at KWIND," he said.

Uncomfortably aware of the sharp intelligence lurking in those midnight dark eyes, it was all Faith could do not to squirm beneath his unwavering gaze.

Focus! she instructed herself firmly.

"I've already explained that. Radio personalities —"

"Use different names in different markets," he said. "I get that. What I don't understand is why it's the only name the station has for you. Your checks are written to Faith Prescott, which means your taxes are being withheld under that same name. But the thing is, sweetheart, you don't exist."

She'd known, from the way he'd worked with the Feds to break up the sexual trafficking case, that Will Bridger was a clever, dogged, even, at times, driven cop. What she hadn't expected was that he'd have any reason to turn all those investigative energies toward her.

Hell. She should just have left town when he first showed up.

Refusing to flinch under his gunslinger's glint, she decided to play the offended-dignity card.

"I'd think, what with all you have on your plate right now, Sheriff, that looking up the background of a small-town radio talk-show host would be rather low down on your priorities."

Still stalling while she tried to figure out how to handle this, she took a sip of her own coffee. "Unless for some inexplicable reason you've decided I'm a suspect in Erin Gallagher's murder?"

"I don't remembering telling you the girl was murdered."

"Actually, you haven't told me anything. Yet."

"Like I said, I prefer knowing who I'm dealing with before I start giving away case information."

He wasn't going to budge. And she had the feeling that if she didn't give him something in return, she wouldn't get her exclusive. Which wasn't an issue any longer, since she was leaving town as soon as she could get rid of him.

At least she'd been planning to leave.

But as she glanced around the cozy kitchen with its wooden countertops, bright blue cabinets, and hammered-tin ceiling, she remembered how, despite all the work needed on it, she'd fallen in love with this house from the moment she'd walked into the door.

And even if she hadn't begun to put down roots, unlike when she'd escaped Nevada in the middle of the night, Faith decided that she was sick and tired of running. Of always looking back over her shoulder. Of never having any kind of real life.

It was time — past time — to take a stand.

"Is there a point to this line of questioning? Some reason you've decided to submit me to the third degree?" She tilted her head. Met his gaze straight on. "Am I a suspect? Can I expect you to bring out the blinding lights and rubber hoses next?"

"You don't have to worry. The Supreme Court says we can't use them anymore."

"More's the pity."

"Yeah. That's pretty much the way I see it." Despite the gravity of the topic, he sounded almost amused. "And, for the record, of course you're not a murder suspect."

"So it was murder?"

"You figured that out for yourself back at the lake. Someone slit her throat."

Faith gasped and unconsciously lifted her hand to her own throat.

He rubbed his jaw and studied her. "How well did you know the Gallagher girl?"

"I told you, we chatted every so often when she was at the station. Obviously, given that we never discussed her scars, we weren't close enough for her to share secrets, but I do know she was determined to make a new start."

"Eighteen's a bit young to feel the need to start over."

"Perhaps it's a different situation when the first seventeen years of your life was totally run by others."

And didn't Faith know something about that? Susan Gallagher and the woman who'd given birth to Faith were so economically and socially apart they could have lived on different planets. But both had used their daughters for their own selfish gains.

"And not all of us have our futures all planned out when we're still in our teens," she said.

He pursed his lips. Seemed to consider that. "How about you?"

"How about me, what?"

"Were you a late bloomer?"

"Absolutely." And wasn't that the understatement of the year? "And I fail to see how my past is at all germane to your investigation."

He jerked a shoulder. "You never know what's germane. Any crime investigation is like a jigsaw puzzle. You put a piece in there, another one here, keep working it, and eventually you're looking at the whole picture. . . .

"Did she ever mention any boyfriends?"

"No. Why?"

"Because Josh said she'd mentioned a guy. She didn't go into details, but he got the impression he was a lot older."

Faith shook her head. "She never said anything to me."

"Okay. Maybe some of her friends will know. Before coming over here, I called the dean of the school, who went online and checked Erin Gallagher's registration records. Turns out she listed false contact addresses and phone numbers for both her parents. I don't suppose you know where I could reach them?"

"Her father's remarried. He lives back East somewhere with his new family. Massachusetts, Pennsylvania." Faith shook her head. "I can't remember which. But I got the impression they weren't close."

"And her mother?"

"She's dead."

When he blinked, slowly, Faith realized that she'd managed to surprise him, which she suspected wasn't easy to do.

"You sure about that?"

"I'm sure that's what she told me." Faith hesitated and gave his question a moment's more thought. "I never saw a death certificate, but I didn't have any reason not to believe her."

"Girl hacking up her wrists suggests she was troubled."

"We can agree on that."

"So, given that she was unstable —"

"Troubled and unstable are not exactly the same things. Especially when you're a teenager."

Along with feeling like a liar and a sneak for not having been open with Will Bridger about her true identity, Faith felt guilty for not having broached the subject of those marks with the obviously troubled teen. She'd told herself that she'd wanted to give Erin time to trust her. In retrospect, Faith admitted she'd also wanted to make sure she could trust the teenager.

"The article in *Sports Illustrated* didn't mention any recent death."

"Perhaps it wasn't recent."

"There was a photo of them together at the U.S. Nationals last year. Susan Gallagher couldn't have been that old; she looked more like an older sister than a mother, so it'd have to be an unnatural cause of death."

He thought about that for a moment as he took another drink. "Given that the girl was a media darling, it seems her mother dying of cancer or a fatal accident would've made the news."

It sounded like a hypothetical question, but Faith answered it anyway. "I'd think so, yes."

"I'll check with the offices of the Olympic committee as soon as they open. See if they have more information."

"That's a good idea."

"Thanks," he said drily.

Faith felt a tinge of heat flood into her cheeks. "Sorry. That sounded . . ."

"Patronizing?" He folded those muscled arms across his chest.

"Well, a bit," she admitted. "But I certainly didn't mean to imply you weren't up to the task."

"Not all small-town cops are Barney Fife clones."

"I realize that. Having witnessed your

work, up close and personal." Too personal.

He had the grace to wince. "We're going to have to work this stuff in our past out."

"I don't believe that's necessary."

"Look, we can't continue to ignore it. This is a small town —"

"Ah, this is where you tell me it's not big enough for the both of us. I seem to recall that line from an old western I saw on the late show."

"Dammit." He dragged his hands down his face. "Would you quit second-guessing everything I'm going to say?"

He paused, as if expecting her to leap in again.

She managed to refrain and only nodded for him to continue.

"We had something going down there, Faith. And because of circumstances beyond either of our control, we never got to see where it was headed. Now, I understand that there's a good chance I'll never be able to make amends for having betrayed your trust. All I'm asking is an opportunity to at least say what I couldn't say back then."

He looked sincere. Sounded sincere. Of course she'd also believed him when he'd told her that he'd never felt the way about any other woman the way he'd felt about her. They'd been on the top of a Ferris wheel overlooking the city. Two nights later, the house of lies he'd built had come crashing down around them.

She'd never been one to blame her bad choices on others. But at times Faith thought the events in Savannah had, in part, contributed to the trouble she'd gotten into in Las Vegas. The mess that had put her in Sal Sasone's crosshairs.

She'd managed to convince herself that she'd moved on. Gotten past it. Now she was wondering if she'd emotionally run away from dealing with it, the same way Diane/Tammy had always done. The idea that she might have anything in common with her mother was more than a little unsettling.

"I suppose closure wouldn't be such a bad thing."

"Closure wasn't exactly what I was thinking," he said. "But if it works for you . . . damn." He snatched the pager off his cop utility belt and looked at the display. "I've got to go. We'll have to pick this up later."

"I'll be at the station at eight."

"That's less than three hours from now."

"You promised me an exclusive, Sheriff," she reminded him, slipping back into the much more emotionally comfortable reporter mode as she followed him through the maze of boxes and handed him his heavy parka. "That's worth losing a little sleep over."

Especially since, now that he'd opened their personal can of worms, or let the genie out of the bottle, or any of the half dozen apt metaphors that came to mind, Faith knew she wouldn't be getting any sleep anyway.

She stood in the open doorway and watched him disappear into the falling snow illuminated by the Suburban's headlights.

The sky over the lake was dark, suggesting that everyone had left the murder scene.

Everyone including the murderer.

Faith's mind reeled at the possibility that the killer might actually have been targeting her. All right, admittedly by running away from Las Vegas she'd run the risk of making Sal even more furious.

But even at the man's very worst — which was not pleasant — Salvatore Sasone wasn't the type to sneak up behind someone with a straight-edged razor and slit her throat.

Was he?

That idea had Faith shivering as she shut and bolted the door.

21

The sun was barely above the horizon, casting a yellowish lavender light over the drifts of powdery snow, as Will drove to the sheriff's office.

The news came on the radio, with a brief, undramatic mention of an unidentified body being found at Silver Lake sandwiched between the weather and sports. It was only a repeat of what Faith had reported last night, but unfortunately, that hadn't stopped the media hounds from descending on the courthouse.

Apparently the celebrity news was getting a little staid this season; nothing like a murder to liven things up.

Wishing that he'd just gone ahead and driven to Jackson, he pulled into the courthouse lot, wishing he had his old Ford truck with the attached snowplow to shove the dark green Explorer parked in his marked spot into a snowbank.

Instead he pulled up right behind it, his front bumper kissing its back one.

Let the asshole figure out how to get out of this one.

The thought gave him a fleeting sense of satisfaction.

They descended on him like a black cloud of Northern grasshoppers attacking a mountain meadow, shouting out his name, his title, jockeying for position, clamoring for answers to questions he wasn't about to stop and listen to.

"No comment," he repeated again and again as he made his way across the lot, frozen snow crunching beneath his boots.

One particular question was called out by a sexy blonde wearing a bubble-shaped jacket in a riot of psychedelic pink, reds, yellow, and purple over sprayed-on, pink ski pants, who managed to shimmy her way through the crowd and shove a microphone into his face.

"Paris Benton, K-KOLT news," she said breathlessly, steam puffing from between collagen-enhanced, bubble-gum pink lips. "Is it true you've got a murder on your hands, Sheriff?"

"No comment." He brushed the mike aside and continued up the stone steps.

"Dustin Kittridge, *Riverton Daily Ranger.*

Are women of Hazard in danger?"

"No comment."

"Madison Johnson, *Jackson Hole News and Guide.* What are your plans to apprehend the killer?"

"There's an idea. Why don't I tell you my secret game plan and you can put it on TV so the bad guy will know what to watch out for."

"Do you expect more killings?" another reporter called after him.

Will didn't bother to respond. Just kept walking, wishing Wyoming Fish and Game gave out hunting licenses for reporters.

"The word is you may be looking for a mythical Indian cannibal," a male voice rose above the din.

O-kay. That one got his attention. He wheeled around and gave the bearded guy — whose salt-and-pepper beard, Willie Nelson braid, and feathered dream-catcher earring gave him away as one of those New Agers who'd established a commune outside of town — a hard look.

"I'll be holding a press briefing at nine o'clock." He held up his hand as they surged forward, appeared ready to charge the door. "Here on the steps."

"Outside?" pink lips asked in disbelief.

"It's colder than a witch's tit," another

reporter complained.

"Fire regulations." He swept a dismissive look over them. "It's against state law to have this many people at any one time in our office conference room."

Will had no idea if that was true or not. If it wasn't, it should be.

"But you are the law," pink lips wheedled prettily.

"I was sworn to uphold the law."

Looking at them now, as they tried to figure out what they were going to do for the next hour, Will almost felt like smiling for the first time since that nightmare and his glitchy heart had jerked him out of sleep.

"I'm not above it."

He continued into the building just in time to meet Trace Honeycutt walking down the hall carrying a cardboard box filled with steaming cups of coffee from the vending machine.

"I'll take those." He lifted the box from the deputy's hands. "You're assigned to guard the door. If any of those reporters even tries to come inside, shoot them."

The deputy's Bambi-brown eyes widened. "You're kidding, right, Sheriff?"

"Probably," Will allowed, deciding all he needed was a cop-shooting-a-reporter story.

Though it was a damn nice fantasy. Not

nearly as good as Faith naked on a bearskin rug, but it'd do for now.

"Do whatever you need to do, short of gunfire, to keep them outside. Did they teach you crowd control at the state police academy?"

"Sure, Sheriff, but —"

"Good." He balanced the box on a palm and patted the deputy's shoulder. "I've confidence in you, Deputy. You'll do just fine."

"Thank you, sir." Honeycutt rose to his full height of five feet eight inches. "I won't let you down."

"If I thought you would, I'd have you out ticketing news vans for parking violations. Hold down the fort, Deputy. I'll be back down to take them off your hands in an hour."

"Yessir." Trace Honeycutt didn't exactly salute. But he came damn close.

The green-as-spring-grass deputy had Will feeling about a hundred years old as he climbed the stairs to his office.

"The barbarians are at the gate," he announced to Sam. "I've got Honeycutt guarding the ramparts."

"I'll bet you made his day."

"Seemed so. Are they making cops

younger these days? Or are we just getting old?"

"Not old." Sam picked up a cup of the sludge, sipped, and made a face. "We're experienced. In our prime. Like good bourbon, we season with age."

"Just keep telling yourself that." Will scowled up at the clock on the wall. He handed Sam the piece of paper with the Explorer's tag number on it. "Would you have someone run this plate? I want to ticket the son of a bitch who parked in my space before I have it towed."

"Will do," Sam said agreeably.

Will glanced at the three empty chairs sitting in the small, unadorned space laughingly called reception. "She's late."

"If you're referring to Faith Prescott, she's waiting in your office. In fact, that's why Trace was down getting coffee. Hers is the one with the double sugar and extra cream."

"Too bad Hazard doesn't have a Starbucks. You could've had Honeycutt run out and get her a mocha frappé."

"The lady might not be a local, but she's real nice. And she must be planning on staying because I hear she's about to buy the old Maxwell place."

"Probably planning to turn it over for a big profit."

"No crime in that. Last I checked the statutes anyway."

"Well, there should be. If all those California escapees keep coming up here with all their big real estate bucks, raising the cost of houses, people whose families have lived here for generations are going to be priced right out of the valley."

"Damn. I hadn't realized the woman was such a threat to society." Sam unfastened his handcuffs from his utility belt and tossed them toward Will. "And for the record, she's from Vegas, not California, but we'd still better get her behind bars, now, before she brings about the ruination of the entire state.

"Hell," he continued, "why don't we charge her with raising the price of gasoline and global warming while we're at it?"

Will managed a faintly sheepish grunt. "Maybe I came on a little harsh."

No way was he going to try to explain that he was pissed off at her for having gotten under his skin. And into his mind when he had no business thinking about dragging her off to bed while a murderer was running loose in his town.

"You've got a murder that's on the verge of turning into one damn mess," Sam said. "Makes sense you'd be on edge. But she's nothing like the rest of those vultures, Will."

"I know that." Only too well.

Sam waved toward the window where a clamor rose from the street below. "Besides, like my dear old Shoshone *hutsi* used to remind us grandkids, 'You can catch more flies with honey than with vinegar.' "

"Now see, no offense to your grandmother, but that's one of those sayings that's never made a lick of sense to me. Why the hell would anyone want to catch flies?"

Not bothering to hang around for an answer, Will carried the carton with the two remaining cups of coffee into his office.

She was standing at the window, her back toward the door, giving him a second to take in the sleek slide of hair that was as dark and shiny as a mink's pelt. She'd changed out of the sweats she'd been wearing when he'd shown up at her house to a pair of gray wool slacks and a short, cardinal red sweater that looked as soft as a cloud and stopped at her waist, accenting her narrow waist and slender hips.

She glanced back over her shoulder as he entered the room. "Good morning."

She'd gotten a bit of color back into her cheeks, but she was still too pale. And there were lavender smudges, like bruises, beneath her remarkable eyes, and either she'd neglected to put on lipstick or had already chewed it off.

She looked exhausted and a lot more fragile than Will knew her to be.

"Morning," he responded with equal formality, as if they hadn't both been drinking coffee in her cozy kitchen a few hours ago.

There was an odd buzzing in the room, like the hiss of electrical wires after a thunderstorm. Or maybe the buzzing was in his head.

"Sorry to have kept you waiting."

"I just arrived myself a couple minutes ago. Besides, I imagine you've been busy," she said in the husky voice he'd never entirely gotten out of his mind.

It was an intriguing contrast — that sultry purr of temptation coming out of a sharply angular face dominated by that generous mouth and intelligent eyes.

Reminding himself he had a killer on his hands, Will tried his damnedest to forget he'd always enjoyed contrasts.

"You could say that." He put the carton on the desk and held out the overly sweetened cup.

"I believe I just did."

She glided across the room on those long, wraparound legs, bringing with her a faint scent that reminded him of summer sunshine on a mountain meadow. It was bright and fresh, but warm, all at the same time. It suited her, but he missed the gardenias of that stolen Savannah summer.

"Took me a while to find a parking spot. The building's surrounded by carrion."

"I assume you're not referring to flocks of the feathered kind," she said as she took the cardboard cup from his hand.

"Apparently the members of the fourth estate have run out of Tinseltown sex scandals to report on."

She shrugged, sending the wide neckline of her sweater sliding off one shoulder. "Murder sells."

"Yeah. So I've heard." Will was struck by an almost overwhelming desire to bite that smooth, exposed flesh. "Anyway, one of the vultures parked his Explorer in my designated spot, so I —"

"What color Explorer?"

"Same color as half the ones in the valley. Forest green." Now her cheeks were decidedly pink. "Why?"

"That explains why the spot was still open." She dragged a hand through her glossy brown hair. "I'm sorry. I suspect the Explorer's mine. But I honestly didn't notice a sign." A sigh escaped those full, unpainted lips. "I should've realized it was too good to be true, but I was rushing so I wouldn't be late, and I guess I just decided it was my lucky day."

"Don't worry about it."

His irritation disintegrated, even as he realized that if it'd had been bald, cigar-chomping Pete Wagner, from the *Hazard Herald,* or even Ms. Bubble-Gum Lips, he'd still be pissed.

"Thank you," she said.

"No problem."

An expectant silence settled over them. "So, how's Josh?" she asked.

"He'll live."

"You do realize that as soon as it gets out he was questioned, they're going to shift their attention from you to him."

"They'll have to find him first."

"Don't tell me. You had your father take him out of town."

"I didn't have him do anything. It's snowing. The stock needs feeding. A ranch kid doesn't have the luxury of sitting around on his butt watching MTV and playing video games."

"Would you have let him leave Hazard if he'd been some other man's son?"

"To keep stock from dying, absolutely," he said shortly. "You may not be familiar with how things work out here on the high range. But it's a cow's job to have a calf as often as she can. It's the rancher's job to get as many of those calves to market as possible."

"Thank you for explaining Western market economy to me." She flashed him a false smile over the rim of the cup. "If I ever get assigned the Wyoming business news beat, thanks to you I'll be ready."

He sat down in the chair behind the desk, leaned back, put his elbows on the scarred wooden arms, and studied her over linked fingers.

"This part is off-the-record. I want it held back to separate the real killer from the nut-cases who decide to confess to crimes they don't do. Or any copycats we might be unlucky enough to get."

"All right."

"The killer left a note."

"Like Jack the Ripper? Or Son of Sam?"

"Sort of. It was a poem."

He could see the wheels turning in her head as she digested that piece of information. "Like the BTK killer," she murmured.

"Don't even suggest that," Will warned. That was all he needed, a serial killer loose on the streets during the city's biggest tourist event.

"Was the poem original?"

"I don't know. Deputy Douchet's going to check it out online as soon as she gets back from escorting the body to Jackson."

"May I see it?"

He considered that for a moment. "I don't see why not. So long as you understand it's off-the-record. The last thing I need right now is for you media types to give him a cutesy name like the Poet Killer."

"I suppose that could fuel his fantasies."

"Sure as hell could. Wacko killers who leave notes and write letters want attention. They're chasing fame and I want to make sure this creep doesn't get it."

"I understand your reasoning, but that plan could backfire. Possibly make him kill again to garner the attention you refused him the first time."

"True. Which is why I have to catch him. Fast."

Will refused to think he wouldn't.

He reached into the manila case file he hoped wouldn't grow all that much. Guys like this were addicted to the rush every bit as much as a crackhead or meth addict. The more they killed, the more they needed to kill. If Erin Gallagher's murderer wasn't caught soon, things were bound to get worse.

The poem had been double-bagged to protect it from outside fingerprints. Unsurprisingly, they hadn't found any prints, indicating that this guy was a more careful planner than some.

She skimmed the lines.

"Creepy, that part about with 'the knife that men use, with the knife of the hunter, I will stoop down for my gift,' " she read aloud.

"It's not exactly a love sonnet," he agreed.

"No, it's certainly not. It's also not original. It's 'Mowgli's Song,' from Rudyard Kipling's *Jungle Book.*"

Those barbed-wire lines across his brow deepened again. "The one about the kid raised by wolves?"

"That's it. I remember reading it in lit survey class."

"So all we have to do is find someone who's taken English 101." Should be a snap in a college town. Yeah. Right.

"Or has access to the internet. You could probably do a search for poems about murders and come up with thousands." She read the entire poem again. "This definitely doesn't suggest a crime of passion."

"Usually slit throats involve preplanning. And practice."

She visibly flinched. "Are you suggesting

she wasn't the first?"

"I'm no profiler. And I only worked Homicide for a couple years, before Vice, but I wouldn't be surprised.

"So, here's what I know so far." He leaned forward, folded his hands on top of the folder.

"Erin Gallagher's throat was slit sometime between midnight and three a.m. Since her clothing appeared to be intact, I'm guessing against sexual molestation, but I could be proven wrong. She could have been raped. Then dressed again."

"Wouldn't that be risky? Given that she was outside where she and the murderer could be viewed . . . Unless she was killed somewhere else and moved?"

"No." Will shook his head. "She was killed there in the woods." He knew he'd be seeing that frozen blood violating the pristine white snow for a long time. "As for the risk, a lot of psychos get off on risking detection as much as the actual taking of a life. It's all a game to them.

"That song, or poem" — he nodded toward the paper she'd handed back to him — "was attached to a clip on the type of lanyard used to hold ski passes."

"I assume you're going to check out where the lanyard was purchased?"

"I already did. They sell them in the ski shop at the lodge. Apparently they can get as many as five thousand people a day on the mountain and go through at least a couple hundred of the lanyards a week. And it's not unique to White Mountain. The same brand's also sold in ski shops all over the country. And online."

"Well, that certainly narrows it down," she murmured. "Should be a snap."

"Like looking for an ice cube in a snowbank," he agreed.

She'd pulled a pen and pad from an oversize red leather bag that looked as if it weighed a ton. "What else do you know? That you can tell me," she tacked on, in a show of cooperation he appreciated.

"The last person we've been able to locate who saw her was Josh. They'd been together at her place."

"I've seen them talking together from time to time at the station, but hadn't realized they had a thing going."

"It wasn't exactly ongoing, if Josh can be believed, which — and this is absolutely off-the-record — I'm not sure he can be. He said they'd just talked before. Until she picked him up at the gas station. Said it was a spur-of-the-moment thing that was totally unplanned."

"Interesting." Faith tapped the tip of her pencil on the paper. "She didn't necessarily seem like the spontaneous type. But I suppose you never know."

"No. He did say she seemed edgy. Wired."

"But he wasn't with her when she was killed?"

"No. Apparently he fell asleep."

"Not while watching any video," she guessed.

"No. It was after they'd had sex."

Will hated sharing something his son would undoubtedly prefer to remain private, but the truth was bound to come out as soon as the autopsy was made public.

"Sleeping with Erin so close to the time of her death could seriously compromise Josh's situation."

"Why don't you tell me something I don't know?"

"Picking up your son doesn't seem like all that risky a thing to do, since beneath all that tough bad-boy bravado, he's a good kid. A little lost, perhaps, but that's not unexpected, given all the changes in his life the past year."

"He'll adjust."

"Better if he has something positive to focus on. Something that boosts his self-confidence."

"Excuse me. Have you had a child since the last time we were together?"

She threw up her hands. "I'm sorry. I didn't realize you're the only father on the planet who's earned his perfect-parenting merit badge. . . .

"Getting back to your case, it was definitely reckless of Erin to go skating alone in the middle of the night with the woods full of strangers."

"Agreed."

"Do you think she might have been meeting someone?"

"It's always possible. But unlikely, unless she was into threesomes, because she'd asked Josh to go with her."

"Poor Josh." Faith dragged a hand through her hair. "He's got to be feeling guilty."

"I'd say that's a given."

"I know you don't want any advice." She leaned forward in her chair to press her point, her fantastic eyes earnest. "But you might want to get him some help. Perhaps have him see Drew Hayworth on a professional basis."

"I thought the shrink taught at the college."

"He does. But he's just an adjunct professor there, which doesn't exactly pay the big bucks, so he also has a small private practice. And he's written a book on survivor guilt."

Will thought about Josh going through the rest of his life thinking about how things could have been different if only he'd stayed awake. If only he'd been at the lake to protect the girl with whom he'd been as intimate as two people could be.

Will thought back on those scars on Erin Gallagher's wrists. Statistics on teenage suicide swirled through his mind. Along with the grim knowledge that although he locked up his Glock every night, if his son was determined enough, he could break into the steel box.

Or buy a gun somewhere else. This was Wyoming, land where it seemed every other truck boasted an NRA bumper sticker while others proudly proclaimed that Guts, Guns, and God were what made America great.

"Christ." He swiped a hand through the hair his father had been after him to cut. Some things, such as father-son hair disagreement, he'd discovered upon returning home, never changed. "This sucks."

"I know," Faith said. "And if it's tough on us, it's got to be a million times worse on Josh."

When she was right, she was definitely right.

"I'm going over to the college to talk with Hayworth about the Gallagher girl after the press conference. I suppose it wouldn't do any harm to see how he thinks Josh is doing. Maybe set up some sessions."

"That's a good idea." She leaned back and crossed those long legs again. He appreciated that she wasn't going to be smug about getting her way. "When will you have the autopsy reports?"

"The body would've been waiting at the morgue when the medical examiner showed up for work this morning. Unlike *X-Files,* where Scully performs those middle-of-the-night autopsies, Heather Jackson pretty much works bankers' hours, from nine to four.

"So, I'd say, absent the drug screening and DNA, by this afternoon." He glanced at the window. The hum of the generators from the news vans could be heard through the glass. As could the increasingly loud drone of voices.

"The damn natives sound like they're getting restless."

"Then you'd better go throw them some red meat." She stood up and closed her notebook. "Thank you, Sheriff. I appreciate your cooperation."

"It's not like you gave me any choice."

"Newsflash, Bridger." She tucked the notebook back into that oversize red leather bag that was nearly the size of his day hiking pack. "I'm one of the good guys. I may still be pissed at you for trying to use me to get to my boss, no matter how noble your end goal. But I wouldn't have climbed over you, your son, or a murdered girl to get even."

"That's good to hear."

"There is just one thing." She flashed him the first genuine smile he'd received from her since the night everything had fallen apart in Savannah. It was no less dazzling than it had been then. "Don't look now, Sheriff, but you've got yourself a new partner."

22

Will stared at her. "What in the hell are you talking about?"

Faith's eyes sparked with a determined glint. "Despite the ten-year gap in our ages, Erin was a friend. I wish I'd been a better one to her, but it's too late to change that now. But I can at least try to make amends by helping you track down the person who took her life."

"That's my job. And in case you haven't noticed, cops and reporters are definitely not natural collaborators. And I don't need a partner."

"I'll bet you had one in Savannah."

"Sure. Another detective, who'd been trained to do police work. The Hazard sheriff's department may not be the largest in the country, but we've got three deputies — Charbonneaux, Douchet, and Honeycutt — working the case."

"And I've no doubt they're not only highly

qualified but efficient. But none of them has a microphone. And a ready-made audience."

He rolled his eyes. "I don't want to hear this."

"I could go on the air, maybe encourage him to call —"

"What part of 'I don't want to turn this guy into some sort of celebrity like Ted Bundy or the Mansons' did you not understand?"

She did her best to contain it, but accustomed to watching for tells — those little personal tics and behaviors that gave away emotions — from suspects, he didn't miss a faint shiver.

It was good that she was scared; she'd stay safer that way.

"Surely you don't think you're after a serial killer. Whoever murdered Erin has only killed one person —"

"That we know of."

He looked out the window, in the direction of the lake, recalling the scene in vivid Technicolor detail. The body was in Jackson, about to be attacked with saws and a claw hammer, and the bloodied snow had been scooped up and stored in ice chests for the lab along with the clothes she'd been wearing.

The snow that had been falling steadily all night would have covered the boot and truck-tire tracks, so that any sledder who happened by would never know that evil had been done there.

But Will knew. And the bitch was that he also knew he'd never be able to get it out of his mind. Which was one more reason he'd disliked working homicide.

Sure, vice often led to murders, but often as not, the victims were just as guilty as the perps.

They were not innocent, young college girls with their entire lives ahead of them.

Nor radio personalities who might just have more heart than sense.

"You will not, under any circumstances, interfere with my investigation," he said through gritted teeth. "If I hear one word that sounds as if you're trying to establish some sort of sick reporter/killer bond with the guy, I will pick you up, toss you into a cell so fast that gorgeous dark head would spin, then throw away the key."

"I believe that just might be against the law. Even here in Wyoming."

"Why don't you ask me if I give a flying fuck?" he exploded.

As if he'd been lingering just outside, Sam Charbonneaux stuck his head in the door.

"Everything okay, Sheriff?" he asked mildly.

"Yeah. Everything's just dandy," Will lied.

"Okay." Solemn brown eyes measured the situation. "Morning, Faith," Sam said.

She managed a crooked, somewhat embarrassed smile. "Good morning, Sam."

"Good program last night."

"Thanks."

"What did you need, Sam?" Will asked abruptly.

"Just wanted to let you know that Desiree got a make on that Explorer parked in your space." Sam was suddenly studiously avoiding Faith. "Maybe I'd better fill you in on that later."

"It's not necessary. I already have a confession. Seems the perpetrator overlooked the sign."

Sam grinned. "Didn't I tell you that sign oughta be yellow? People notice yellow. That blue and white blends right in with the snow."

"I'll make a note to have the county maintenance crew repaint it."

"Good idea. I also wanted to let you know that I finished checking out Erin Gallagher's apartment."

"Find anything?"

Sam glanced pointedly at Faith.

"She's okay," Will said. "Since everything you say is off-the-record."

Sam seemed a little surprised by that, but Will knew he was far too professional to ever question a superior officer in front of a civilian.

"Nothing that points to a reason she was murdered."

"No indication of drugs?" Although drugs weren't the problem they'd been in the city, Will knew that small towns weren't immune.

"Nothing illegal, but apparently she wasn't exactly the happy, carefree girl she appears to be on all those commercials, because along with some birth control pills, I found a bottle of Prozac and another of Clonopin. I know the first's prescribed for depression, but I don't know what the second one's for."

"It's an antianxiety drug," Will said. The doctor who'd diagnosed his glitchy heart had suggested he try it. He'd refused. "Had they been filled locally?"

"No. It's one of those mail-order drug companies. And the doctor's from Park City, where I guess she used to train. I've got a call into his service, but he hasn't gotten back to me."

"Interesting," Will mused.

"Yeah. I thought so, too. Funny thing, she

didn't have any skating memorabilia around."

"She referred to skating as being her previous life," Faith said.

"Odd she'd make that much of a separation," Will observed.

"Maybe it hadn't been as positive an experience as it appeared to outsiders. After all, we just see the glittery costumes and the glamour. The Olympic TV cameras never show young girls moving away from home, the hours of practice, the injuries, the pressure to constantly succeed. The isolation."

"Doesn't seem like much isolation when you're appearing in front of millions worldwide," Sam said.

"Millions of strangers," Faith pointed out. "From the little Erin had dropped about her past, I had the impression that she didn't know anyone — or about anything — outside of skating. She didn't even go to public schools. She had a tutor four hours a day from the fourth grade. That was why —"

Unshed moisture welled up in Faith's eyes. She swallowed, choking back tears.

"Why what?" Will asked. He reached into his breast pocket and pulled out a snowy white handkerchief.

"Thanks."

Faith dabbed at her eyes. Her teeth were worrying that lush bottom lip he'd been fantasizing nipping at only minutes ago.

"Everything was new to her," she managed once she'd composed herself again. "There were times when she seemed like a two-year-old, who was just discovering that there was a world outside her previously small comfort zone. She was driven to experience everything. I suspected, to make up for all she'd missed." Faith drew in a breath. Let it out. "Now she'll never get the chance."

"We'll get the guy," Will promised her yet again, just as he had Josh last night. "Why don't you go start interviewing her friends and classmates at school," Will told Sam. "I'll get rid of the vultures and tackle the shrink."

"Good idea," Sam agreed.

The deputy said good-bye to Faith, then left them alone again.

"So." Will rubbed his hands together, easing out stress-induced kinks. "Where were we?"

"I believe you'd just threatened to throw me in jail."

"Right. I was also about to remind you that I said I'd get the guy. And I will. A lot faster and easier if I don't have an amateur screwing up my investigation."

"Now we're getting to the heart of the matter."

"Dammit —" He raked a hand through his hair again. Rubbed his heart, which was suddenly on the verge of doing backflips.

"There's more involved than your ego, Sheriff. And I have a question."

"Why am I not surprised?"

He was beginning to remember another reason he'd realized right off the bat she wasn't involved in that crooked congressman's illegal activities. The guy, like so many other politicians Will had met, had surrounded himself with yes-men. Faith had a mind of her own, and if they hadn't arrested the guy, he figured she would've only lasted another week or so working in the smoke-filled backroom deal making that seemed to be the norm in political life.

"I'm a reporter. Asking questions is what we do. If I'm not allowed to speak with Erin's murderer, what do you expect me to do if he calls out of the blue?"

"I expect you to keep the tape running — you do tape the show, right?"

"Sure."

"Good. Then have Mike call me the second the call comes in."

He reached into the breast pocket of his

starched shirt and pulled out a business card with his office phone, cell phone, and pager numbers on it.

"And try to keep the guy on the line."

"Ah." Another nod. "So, I am allowed to actually talk with him?"

He ignored her faint sarcasm. "Only if he calls." A thought occurred to Will. "I'll want to tap your phone. Just in case."

"My home phone? Or the station's?"

"The station's for starters. If he does decide to call, we'll include yours."

"I can't make a decision about something that important for KWIND. I don't even know if it's legal."

"Okay, then I'll call Fred Handley and get his okay."

She scowled. "You know Handley?"

"Sure. He grew up in Jackson Hole. We both played football, him for the Broncs, me for the Timberwolves."

"Please tell me you won."

"We stomped them four years running."

"Good." She folded her arms and nodded decisively.

"Sounds as if he's still as much of a jerk as he was back then."

"I've no idea how bad he was in high school, but he's a narrow-minded, chauvinistic jerk now. Part of the reason I really need to do this story," she revealed, "is because he doesn't believe women can do news. I intend to prove otherwise."

"Sounds like old Fred. If his dad hadn't been a mining bazillionaire, he would've gotten himself kicked off the team, and possibly expelled for sexually harassing cheerleaders. I heard one encounter beneath the bleachers after a game was a lot more rape than seduction."

"I'm not surprised. He made my skin crawl."

"Yet you went to work for him."

"I needed a job." The scarlet sweater dipped again when she shrugged. "Besides, he's in Cheyenne. So far he hasn't been moved to make the drive up here, and with any luck it'll stay that way. What makes you think he'll go along with tapping the station phone?"

"The valley doesn't have any local television outlets and the paper's a weekly, which makes you the only media game in town. If he decides he wants some press and decides to call KWIND, that tape could prove a PR bonanza for Handley. Which would be especially helpful if rumors of him running for Congress are true."

"Reflected fame."

"Absolutely." It did not escape Will's

notice that their thoughts were in sync. The only other person he'd ever met he didn't have to explain himself to was Gray.

"I'll walk out to the parking lot with you," he said. "Unless you want to stick around while I throw some raw meat to the vultures."

"Are you going to tell them anything you didn't tell me?"

"I'm not telling them as much as I told you."

"Then I may as well go. But you don't have to see me out."

"Actually, I do," he said as he walked out of the office with her to the elevator. "Since I'm parked behind you."

As soon as the metal elevator door closed behind them, Will jabbed the red emergency button, stopping the elevator's descent.

23

"What are you doing?" Faith asked.

"Here's the thing. I've been thinking about you. Too much, dammit." He ran his palm over the shoulder of the white parka. "Back there, in my office, when your sweater slid off your shoulder?"

"It did?"

"Yeah. It did. And I wanted to bite you. Right here." His hand tightened. "Not hard," he assured her when her eyes widened with what oddly looked like fear. "Just enough to get your attention."

"You already had my attention."

"You don't sound happy about it."

"I'm not. I want to really, really hate you."

"I don't blame you." His gaze locked with hers, wanting, needing her to believe him. "It would serve me right if you never wanted to have anything to do with me again."

"That's what I should do."

“Maybe.” His hand trailed down her arm. She stiffened when he linked their fingers together, but Will was encouraged when she didn’t pull away. “My dad has this saying.”

He turned their joined hands over, unfolded her fisted fingers, touched his mouth to the center of her palm, and was amazed when her warming flesh didn’t sizzle.

“About not cutting off your nose to spite your face.”

“I’ve heard it.”

The air surrounding them was so charged Will could feel the electricity sparking beneath his skin. Fortunately, the building was old, the elevator small. Which meant that he had her just where he wanted her.

With her back against the wall.

“Tell me you don’t feel it.” He skimmed a kiss along her jaw, knowing just where to nip to make her moan. “That connection we’ve had from the beginning. When I walked into that campaign office and felt as if I’d been poleaxed.”

Gripping his shoulder for balance, she tilted her head back. “It doesn’t matter what I feel. . . . Oh, God,” she nearly whimpered as his lips trailed down her throat. “I spent the drive into town worrying you might try something like this.”

Sighing, she linked her arms around his

neck. "And worrying that you might not."

His answering laugh was rough, relieved.

He dipped his head down, planning — despite that they were in an elevator between floors, with a horde of reporters gathered outside waiting to attack him with a barrage of questions — to take his time. To savor what he'd been thinking about, fantasizing, since returning to Hazard.

No, longer than that. Since he'd watched her walk out of that Savannah courtroom and out of his life.

But the moment his lips touched her, the tight rein he'd been keeping on his emotions snapped.

Every nerve, every atom in his body, instantly spiked; he wanted her, so badly he ached.

Worse yet, he needed her.

Without taking his mouth from hers, Will hooked an arm around her waist and dragged her up onto her toes.

Her head fell back on a low, throaty moan of pleasure that vibrated from her mouth to his, shooting directly down to his groin. Her long, lean, sexy body arched against him as Will feasted on her. And she on him.

Her leg twined around his thigh, she was plastered against his erection, her hips writhing, bucking, desperate.

He was actually considering dragging her down to the floor, sinking deep into her, taking them both to oblivion, and beyond, when some tattered vestige of sanity kicked in.

He pulled back. Struggled to breathe. To think.

"We're going to finish this."

Lingering passion swirled hotly in her eyes, her lips were parted, her cheeks flushed. He braced for her to deny what had just happened.

"Yes."

On second thought, he wasn't surprised she didn't play coy. Faith had never been one to play games. That'd always been his thing.

Now, wonder of wonders, despite his having betrayed her in the worst way, it looked as if she was going to give him a second chance.

This time, Will vowed, as he punched the button to send the elevator continuing on its way, he was going to get it right.

24

Okay, another thing Sal hated: hospitals.

He hated the odors of disinfectant, disease, and despair; he hated the lights, which blazed twenty-four hours a day, the indecipherable announcements coming over hallway loudspeakers, the moans, the weeping, the incessant beep beep beep of the machines monitoring various bodily functions.

Speaking of which, what he was discovering he hated most was bedpans.

"I just wanna take a damn leak," he complained to the Nurse Ratched clone.

"Which you're welcome to do," the blond ballbuster said with a steely smile as cold as her heart. "You're just not going to get out of bed to do it."

"I realize, not having a penis yourself, you don't quite grasp the concept that men — real men — piss standing up," he ground out from between clenched teeth.

"Really?" Glacier blue eyes widened.

"Gracious. Next time I meet a real man, I'll have to ask him about that."

Sal nearly bit his tongue off as he forced himself to count to ten, slowly, taking a deep breath between numbers, the way the anger-management counselor had taught him to do.

Unfortunately, it wasn't, he found, nearly as satisfying as the fantasy of strangling the bitch.

"Look, sweetheart, if you want a pissing contest, we'll go outside and see which of us can write our name in the snow."

He'd never met a chick who personified Freud's penis envy theory more than this one.

"Meanwhile, if I were you, I'd get the hell out of my way." Fed up, he yanked the IV needle from the vein in the back of his hand.

"That's it," she shot back. "I'm calling security."

When she lunged for the call button pinned to the overly starched, pink pillowcase, Sal made his move. Grabbing the front of her shirt, he yanked her onto the bed, and before she knew what was happening, he'd rolled over on top of her, effectively pinning her to the mattress.

At which time Ratched began cursing like

a sailor and jabbed a bony elbow into Sal's rib cage.

"That's it," he grunted. "You've just lost any chance you might've had for this year's Florence Nightingale award, sweetheart."

Her response was to bite his earlobe.

"Do we have a problem?" a calm voice asked from the doorway before he'd backhanded the bitch across the room.

If the white-jacketed doctor was at all surprised to see a patient and a nurse playing WrestleMania on the narrow hospital bed, he didn't reveal it.

"Mr. Sasone was trying to get out of bed," the nurse said with a great deal of dignity for someone whose blue scrub pants had somehow been yanked down a good six inches on her scrawny scarecrow hips.

She scrambled off the bed, pulled the pants back up, and retied the waistcord. "I was merely attempting to restrain him when he pulled me over the railing."

"That must've taken some doing, given that he only has one good arm at the moment," the doctor observed mildly.

"I've played a little semipro ball. And I still work out." It was important, in the bounty hunter business, to stay fit.

"Well, it's an impressive move, though a bit ill-advised, given that you could have risked reinjuring your elbow." The doctor, whose name tag read jack dawson, m.d., turned toward the nurse. "I believe we have everyone under control now, Nurse Hoffmann."

"Yes, Doctor." She shot a final killing glare at Sal, then marched from the room.

"I would've expected a goose step," Sal muttered.

"Nurse Hoffmann is one of our most senior floor nurses. She runs the surgical ward with admirable precision."

"Yeah, and Mussolini got the trains running on time, too. But look how he ended up."

The orthopedic surgeon called in by the ER physician after the sheriff had dropped Sal off last night wasn't about to be drawn into the fray between nurse and patient.

"How are you feeling, Mr. Sasone?" He plucked the metal chart from the holder on the foot of the bed.

"Other than my back teeth floating up to my eyeballs from all that saline solution being pumped into me, I'm doing great, Doc," Sal lied.

If he ever found that guy on the snowmobile who'd caused him to run his rental SUV into that tree, he was going to shoot him. Then run over him like he should've last night on the way to the radio studio.

Gray eyes scanned the chart. "All your vital signs seem normal."

"That's me. Mr. Normality. So, if you'll just sign a release form, as soon as I take a leak, I'll be out of here and free up the room for another victim. Uh, patient."

"You've only been out of surgery three hours."

"Yeah, but I've got a constitution like a horse."

"Hmmm." More perusing of the chart.

Having been a good cop, hell, better than good, one of the goddamn best, Sal knew enough not to push too hard. Finesse had never come naturally, but he could, when necessary, employ it to his advantage.

"Let's get that bladder taken care of," the doctor decided. "Then we can discuss our options."

Sal didn't like the sound of that, but also wasn't about to argue when at least one thing was going his way.

At least he thought it was. Until his feet hit the floor. And his head began to spin.

"Feeling a bit dizzy?"

"Nah." Black and white spots were doing the tango in front of his eyes.

"Because, if you are, I can help you back into bed."

"I can make it to the can."

"Okay. But since the hospital attorney gets a little uptight about malpractice lawsuits, why don't you let me call for a wheelchair?"

"I don't need any . . ." The specks were now a damn shitstorm of a blizzard.

"Sorry. It's either the chair or the bedpan."

Sal sagged back against the bed. "Since you put it that way, Doc, I'll take the damn chair. But I'm standing to pee."

"Fortunately, there's an orderly on this floor who used to play defensive linebacker for UW and still holds the school record for blitzes in a season. He's more than capable of providing support. Don't go away; I'll get him."

Like he was capable of going anywhere.

Sal realized he'd been expertly played when, five seconds after he'd left the room, the doctor returned with a six-foot-five moose wearing size triple-X, butter yellow scrubs who was pushing a wheelchair.

"Quite the coincidence, him being so close by," Sal observed.

"Isn't it?" Jack Dawson smiled with satisfaction.

Admiring the way the doc had manipulated the situation, although he'd ended up on the losing side, Sal tipped a slight salute as he was wheeled away.

While he'd throw himself off the top of that mountain looming over town before admitting it, Sal was grateful for the moose's assistance in holding him upright so he could pee standing up like a man.

The doctor was waiting when they came out of the adjoining bathroom.

"You may as well get comfortable," he said. "Given that you're going to be here for a while longer."

"I've got business to take care of."

"Which will have to wait." The doctor folded his arms across the white lab coat. Beneath the unbuttoned coat he was wearing a brown T-shirt announcing dances with moose.

"Most people don't pay all that much attention to their elbows, until they have a problem," Jack Dawson said. "But in fact, it's a very complex joint.

"What you have, Mr. Sasone, is a radial head fracture, which is a fairly common fracture resulting in approximately twenty percent of acute elbow injuries. A common cause of radial head fractures is dislocation.

"When the upper-arm bone slides back into its appropriate place after a dislocation, it can chip off a piece of the radial head, which is shaped like a round disk, resulting in a fracture, which I believe is probably what happened in your case."

"Yeah. That's what you said."

Having been in the kind of pain that was threatening to take his head off when the sheriff had brought him to the ER, Sal didn't remember a lot about their presurgery talk, but he did recall that much.

"In your case, the bone fragment was large enough to fix it with metal screws. I also repaired some soft-tissue ligament tears."

"So, I'm good to go."

The doctor shook his head. "Not exactly. Not yet. Even if I were to release you while you're still under the influence of a narcotic — which, to save you breath on making an argument, I'm definitely not — you need to understand that if you're not extremely careful for the next few weeks, you can experience malunion."

"You want to explain that, Doc?"

"Sure. It's merely a two-dollar medical word meaning the bones might grow back together in an abnormal way, which would require another operation to repair them."

"I'm willing to take my chances," Sal said grumpily.

"That's quite a gamble. Let's try this: you also have three nerves running through the elbow that can be cut, kinked, or pulled by an injury, which could cause damage."

"Which could be fixed, right?"

"Not necessarily. The damage could be permanent. Believe me, Mr. Sasone, this is not something you'd want to happen."

"I'm right-handed. I can handle a little nerve damage in my left arm."

"I've no doubt you're an iron man," the doctor said drily. "However, there's one last thing I believe you should understand." He took a pen from his jacket pocket, pulled out a notepad, and quickly sketched a diagram.

"This is your elbow. This line here" — he tapped the point of the pen against the paper — "is an artery that runs very near your elbow joint, which supplies blood to the forearm. Certain injuries can cut or kink this artery. Which in turn cuts off the blood flow."

Okay. He'd finally gotten Sal's unwilling attention. He also didn't have to draw another damn picture.

"Are you saying I could lose my arm?"

"I'm saying that's a remote possibility. And, I wouldn't think, a very appealing one."

"Christ on a crutch." Sal flopped his head back against the rock-hard pillow. "You win this round, Doc."

"The goal is for you to come out the winner, Mr. Sasone."

Damn. Could things be more screwed up? Sal took another deep breath and reminded himself that this doctor, who may have saved his arm, wasn't responsible for the fact that he was up shit creek. Seemingly without a good arm to paddle.

"How long do I have to stay here?"

"At least until the Demerol wears off. Perhaps, if the pain is manageable, later this evening I'll sign the release form then."

"Nobody can stop me if I decide to walk out without a damn piece of paper."

"That's true. But I believe the operative words are *walk out.* I don't know what business you have here in Hazard that's so urgent, Mr. Sasone. But I doubt you'd be very effective when you can't even stand up without risking falling on your face."

Sal hated that the guy who looked like he could've played a doctor on some TV soap opera was right. He was trying to think about what to do next when Dawson came up with a new suggestion.

"Let me offer a compromise. Stay here for another four hours. That should give us time to ensure you're not going to have any complications from the surgery. Then, after I check your elbow one more time, I'll have one of the interns drive you back to" — he flipped to the front page of the chart — "the lodge."

It wasn't Sal's first choice. Hell, it wasn't even his second or third. But the doc had a point. How effective would he be dealing with Faith if he couldn't stay on his damn feet?

"Four hours," he agreed reluctantly.

"You won't regret it, Mr. Sasone."

Now that's where the doc was flat-out wrong.

Because Sal was already regretting everything about this trip.

Beginning with the cockamamy idea to come to Hazard, Wyoming, in the first place.

25

"So, how did things go with Bridger?" Mike asked Faith when she arrived at the station.

"Fine."

Feeling the heat flooding her face, Faith glanced around the small break room trying to remember having driven here. She'd been operating on automatic pilot ever since leaving that elevator.

"So what did he say?" Mike was sprawled out on a bark-brown leather couch that had definitely seen better days. "Did he give you anything that'll make a splash?"

"Actually, he didn't give me much more than we already knew."

Faith crossed the room and took an Earl Grey tea bag from a green plastic basket that had once held take-out fries from The Branding Iron café.

"The body has been tentatively identified as Erin." She turned on the tap at a small sink, filled a red-and-white KWIND mug with water, and stuck in into the microwave on the counter.

"The autopsy is being held in Jackson, and so far nothing that Sam Charbonneaux found in her apartment suggested a reason for anyone to kill her."

"So it was a random murder?"

"It appears so."

"The sheriff did reveal that Erin's throat was slit." She had to push the words past the lump that had risen in her own throat. "And that it appeared to have been done by someone who knew what he — or she — was doing."

"So he thinks it could be a woman?"

"I don't believe he has any ideas at this point. And although the violence points to a man, I suppose he's not going to rule out a female killer."

"Christ." Mike shook his head. Scrubbed a hand down his face. "What a mess."

"That's putting it mildly." The microwave dinged. "He hasn't located Erin's parents yet."

"She never did talk much about them. At least not to me."

"Me neither. Did she ever mention her mother being dead?"

"Nope."

"She did to me. Just in passing; it wasn't

like she made a big deal of her having died."

"That's freaking strange."

"Do you think so?" Faith paused from dunking the tea bag into the water to glance back over her shoulder.

"Well, sure. Having your mom die would probably be rough on anyone. But from what I'd read in that *Sports Illustrated* cover story, Erin and her mother were like this." Mike crossed his fingers. "Seems if she'd died, it would've been a big deal."

"I suppose so." This was a subject Faith could not relate to.

"Specially given that girls tend to be so connected to their mothers. Hell, my older sisters are thirty-eight and forty, but they were both emotional wrecks when Mom went in to get what turned out to be a benign lump removed from her breast."

"Really?"

"My brother-in-law Dave said Melody kept bursting into tears at the drop of a hat, even a week after the surgery. And Meredith lost ten pounds because she was too nervous to eat."

"That's . . ." Faith paused, looking for the proper word. "Surprising."

"Not if you knew them."

He was looking at her a bit curiously. A look she remembered all too well from childhood. A look that revealed he'd pegged her as an alien outsider. Like a pod person. Someone who may look human, but wasn't quite.

"Guess you didn't exactly have that same relationship with your mother, huh?"

"No." Her fingers tightened on the mug as memories of cruel hands and hurtful words washed over her. "I didn't."

She went over to the window and looked out over the rolling fields of white. The sun glancing off the fields of snow was blinding.

"It's so beautiful out there, isn't it?" she murmured in an attempt to shift the conversation before Mike got it into his head to ask any more questions.

"That's what you say now. Let's hear if you feel the same way come March."

"I made it through last winter okay." If you discounted jumping every time the phone rang or a strange car pulled up outside her apartment. "Besides, you can't appreciate spring without going through winter.

"It seems it would have to be a man," she said, returning to their original topic. "Will — the sheriff — said she was attacked from behind and didn't put up any struggle, which suggests either she knew her killer, or he was a great deal taller and stronger."

"The girl was no bigger than a minute," Mike pointed out. "Hell, you're what, five-six?"

"Seven."

"See? That's nearly half a foot taller than Erin was. I'll bet you could've taken her."

"I suppose so. Physically. But there's no way I could ever kill anyone."

Unless, perhaps they were trying to kill her. A possibility Faith had been forced to consider. Which was what had brought her to Wyoming.

"I didn't mean you had it in you to do murder. I was just stating a possibility. Like they do on *CSI*."

He pushed off the couch and poured a mug of coffee from the carafe and snagged a sugar-frosted donut from the pink cardboard box in the center of the table.

"So, since Bridger hasn't found her parents, I guess we're still holding back her name."

"No. He was pragmatic enough to realize news travels like wildfire in a town this small."

Immediately after that breath-stealing kiss, he'd shifted immediately back into cop mode and given her permission to tell that much about the case.

"He's decided at this point, perhaps going

public might result in some people coming forward with information." She glanced down at her watch. "In fact, I suppose we shouldn't be waiting for the top of the hour if we want to be first with the facts."

Mike jammed the donut into his mouth. "I've already asked Marty to give you some airtime," he revealed around the sweet, fried dough.

Marty McBride was the morning man who hosted *Trash to Treasure,* a popular barter show drawing callers all the way from neighboring Idaho and Montana looking to swap everything from antique tractors to kitchen-sink plungers. Last summer two callers had even traded a two-bedroom, 1960s ranch house for a motor home.

White confectioners' sugar drifted down to the vinyl floor like falling snow as Mike brushed his hands together. "Let's go scoop the big guys."

26

Wind River College was an eclectic collection of block and frame buildings dating back to the school's founding in the late 1970s.

The ten-acre campus might not be as famous or as visually appealing as some of the Eastern Ivy League colleges, or Vanderbilt in the South or Stanford in the West, the fraternity and sorority systems were pretty much nonexistent, and the sports were nothing to shout about, but thanks to endowments from local oil-rich sponsors, the administration could afford to bring in high-caliber professors, which, to Will's mind, was what college should be about, anyway.

The Social Sciences department was housed in a two-story, rectangular frame building that someone had decided to paint an unfortunate shade of yellow. While it would never win any awards for architecture, north-facing windows offered a million-dollar view of White Owl Mountain.

Although he'd learned early in his career the dangers of pigeonholing people, if asked, Will would've had to admit that in his mind he was picturing Dr. Drew Hayworth along the lines of Freud. A small, rather fussy-appearing man with a tidy goatee wearing a three-piece tweed suit. Or perhaps a sports coat with leather patches on the elbows.

The office would be minimalistic, the upholstered pieces wrapped in a pewter gray suede; the art on the wall would be stark black-and-white, perhaps with a few shades of gray, framed in narrow, black metal. Nothing that could be recognized as anything in real life, but more like a Rorschach inkblot test.

He would've been wrong on all counts. The man who greeted him was about his own height of six feet two inches, with blue eyes and an open, almost boyish grin. Rather than a suit, he was wearing a navy cashmere, V-neck sweater worn over a blue oxford-cloth shirt, perfectly creased jeans, and hiking boots, which, from the scuffs, appeared to have actually been worn for hiking.

He looked younger than Will's own thirty-six, but Will figured the guy must be at least that old to have written as many books as he had. There were two bookcase shelves of them, all, from what Will could tell at a glance, clinical studies of psychological disorders.

Including, he couldn't help but notice, anxiety attacks. A couple had the bright and flashy look of commercial self-help books — one, as Faith had mentioned, on moving past grief; the rest appeared to be more scholarly.

The furniture — the requisite shrink couch and a grouping of wide-armed, oversize leather chairs — appeared comfortable and designed to invite patients to put their feet up on the heavy wooden coffee table.

Rather than inkblots, the wall was covered with Western oil paintings and old sepia photographs, including one Will recognized from the late 1800s, of Arapaho women doing the Ghost Dance. A Native-painted rawhide drum depicting a buffalo hunter on horseback claimed the spot of honor atop a low bookcase.

An eight-foot, perfectly shaped native blue spruce, adorned with white lights and hand-beaded native art, took up the far corner of the room.

"You've certainly settled into the spirit of the valley," Will observed after they'd shaken hands.

Drew Hayworth put his hands into the back pockets of his jeans, rocked back on his heels, and swept a satisfied glance around the office that could've been lifted from the State Art Museum in Cheyenne.

"I'm a psychological anthropologist," he said. "As such, my work seeks to understand the relations between personal and sociocultural phenomena — between such things as innate personality and mind on one hand, and society and culture on the other."

"I knew a professor of cultural anthropology at Savannah State University," Will said. "Her work was certainly eye-opening."

It had also, in a way, helped him fit into the underworld culture where he'd lived and worked for months at a time.

"Cultural anthropology is very close to what I do. But psychology brings in the additional question of how our minds are involved in the world we live in.

"As for my collection, I'm a greedy man," Hayworth divulged easily. "If I were to analyze myself, I'd describe me as a classic overachiever, competitive, compulsive, with a driving need to experience all life has to offer.

"Given that we're only granted a finite number of years to experience our mortal existence to its fullest, I enjoy a change of scenery every few years."

"I suppose there's something to be said for change." Wasn't that what Will had enjoyed about working vice?

"Absolutely. And whenever I move to a new location, since I know I won't be staying all that long, I enjoy immersing myself fully in the local culture."

He'd definitely done that. Will was drawn to the tree. "This is an impressive collection."

"Isn't it?" Lines crinkled around the doctor's eyes when he smiled.

His all-American looks resembled Redford back in his Sundance Kid days. His skin was deeply tanned, the better to showcase eyes as clear and blue as a Wyoming sky, and his body was lean, but built. If you didn't know better, you might actually believe the shrink was a native. Even his gravelly, Western voice was pure cowboy.

"The Native American culture is so rich, so filled with marvelous tradition and symbolism, it was difficult to choose what to focus on. But after some study, I decided to concentrate on the Plains tribes' spiritual beliefs in the magical properties of herbal medicines and hallucinogenics."

He opened the cabinet and took out a long, soft leather bag depicting a beaded turtle.

"I'm particularly pleased with this medicine bag," he said. "I suspect it could have been used to carry the red mescal bean that was used for ceremonies.

"We know it belonged to a woman, given the Arapaho creation story that tells of a turtle diving to the bottom of the ocean and retrieving a mouthful of clay from which the earth was created."

He traced the orange-and-green, geometric turtle design with a fingertip, the gesture almost reverential. "Although I haven't acquired one yet, I'm told the boys received lizards."

"A symbol of long life and wisdom," Will said.

Will's grandmother had made him a lizard amulet to take on his vision quest when he'd turned twelve; twenty-four years later, he still carried it with him.

"Exactly." Hayworth seemed pleased to have someone to share his new interest with. He skimmed a glance over Will's face. "But of course you'd know that, being of Arapaho descent."

"I didn't realize it showed."

"Oh, it does if one knows what to look for — the faint epicanthic fold to your eyelid, the aquiline bridge of your nose, your broad chest. . . . But to be honest, I already knew from stories I've heard about you."

"All lies."

The doctor's laugh was so warm and genuine, Will understood why students, most importantly Erin Gallagher, had been drawn to him. Had he, Will wondered, been the older man in her life?

"And as much as I'd like to spend the rest of the morning admiring your collection and discussing Native American art, I'm here in an official capacity."

"Of course." The smile instantly disappeared from the doctor's face. A line furrowed between his brows. "You're here about poor Erin."

"You know?"

"I heard Faith Prescott break the news on the radio a few minutes ago." He shook his head. "What a tragic thing to have happened to such a sweet, lovely young woman."

"Death is always a tragedy."

"Of course," Drew Hayworth agreed swiftly. "But she was just a child, Sheriff. It just seems particularly sad to have her life cut short just when she'd starting living it."

"That's pretty much what Ms. Prescott said."

"Did she now?"

"She mentioned everything seeming new to the girl."

"That's exactly right." Hayworth nodded in confirmation. "She was like an eighteen-year-old toddler. Drinking in all the sights and sounds and tastes of her world."

"Would that include sex?"

"I wouldn't know, although it certainly wouldn't be unexpected. College is a time of discovery. Of experimentation. Which would undoubtedly include sexual experimentation."

Hayworth turned thoughtful. "Are you suggesting if she did have a lover, he — or she — might be the one who killed her?"

"I'm not suggesting anything. I'm just collecting names of people she knew; friends, acquaintances, enemies —"

"Erin didn't have any enemies," he said quickly. "Although she hadn't had the opportunity to make any close friends yet, she was uniformly liked, which, when you think about it, was a bit surprising, given her fame and looks. A lot of people would have generated jealousy among their peers. Or at the very least envy.

"However, as I said, everyone who knew

her loved her."

"Including yourself?"

"Of course."

"What was your relationship to Erin Gallagher?"

"Employer, friend, and, more recently, her therapist."

"Not her lover?"

A muscle jerked in the psychologist's tanned cheek. His formerly friendly eyes hardened to stone.

"Because I want you to find her murderer and understand how important it is not to overlook anything or anyone in your investigation, I'm going to resist taking offense at that suggestion, Sheriff," he said stiffly.

"I'm a licensed psychologist. It would be both illegal and unethical for me to have sex with a patient."

"Yet some doctors have been known to do exactly that."

"Unfortunately, that's true. In fact, there was a study that found eighty-seven percent of therapists reported sexual attraction to a client."

"That's quite a high percentage." Surprisingly high, Will considered, which had him rethinking turning his son over to a shrink.

"Granted."

"Have you? Been attracted to a patient?"

"I'm a man before I'm a psychologist, Sheriff. I have desires just as any other male and can't always prevent having feelings for a female patient. I can, however, refrain from acting on that attraction.

"Particularly since that same study indicated that ninety percent of patients who engaged in sexual relationships with their therapists ended up being emotionally harmed."

Hayworth folded his arms across the front of the sweater. "I have never had sex or engaged in any other untoward sexual activity with a patient. And I'm more than willing to take a lie detector test, if necessary."

"I'll let you know. So, this attraction thing," Will pressed on. "Were you attracted to Erin Gallagher?"

Unlike the earlier friendly smiles, the one Hayworth offered Will was brittle and false. "If I had been, it would certainly be a mistake to tell you, when you're obviously trying to decide whether or not to put me at the top of your suspect list."

He drew in a breath seemingly meant to calm the irritation Will's question had stirred. "But the answer is emphatically no. Erin was a lovely, bright young woman. Anyone — man, woman, or child — couldn't help be attracted to her enthusiasm and zest of life. But there was absolutely nothing sexual about my feelings."

"What about her parents? What do you know about them?"

"I'm uncomfortable discussing what she told me in confidence. There is such a thing as doctor/patient privilege, Sheriff."

"I understand that, Doctor. But withholding personal information only makes sense if the patient is alive. Which the victim isn't."

"Point taken." Hayworth blew out a long breath. "Her parents divorced several years ago. Apparently over an ongoing disagreement over the emphasis Mrs. Gallagher put on their daughter's skating. Her father remarried, and from what I gathered, he's chosen to remain out of her life."

"How did she feel about that?"

"How do you think she'd feel, Sheriff?"

Will remembered the former stripper turned shrink's trick of always answering a question with another question. He hadn't liked the technique then and he damn well didn't like it now.

"Lousy."

"That's pretty much how she felt."

"Is that why she was on mood-altering drugs?"

"Part of the reason, I suppose. The mind is very complex, Sheriff. We hadn't known each other long enough for me to get to know her very well, but apparently she'd been on a fruit cocktail of medications for several years. I was hoping, with time and proper therapy, to wean her off them.

"It's very difficult for athletes," Hayworth said. "Especially female athletes. We put them up on gleaming pedestals, where they're expected to be poster children, while at the same time they're facing so many difficult issues. Like self-esteem problems, eating disorders, depression, the constant need not only to succeed, but excel. They live with pressures we adults would find difficult to handle day after day. Which is why so many attempt to self-medicate with drugs, alcohol, and sex.

"And while the athletic community is very proactive when it comes to handling physical problems, they're often far less knowledgeable about emotional and psychological problems.

"Coaches expect athletes to be able to tough things out. Which is, of course, impossible when you're talking about profound clinical depression."

"Do you think she could have been depressed enough, or unstable enough, that she'd enter into an affair with a father figure?"

"Anything's possible. Especially in the skating world where coaches control every waking moment of their students' lives."

"Did Erin Gallagher's coach control every aspect of her life?"

"From what she told me about Fyodor Radikorsky, absolutely," he said with conviction.

"Including the nighttime hours?"

"If you're asking if the man was guilty of sexually harassing Erin, or even molesting her, I'm not certain, because we'd just begun broaching the topic last week. But, from the way she'd become tense and distracted whenever his name came up, I wouldn't be at all surprised."

Damn. Just when they were getting somewhere, Will's cell phone vibrated. He took it off his belt and shot an irritated glance at the caller ID screen.

"I've got to take this," he said when he saw Sam's name.

"Of course." Drew Hayworth waved him to go ahead.

"Bridger."

As always, Sam got straight to the point.

"We found the mother."

"How?"

"She heard about her daughter on the news and called in."

Shit. That was exactly what Will had been trying to avoid.

"How soon can she be here?"

"Well, that's the thing. She's already here."

"What?"

"At the lodge. She checked in this morning. I offered to go over there and bring her in, but she insisted on using her own car and driver. She's on her way."

"I'll be right there." Will cut off the call. "I've got to get back to the office."

"Of course." The doctor stood up. "Have you gotten a break in the case?"

"I don't know yet. But it turns out that Mrs. Gallagher's a guest at the lodge."

"Well." Hayworth tapped his finger against his lips. "Susan Gallagher's in Hazard?"

"Apparently she arrived a few hours ago."

"That's quite a coincidence."

"Yeah." Will had never trusted coincidence.

"She's undoubtedly going to be in an emotional state."

"I expect so, since it can't be easy losing a child."

He'd only been a father — or at least known he was one — for three months, but Will certainly couldn't imagine anything worse.

"No. Especially a child you're estranged

from." Blue eyes shadowed. "She'll undoubtedly go through life regretting that she didn't make a greater effort to reconcile with her daughter." He shook his head. "Perhaps I should go to the station with you."

"Why?"

"I've done some work on survivor guilt," he said, revealing what Will already knew. "In fact, I recently wrote a book on the impact it had on a Guatemalan village that was devastated by an earthquake. With everyone in the village being related to dozens of the dead, you can imagine the emotional aftermath was catastrophic."

"Yeah. I imagine so." Will figured, what with Faith insisting on being involved in the investigation, the last thing he needed was another civilian partner. "But I don't know if it's really necessary that you meet Mrs. Gallagher right now."

"She may know things about Erin's emotional state."

"The fact that the Gallagher girl was telling people both her parents were dead doesn't point at them having been real close lately."

"True. But before their rift, they did spend seventeen years together in a symbiotic relationship much stronger than that of most mothers and daughters. She was obviously in Erin's life when the girl cut her wrists. Knowing what triggered that emotional outburst could help your investigation. Take it down a new path.

"Listen to me." Hayworth raked a hand through his hair. "I'm not suggesting I know anything about police investigations. I do, however, know a great deal about human behavior, Sheriff. And I'd like to do whatever I can to help you find the man who so cold-bloodedly snuffed out an innocent young life."

Will's first thought was to wonder why the hell Hayworth was so eager to help out. In his experience, most people tended to behave just the opposite when they found themselves involved — even peripherally — in any kind of crime.

Then again, maybe he'd just spent too many years in Savannah's dark crime underbelly. Cops tended to be suspicious of civilians, anyway, and vice cops were admittedly worse.

Besides, Hazard was nothing like the city. A Western version of a Norman Rockwell painting, it was a place where people still didn't lock their doors, where kids were allowed to ride their bikes blocks from their homes to school or the park, where people attended the Friday-night fish fry at the VWF and gathered in Pioneer Park for the annual Christmas-tree lighting ceremony.

On second thought, since time was running out and it was difficult, if not impossible, to get information from a hysterical person, perhaps it wouldn't hurt to have an expert on grief counseling on standby, just in case Susan Gallagher fell apart on him.

"I'll meet you there."

The doctor readily agreed. "Oh, Sheriff," he called out as Will was nearly out the office door.

Will glanced back over his shoulder. "Remember something?" he asked mildly as the back of his neck itched, a sign he'd learned to pay attention to.

"On the contrary. It's something I'll undoubtedly never forget." Hayworth pinched the bridge of his nose. Looked pained. "I saw her last night."

"Define last night."

"Around nine. She came by my office just as I was leaving. Wanted to know if I had any work that needed doing." His fingers moved from his nose to press against his eyes, as if, Will thought, trying to block an image. "I had papers to grade and I'm afraid I may have been a bit curt with her."

"It happens." Will wouldn't want to count

the times he'd been brusque with Josh over the past trying months.

"True. But I'm trained to notice things other people might not catch. I realize now that she seemed unsettled. Restless, at loose ends."

Hayworth's voice drifted off as he seemed to be lost in the memory. "If I'd only stopped to talk with her, she'd be alive now."

"You can't know that," Will said.

"No." Hayworth shook his head, harder this time, as if attempting to shed unpleasant thoughts. "But I can't help thinking it's ironic that while I've made an in-depth study of survivor guilt, here I am destined to suffer it myself."

Ironic, Will agreed as he drove away from the college.

Physician heal thyself.

27

Susan Gallagher arrived at the station on the arm of a hunk who looked like a ski bum turned professional escort-service gigolo. Will figured the black ski sweater and snug acid-washed black jeans were a casual take on the chauffeur's uniform.

The woman's hair had expertly been colored the pale shimmering hue of corn silk; her body, save for full, high breasts, was as slender and fit as it had undoubtedly been when she was a young teen skating competitively.

She was wearing a red sweater beneath a mink bomber jacket, a short, tartan-plaid, pleated skirt, black tights, and shiny black boots with high heels, which might look real snazzy at some Olympic Village club, but were highly impractical for Hazard's ice and snow.

Desiree, who was the department's internet expert, had downloaded several articles on Erin Gallagher as background. Having read that the girl's mother had married a financial counselor after a career-ending injury, Will did the math and realized that she had to be thirty-eight.

If he'd had to guess this woman's age, without knowing she was the mother of a teenage girl, Will would've guessed she was in her late twenties, tops.

"Better living through plastic surgery," Desiree Douchet murmured as he started to head out of his office to the reception area to meet her.

"What?"

"That woman's a walking billboard for the Botox and implant industry."

"That woman just lost a daughter."

"Every mother's worst nightmare," she agreed. "But I'll bet you a dinner at the restaurant of your choice that we're about to meet the exception."

"No way am I betting on a dead girl. Or her grieving mother."

Desiree shrugged. "And here I was looking forward to the buffalo prime rib at the Gun Barrel."

Desiree Douchet had worked three years in Denver's sex crimes unit before moving here to live with a ski instructor she'd met white-water rafting on the Snake River.

The two had broken up within six weeks of moving in together, but her romance with White Owl Mountain's five-hundred-plus inches of white powder each winter had kept her in Hazard for three years.

Desiree was a damn good cop. And like almost every other cop Will had ever met — with the exception of boyishly eager Trace Honeycutt — she was unrelentingly cynical of everyone and everything.

"Where is she?" Susan cried out, grabbing the hands of the first person she came to. Which, as luck would have it, was baby-faced Honeycutt. "Where's my precious girl?"

"Mrs. Gallagher." Will crossed the office. "I'm Sheriff Will Bridger. I'm sorry for your loss."

"Are you certain it's my Erin?" Her eyes were moist and red-rimmed. "Who identified her body?"

"A friend," Desiree said, jumping in to save Will from having to decide how much he needed to share with the victim's mother at this stage of the investigation. "There was also a driver's license and student ID at the scene. Plus, there was physical evidence —"

"Evidence?" Susan released the deputy and pressed her perfectly manicured fingers against her throat. "What evidence?"

"Why don't we go into my office and I'll fill you in," Will suggested, deciding it'd be better to segue into those thin white scars.

"It must be a mistake," she insisted. Will wondered how many times a day, in police stations all around the world, those words were spoken. "My daughter is young. Vital. She was about to make a comeback." Her eyes brimmed over, tears trailing down alabaster-pale cheeks.

"Really?" Desiree asked. "I'm a huge ice-skating fan." Which, Will knew, was only true if you were talking about guys on skates slamming a puck around the ice and occasionally high-sticking each other. "But I hadn't heard that news."

Susan Gallagher paused. It was only an instant's hesitation, but as Desiree flashed him a gotcha look, Will knew he hadn't been the only person in the room to catch it.

"We didn't want to take any of the spotlight away from the Olympic athletes," Susan said with a delicate shrug. "She was planning to begin training again after the Torino closing ceremonies."

Her voice caught in a little hitch that suggested she might just be on the verge of a crying jag.

"Why don't we go into my office," Will again suggested gently. "Can I get you some coffee? Or tea?"

She looked up at him from beneath her lashes in an oddly flirtatious way Will suspected was second nature. "I don't suppose you have something stronger? Perhaps brandy? Or even Scotch?"

"Sorry."

"That's all right." She managed a watery smile. Then looked over at Desiree. "I'll take tea. English breakfast, if you have it. Earl Grey will also do. Black. No sugar."

Her tone was that a queen might have used with a servant whose name she'd never bothered to learn.

"I'm sorry," Desiree said with a politeness Will knew cost her. "We're flat out of the fancy stuff. Would Lipton do?"

"I suppose. If that's all you have." Her words were directed at Desiree, but Susan was looking up at Will as she drew in a deep, shuddering breath that caused her allegedly enhanced breasts to rise and fall. "Thank you."

"It's my pleasure," Desiree said, rolling her eyes behind the older woman's back.

"May Chad come with me?" Susan asked Will. "He's more than my driver. He's my strength and my rock." This time the wet smile was directed up at the young man who did, indeed, appear to be holding her on her feet.

"Perhaps the sheriff needs to speak with you alone." Chad risked a sideways glance at Desiree that couldn't quite conceal his interest. "Why don't I show the deputy how you like your tea?" he suggested. "Then I'll catch up with you."

There was another of those little hesitations as the woman's gaze flicked from Chad to Desiree and back again. Will suspected Susan Gallagher was calculating the risk of letting her paid-for hunk disappear with a woman who'd been known to have grown men walking into walls.

"We'll be right inside," Will said, gesturing Susan Gallagher into the office. "A friend of Erin's has offered to join us."

"A friend?"

"Dr. Drew Hayworth," Drew said, rising from one of the chairs on the visitor's side of the desk. "It's good to meet you, Mrs. Gallagher. I'm just sorry it has to be under such tragic circumstances."

She made a little sound in her throat that could have been agreement. "You're a doctor?"

"A psychologist."

"Oh?" Vermilion lips pulled into a tight frown.

"Your daughter has told me a great deal about you, Mrs. Gallagher."

"Did she now?" A blond brow quirked, just a bit, but her smooth-as-porcelain brow didn't move, making Will suspect Desiree might have been right about the Botox.

"Absolutely. She spoke very highly of all your sacrifices."

"Well, one does what one must," Susan Gallagher said on a shimmering little sigh. "It's gratifying to hear that my daughter actually appreciated all I'd done for her. Sometimes parents are the last to know what their children are thinking."

"Isn't that the truth," Will agreed.

"Was my daughter a patient, Doctor?"

"We'd recently begun sessions," he allowed. "Which were unfortunately cut short by her untimely death. She also did some part-time work for me. Filing, typing, researching articles on the internet, that sort of thing. She was a wonderful help. And a very sweet girl."

"Sweet." Susan Gallagher tried the word out, as if the description were a new thought. "Of course she was."

She reached into a small black bag and pulled out a tissue she used to dab at her eyes, which had begun to fill.

"I don't know what we'll all do without her."

"All?"

"Her coach. All the people who've worked so hard to help her get to where she is. The skating community. She was much beloved, you know."

A single tear rolled down her cheek. She brushed it away with a flick of a crimson fingertip.

"What about your former husband?" Will asked.

"Dennis?" She pursed her lips. Looked surprised. "What about him?"

"Was she close to her father?"

"No. My ex-husband is an egocentric, selfish individual, Sheriff." Her voice was cold as ice, as sharp as barbed wire. "He was always jealous of Erin. Which, I suppose, is why he abandoned me. Us," she corrected.

"So he hasn't been involved in her life?"

"Not since she was eight. Erin and I only had each other. However," she tacked on, "we were all either one of us needed."

"What about boyfriends?"

"She had friends, of course. But no beaux. Now that she's returning to skating, she won't have any time for dating and boys."

A stricken look crossed her face, as if the reality of her daughter's death had hit home.

"Wouldn't have had time for boys," she corrected. She pushed her hair back from her face. "Oh, G-G-God, if only I'd gotten here a day earlier. She wouldn't have been out skating on some frozen lake in the middle of the night."

"You arrived today?" Will asked.

"Just this morning." Her voice hitched. "We were planning to spend New Year's together." She drew in a deep breath. Let it out on a soft, stuttering sigh. "I'm her mother." She clasped her hands together against her breast. "I could have kept her safe."

"That's a perfectly normal emotion," Drew Hayworth volunteered. "Unfortunately, we can't keep our children in cotton batting all their lives."

"We're parents." Her eyes were brimming with tears. "It's our responsibility to try. I'll feel guilty for the rest of my life."

"Survivor guilt is a common occurrence for anyone who's suffered a traumatic life event," Hayworth soothed. "But counseling can help you look at your situation more realistically, to better assess your role in what happened to your daughter.

"And I believe you'll find that the destructive aspect of your guilt will lessen over time and some of the energy currently bound up with your grief can become the source of a more vital and meaningful life."

Her eyes cleared. Narrowed to slits. "Are you trolling for business, Doctor?"

"Of course not." A tinge of red stained his cheekbones; his jaw tensed. "I was merely attempting to ease your pain, Mrs. Gallagher."

"No offense, Doctor, but there's only one thing that will begin to make my life worth living again."

She leaned forward, giving Will an up close and personal view of cleavage that would put the Tetons to shame. "I want you to find the monster who did this, Sheriff."

"I intend to."

"Good. And when you do, I want to cut his fucking balls off with a rusty knife."

28

In room 336 at the Red Wolf Lodge, Fyodor Radikorsky was throwing clothes into an Olympics duffel bag.

A hockey game was playing on TV. The Toronto Maple Leafs had just scored against the Colorado Avalanche when the network broke in with a news bulletin about former champion figure skater Erin Gallagher's death.

He took another hit from a silver flask, savoring the full-bodied vodka burn as he considered what to do about this latest development in a situation that had seemed so easy in the beginning. But had gotten so fucked-up.

A fatalist to the core, Fyodor was not, as Americans were so fond of saying, going to waste time crying over spilled milk.

Still, to quote another popular Western bromide, it was time to get out of Dodge before the sheriff showed up at his door.

"Well," Desiree said after Susan Gallagher and her driver/rock left the office. "Keira Knightley and Charlize Theron and all those other actresses who might be Oscar nominees this year may as well not bother shopping for a kick-ass dress, because we've just witnessed the award-winning performance."

"You didn't believe her?" Will asked with a sardonically arched brow.

"Hey, even if I wasn't creeped out by the stuff I read about her and her kid, I'd still think the woman is a piece of work."

Will couldn't help but agree. He glanced over at Drew Hayworth. "What's your professional take on the situation?"

"Obviously I'd need more time to make a professional diagnosis. But I certainly didn't pick up on any real grief that needed counseling."

"Anyone believe that the girl was going to return to skating?"

"Only in her mother's sicko, greedy dreams," Desiree said. "Did you see her bag? It was Chanel. I saw that online for fifteen hundred bucks."

"Didn't the gravy train stop when her daughter walked away from skating?" Will asked. "Maybe that's what had her moved to tears."

"There's undoubtedly still some endorsement money coming in she's managed to glom on to. But that's probably what had her come to town. To pressure her kid to get back onto the ice."

"She could've honestly been trying to reconcile for family reasons," Will suggested, not believing it for a moment, but feeling the need to explore all possibilities.

"If that woman has a heart, it's stainless steel," Drew Hayworth said. Will figured part of the banked anger in his voice came from the way he'd been personally and professionally attacked. "The only loss she's suffering from is the loss of an easy income and the reflected fame that comes with being the mother of America's Ice Princess."

"There's always the insurance," Sam, who'd thus far remained silent, offered.

"Shit." Desiree slapped her head, immediately jumping onto that idea. "I should've thought of that first off. Considering murder for money is one of the top three motives for homicide."

"Do we even know there was a policy written on Erin Gallagher?" Will asked Sam. "Did you find any legal papers in her apartment?"

"Not a thing." Sam shrugged. "But the girl was a financial asset. She may have only won silver in the last Olympics four years ago, but a lot of people thought she should've won the gold."

"Didn't I read something about her mother and coach claiming collusion?" Will recalled.

"It was more than just a claim. There was solid evidence of a scoring fix."

They all stared at Sam. "You watch figure skating?" Desiree asked in obvious disbelief.

"I read about it in the paper, back when it happened," Sam responded, somewhat defensively, Will thought, as if Sam didn't want people to think he might ever watch such a chick sport.

"Endorsement-wise, not winning gold might've been the best thing that could've happened to her, since she picked up a huge sympathy vote. Before she walked away from skating this year, you couldn't turn on the TV without seeing her pitching something.

"My initial point was that most people, especially ones as into conspicuous consumption as that mother seems to be, insure their assets."

"That's cold," Trace Honeycutt, who'd been standing at the back of the room soaking in the murder discussion, said.

He colored a bit as every eye in the place turned from Sam toward him. "Well, it is."

"Don't look now, Honeycutt," Desiree said, "but with the exception of temper-fueled rage killings, murder usually is damn cold. And whoever killed Erin Gallagher has a stone where their heart should be."

"There are Native American tribes who believe that the conscience is a three-cornered stone residing in the middle of the chest," Drew Hayworth volunteered.

"Each time you do something wrong, the stone turns. The more wrong you do, the more the stone wears down, until finally the edges are completely worn off, then the stone is smooth and no longer hurts when it turns."

"Well, if that's the case, Erin Gallagher's killer's walking around with a stone as smooth as glass," Desiree said.

Will couldn't disagree. "All the more reason to get him before he decides to branch out."

"Why don't I run over to the lodge and ask Susan Gallagher flat out if she had a policy on her daughter," Desiree suggested. "Maybe the element of surprise will cause her to spill the beans."

"She didn't seem to like you very much," Sam said.

"Boy, and doesn't that break my heart?"

"Sam's got a point," Will decided. "She's going to be less likely to be on the defensive if we send someone she can better relate to."

"Honeycutt," Sam and Desiree said at the same moment.

"Great minds," Will said.

"You want me to question her?" the deputy asked. "Alone?"

"Gotta get your feet wet sometime."

Will also decided to get Desiree on the computer and phone and start trying to track down anyone who might know about a policy having been written. Not that it would be easy to find anyone even working this week, but sometimes you got lucky.

"I won't let you down, Sheriff. Though," Honeycutt tacked on, "Mrs. Gallagher sure didn't seem big enough to physically slice anyone's throat. Even someone as tiny as her daughter was."

"Ah, but she's got Chad," Desiree pointed out. "Who obviously provides a helluva lot more personal service than merely driving Susan Gallagher around the valley.

"And," she tacked on significantly, "conveniently happens to have a wandering eye."

"Not that you'd take advantage of any man's weakness," Will said drily.

"Hell, no." She winked and fluffed her wavy cloud of dark hair. "I already agreed, when we were off getting Her Highness tea, to stop by the lodge for a drink on the way home. I'll change into some civvies, maybe flash a little cleavage, see what good old Chad volunteers."

"And how is that not entrapment?" Drew asked.

"All's fair in the war on crime," Desiree countered. "Besides, the Supreme Court allows cops to dupe a suspect to get to the truth."

"Convenient," Drew murmured.

Desiree flashed a brilliant, expectant smile. "Isn't it, just?"

29

The man who was once the boy raised by wolves was not happy. He'd prepared so carefully, seeking out his hunting ground, choosing his kill site, stalking his prey, learning her routine, making copious notes of her every behavior, visualizing the kill at least a thousand times until he could probably have slit her slender white throat in his sleep. He'd planned for every contingency. But one.

The unpredictability of human nature.

Frustration bubbled close to the surface. He took a deep breath. Another. Reminded himself that anger clouded the mind. Dulled the senses.

Something he could not, would not allow.

All right. So things with the girl hadn't gone entirely according to plan. A good hunter improvised. Adapted to his situation while staying cool. Calm.

And most important of all, he stayed focused.

But, of course, that didn't mean he couldn't enjoy his work.

As he raced the black snowmobile across the fields of powdery white snow and through the still and deeply shadowed woods, he imagined how his prey would react when he first cornered her.

She'd be startled. Her amber eyes would go wide. Like a doe in the headlights. A clichéd turn of phrase, perhaps. But one that suited this situation perfectly.

Perhaps she'd be irritated that he'd frightened her. Embarrassed that she'd revealed her fear.

She might even open her lovely red mouth to scream. They usually did. But he was faster, able to slice through her larynx before she could let out so much as a squeak.

One possible problem: he doubted she'd be as passive as Erin Gallagher.

She wouldn't just go limp — and hadn't that been a pain in the ass, having to hold the girl up when she couldn't stand on her own two feet? — and allow her throat to be slashed to the bone.

No. Tonight's prey was, while not nearly his equal, still a fighter. She would not go gently into that good night.

But go she would.

30

The sun was riding high in the sky when Faith returned home from the studio, planning to finally try to catch a few hours' sleep before having to return to KWIND for *Talking After Midnight.*

The drive from the station to her house had taken her by the courthouse, and she wasn't surprised to see that there were even more news crews than there'd been this morning.

She certainly didn't envy Will. Always before she'd been on the other side of a news situation, trying to extract information from cops and public officials who were, more often than not, frustratingly close-mouthed.

Now, forced to see this situation through his eyes, she realized how difficult his job was. Which was, she assured herself, the only reason she hadn't leaked Josh's name yet.

It had nothing to do with the fact that she'd become emotionally involved with both father and son.

"And if you believe that, I've got a ski resort on Maui to sell you," she muttered as she pulled into the garage.

The good news was that there was no sign of Sal.

The bad news was the red light flashing on her cordless telephone's base unit.

One of the calls was from Fred Handley, actually congratulating her on scooping the other news organizations and suggesting that if she played her cards right and continued to stay ahead of the pack, he might consider giving her Brian Kendall's spot, now that Brian — or, as Handley put it, "that disloyal, lying weasel sumbitch" — had accepted a job in Boise.

Two calls were from phone companies wanting her to switch her long distance, and three were from Sal Sasone, assuring her that she might be able to run, but she could not hide.

"I'm at the Red Wolf Lodge," he growled into the phone. "And there's no point in continuing to try to hide from me, because in case you haven't noticed, sweetheart, this place only has one stoplight. You're not going to be that hard to find. And I'm not going away until I settle what I've come here to do."

She did not doubt him.

Part of her wanted to run as far and as fast as she could. The trouble with that idea was that she'd already tried it. Unfortunately, what had once made Sal a helluva good cop, and more recently, she suspected, also made him an effective bounty hunter, was that the man was indefatigable. He'd always reminded her of Marshal Sam Gerard, Tommy Lee Jones's character from *The Fugitive.*

He simply would not give up the chase.

She'd never foreseen that what she'd once considered his best attribute could turn so deadly.

"Damn you, Sal Sasone," she muttered. "And the horse you rode in on."

She went into the bathroom, turned on the shower, in the narrow stall next to the claw-footed bathtub, stripped off her clothes, and stood beneath the pounding hot water, trying to ease out the stress and tension that was tangling with her exhaustion.

She shampooed her hair, then squeezed some liquid soap from the dispenser. When she imagined the hands smoothing it over her body were Will's, not hers, an entirely different, delicious tension uncurled inside her.

They were no longer the same people. Their lives had drastically changed since that seemingly halcyon Savannah summer. But some things were still the same.

Will Bridger was still able to throw her emotional equilibrium out of kilter with a single look. He could still leave her shaken with a touch, desperate with a kiss.

And she still wanted him more than any other man she'd ever met.

Or, Faith feared, would ever meet.

So where did they go from here?

She'd have to tell him. About the past she'd been so diligent in hiding these past years that he hadn't even discovered her secret, shameful past back in Savannah.

Of course, he hadn't known where to look. Nor had any reason to go back that far. But now she knew he was an intensely thorough detective. Given a bit more time . . .

She rubbed her eyes, which, from being up all these hours, felt as if they had sand in them.

You'll have to tell him the truth, her conscience warned. *Soon.*

"I know."

Now she was talking to herself. The ironic thing was that having fallen madly, impossibly in love with him, she'd been planning to tell him the entire, unvarnished ugly truth that night in Savannah.

She twisted off the water with more strength than necessary, wishing she could turn off her guilt so easily.

"Soon."

Fyodor Radikorsky had just turned off the television when there was a hard, determined rapping on the door.

Surprised that room service had arrived so soon with the elk burger and beer he'd ordered shortly before the news announcement, he went to open the door. No point in wasting good food, and he could always eat the burger on the way to the airport.

"Khuy." He ground out the Russian curse on a harsh gargle as he pressed his eye up to the judas hole and viewed the person standing in the hallway.

And wasn't this just what he fucking needed? Deciding that the Russian proverb about the tongue always returning to the sore tooth was all too true, he opened the door.

Steam was practically pouring from Susan Gallagher's ears as she stormed into the room and, without any warning, slammed a knee upward between his legs.

A lightning jolt of pain shot from Fyodor's groin to scorch into his brains. Like a tree downed by a lumberman's ax, he fell to the floor, where he writhed atop the Indian rug, struggling to extract his balls from his tonsils where they'd lodged.

His stomach roiled, his head felt as if the top had blown off.

The room blurred.

Tilted.

"What the fucking hell have you done now?" his nemesis demanded.

She was standing over him like a blond avenging angel. But not one who'd ever reign in heaven. No, from what he'd witnessed over the past decade, this vicious, ice-hearted female had been created for hell.

"That's what I get." She pulled her leg back, then kicked his ass. The wildfire raging through his groin prevented him from fighting back. "Trusting something this important to a fucking brain-sodden alkie!"

Although he outweighed her by a hundred pounds, all he could do was curl into a fetal position and pray for mercy.

Not that Susan Gallagher knew the meaning of the word.

He screamed when another kick grazed his knee.

Retched. Then vomited atop her shiny

black boots.

"Dammit, now look what you've done! These are brand-new Jimmy Choos!"

Still curled into a tight ball on the floor, he watched, unable to move as the soiled boot pulled back. Screeched like a skinned cat as the needle-sharp pointed toe scored a direct hit to the kidneys. He knew, if he survived the attack, he'd be pissing blood for a month.

A moose-shaped lamp with a heavy wood and iron base stood on an end table. She yanked the cord from the wall, snatched the lamp up, and held it over her head. "I know you killed my daughter, you fucking Russian pervert!"

As the lamp came crashing down on his head, Fyodor escaped into a deep, dark void.

31

Faith had just gotten out of the shower when someone began knocking at the door. All too aware that she was naked beneath her thick flannel robe, she grabbed the red bag with the gun from the countertop, and went into the living room.

This time, given it was daylight, she looked out the window. When she saw Will standing on her porch, she felt a little zing of anticipation.

"Hi." Was that breathless voice really hers?

"Hi." He was holding the black felt Stetson he'd gone back to in his hands. "KWIND's been running your report about every two minutes. I wanted to thank you for holding back Josh's name." He was turning the hat in his hands. Could he possibly be as nervous as she was?

"You're welcome. But I didn't do it for you." Well, not entirely.

"Whatever the reason, I'm grateful. It's

definitely going to have to come out, but I'd like to be able to give the vultures the killer when it does."

"No one who knows Josh could believe he'd hurt a fly."

"Well, yeah, but the thing is, he hasn't been here long enough, and my less than spotless teenage reputation probably isn't going to help."

"If we're going to be judged by our teenage days, we're all going to be in trouble," she murmured.

"And isn't that the truth." They were standing there, her looking up at Will, him looking down at her.

"Do you have time to come in? I've made coffee."

"I'll make time."

She moved aside, letting him into her house again. And this time, she knew, into her heart.

His boots were encrusted with snow. He yanked them off, leaving them in the box by the front door.

He shrugged out of his parka and, as he had earlier — had that only been a few hours ago? — hung it, along with his hat, on the wall rack. Faith knew it was ridiculously romantic, but seeing their two jackets side by side on her living room wall made them seem almost like, well, a couple.

"So," she said. "Do you have the coroner's report?"

"Nope. I'm still waiting. Seems some congressman's kid got drunk and took a header off his third-floor Jackson condo balcony and landed on the roof of a Jeep parked on the street. The DA's worried the congressman's going to start calling for an investigation, so he's trying to get ahead of what could turn out to be a red-ball case. So, my homicide just got bumped to second place."

"An Olympic athlete isn't a potential red-ball?"

"Not as much as a kid whose dad is about to be indicted for shady casino dealings and suspect foreign oil deals."

"Do they think he was murdered?"

"Beats me. Since it happened within the town limits, it's not my jurisdiction. Nor my case."

"Still, another dead teenager —"

"There aren't any similarities. The kid was kicked out of two bars for being drunk and disorderly before going on to a private party where he got in a fistfight over some UW coed.

"Now, maybe someone did go home with him and kill him. Maybe he and the coed decided to have sex outdoors and things got a bit too gymnastic for safety and she took off. But either of those scenarios would be acquaintance murder. Which, unfortunately, is all too common when you add testosterone and alcohol.

"Still, I've touched base with the police chief. He's a good cop; if he finds any connection between my dead kid and his, he's going to call."

"So, if you don't have the coroner's report, why are you here?"

"Why do you think?"

He drew her into his arms. Just as she'd been hoping he would. The kiss began as a subtle persuasion — a feathering brushing of his mouth to hers, a slow stroking of his tongue against her lower lip.

When his tongue slipped between her lips, then retreated, Faith wondered how it was that her body could be so exquisitely alive even as her brain grew more and more clouded.

"Nothing's changed," she murmured as Will abandoned her lips to press stinging kisses against the line of her jaw. "The timing's all wrong."

"It sucks." He smoothed a hand down her hair, which was falling wetly over her shoulders.

"You have a murder to solve."

"Which I intend to do," he vowed, burying his lips in her hair. "Later." His palms skimmed over her shoulders, down her back, to her hips.

Will had come here to thank her for protecting his son. That had been his honest intention. Yet he'd had a second motive, one that had nothing to do with work and everything to do with the hormones that started bouncing around like a pinball in an arcade machine whenever he got anywhere near this woman.

She was wearing about the ugliest piece of women's clothing he'd ever seen. But even with her body covered up by that heavy, red flannel robe, with her hair tangling like wet seaweed over her shoulders, and not a speck of makeup, he still found her drop-dead gorgeous.

"I want to taste you." He slipped his hand into the front of the robe. Her heart pounded furiously against his palm. "All over."

He yanked the hastily tied knot loose, then pushed the flannel off her shoulders. "My lips on every fragrant inch of that long, lean, sexy as hell body."

"Oh, God," she murmured on a helpless, throaty laugh as her hands got busy on the buttons of his khaki shirt. "I want that, too."

"Then I want to be inside you." His mouth skimmed up her cheek, lingering at her temple. "I want you, Faith."

His lips moved back down her face, pausing to drink deeply from hers before moving down her throat. "In every way a man wants a woman. Some that are undoubtedly illegal in half the jurisdictions in this state."

Her pulse, beneath his mouth, was pounding; Will could feel the pleasure rising, heating her skin as his tongue caressed her breasts in slow, tantalizing strokes.

Her fragrant flesh was even silkier than he'd remembered. She was everything he'd ever wanted, without having realized he'd been wanting.

Everything and more.

"Then, once I've had you, being the generous sort of guy that I am, I'll let you have me."

His caressing touch moved lower, down the center of her body, over her rib cage, her stomach, the silky, dark curls at the apex of her firm, smooth thighs.

"And then, just when you're convinced you can't take any more, I want to start in all over again."

She was trembling, her skin so hot he would not have been surprised if she'd burst into flames. With him right after her. "Do you always get everything you want, Sheriff?"

"Hell, no." Talk about your vast understatements. "But I'm damn well going to have you." He rubbed his thumb over her bottom lip. "And you're going to love it."

"I've missed this," she admitted as her hands fretted down his back. "You." Lower. "And me." Her hips moved in erotic little circles. "Together like this."

"You and me both, babe." He dug his fingers into her hips, ground her against his aching erection.

Once.

Twice.

Three times, until he was on the verge of popping all five metal buttons on his jeans.

"You've been driving me crazy ever since I got back to town. Just about all I've been able to think about is all the things I've wanted to do to you." His fingers caressed the soft, slick folds hidden in the downy nest of black curls. "With you."

"Show me." She writhed against his erotic touch. "I want to know everything," she said on a ragged moan as his fingers slipped into her, savoring her moist readiness. "I want to do everything."

She was so hot. So wet. His fingers thrust

deeper. Stroking, caressing the very heart of her. And, amazingly, all that heat was for him.

He could take her. Here, now. On the floor. Up against the wall. But he wanted more.

What he wanted, Will realized, was everything.

He swept a glance around the room, taking in the boxes she'd yet to unpack and the absolute lack of furnishings.

"I'm more than willing to improvise, sweetheart, but tell me you bought a bed."

"It's upstairs," she said breathlessly, as he nipped at her lips. "Down the hall. Third door to the left." She trembled as he bit the cord at the base of her neck, then dragged her onto her toes.

He put his hands beneath her bare bottom. "Put your legs around me."

She did as instructed, wrapping those long legs around his hips, bringing them chest to chest. Groin to groin. God help him, he'd be lucky if he didn't come before he made it to the upstairs landing.

"You don't have to carry me all the way."

"If you think I'm going to let go of you now, just when I've got you where I want you, you have another think coming," he said as he carried her from the room, head-ing toward the stairs.

The bed was lacy wrought iron, the delicate swoops and swirls and white rosettes reminding him of a wedding cake.

Will pulled back the thick comforter, laid her on the mattress, then stood looking down at her.

"What?" she asked.

"I was just thinking how exquisite you are." He trailed a finger delicately from the hollow of her throat, down over her small, perfect breasts, circling the rosy tips. "You always have taken my breath away," he murmured.

His caressing hand stroked her stomach, her hips, her taut, satiny thighs.

"You're not so bad yourself, cowboy. . . . I want to see you," she said, arching against his intimate touch. "Feel you."

"Sweetheart, I thought you'd never ask." He unbuttoned his cuffs and peeled off the shirt she'd already opened, letting it drop onto the polished heart-of-pine floor.

With fingers that were not as steady as he would have liked, Will unfastened his jeans, then shoved them, along with the gray knit boxer briefs, down his hips and stepped out of them.

The way she was staring up at him made him feel like a god.

If the wags who'd been speculating about her love life were even halfway accurate, she'd been living the life of a nun since moving to Hazard. Not wanting to risk her not having any protection handy, he'd come prepared.

He retrieved a condom from the small extra pocket of the jeans; the mattress sighed as he lay down beside her on the bed.

Although the need was almost intolerable, Will forced himself to slow the pace, hands stroking, lips taking slow, leisurely tours over her body, which flushed a deep rosy red beneath his caressing touch.

She flowed like a river beneath him, going wherever he took her.

Until he parted the slick pink folds of her lower lips. And she tensed.

"Did I hurt you?" he asked.

"No." The fever flamed even hotter in her cheeks. Her eyes were oddly shadowed with something indecipherable. Something Will decided he'd think about later. When he wasn't being bombarded by out of control hormones.

He captured both her wrists and lifted her hands above her head.

"Hold on tight," he said, wrapping her fingers around the lacy iron scrollwork of the headboard. "Because you're goin' on an

E-ticket ride, sweetheart." He scraped a fingernail up her inner thigh. "And I'm going to watch you."

She bucked against him when he put his mouth on her, then cried out in stunned shock as the climax ripped through her.

"I wanted to take this slow. Make it last."

She was trembling. She wasn't alone. His own muscles were quivering and his lungs burned as he braced himself over her.

"But I need you." Her back bowed, her hands released their hold on the bed frame to grab his ass, seeking completion.

He gritted his teeth, forced himself to hold back for one last, all-important detail. "Your name."

"What?" Her unfocused eyes blinked.

"What the hell is your name? Your real name."

"Oh." She blew out a short, sharp breath. "It's Faith." Then, as if sensing he might still doubt her, she tacked on, "I swear. Faith Fletcher."

"Faith."

He thrust into her, claimed her. Then plundered, driving her deeper into the mattress with each long stroke.

This time she screamed when she came, her hand fisting the sheets.

"Will." It was half-sob, half-plea. "Please."

Her hands clawed at his back, and lower. "Now."

"Not yet."

When he put his hand between them, his thumb flicking against her ultrasensitive flesh, she poured over his hand.

And then, and only then, did he surrender to his own release.

32

It was driving Sal crazy. What the hell was it about that young murder victim's name that kept ringing a bell somewhere in the back of his drug-numbed brain?

He knew who she was, of course. You couldn't turn on a TV without seeing that teenage chick spinning across the ice advertising everything from cereal to soup. But it was more than that. Something he couldn't quite put a finger on.

Giving up on the problem for now, he pushed himself off the bed and made his way on still unsteady legs across the room to the entertainment center in the bedroom armoire and stuck in the DVD he'd watched so many times he had every line of dialogue memorized.

When he'd first met the woman currently going by the name of Faith Prescott, she'd been doing weekday-morning, drive-time news and a half-hour, Saturday pre-baseball-game call-in show. But a guy'd have to be queer as a three-dollar bill to be able to keep his mind on box scores while listening to her smoky, sexy-as-sin voice.

Which was, of course, how she'd ended up being stalked by that whacked-out guy who'd created a barred, six-by-eight-foot cage in his basement, just for her. Fortunately, Sal had apprehended the sicko before he could pull off his cockamamy scheme to make Faith Fletcher his personal love slave.

Sal had wanted her from the start. But, being a professional, he'd managed to rein in his rampant hunger. After all, he'd always prided himself on being one of the good guys.

Back when he'd been in uniform, patrolling the streets, he'd never once stooped to accepting quickies from cop groupies in the back of his cruiser.

He'd also turned down more blow jobs from hookers looking to avoid arrest than he could count, and although it had taken every damn bit of self-control he'd possessed, there was no way he'd been willing to sully his hard-won detective's shield by fucking a crime victim he was supposed to be protecting.

But once Faith's stalker was behind bars,

three months after the case had first landed on Sal's desk, he'd driven straight to her suite at the Bellagio, where, having done security work on the side for the luxury casino hotel, he'd been able to arrange for the round-the-clock protection the cops hadn't been able to provide.

She'd certainly seemed grateful when he'd broke the news about the arrest and assured her she wouldn't have to be looking over her shoulder all the time anymore. Grateful enough to go to bed with him.

Okay, so maybe it hadn't been the wild chandelier-swinging, down and dirty monkey sex he'd been fantasizing about for the past three months, but as he'd assured her afterward, first times were never all that hot. It'd just take time for them to get to know what the other person liked.

As his court-appointed anger-management therapist had recently pointed out, it had been an emotional time for both of them. He'd marched into the suite, higher than a kite on adrenaline, testosterone, with the creep's blood still on his bruised and swollen knuckles and carrying a magnum of Dom he'd bought downstairs in the Caramel bar.

As much as he'd thought about her, dreamed about her, fantasized spending the rest of his life with her, Sal had surprised himself by proposing afterward.

Faith had surprised him a helluva lot more by actually accepting, and not wanting to give her time to back out, he'd maxed out his already overburdened Visa card by paying nearly two thousand bucks for a long, white limo from the hotel to the Clark County courthouse, an hour of chapel time, an officiant who — thank you, Jesus! — didn't look anything like Elvis, a bridal bouquet and boutonniere, a bottle of sparkling wine, a gilt-wrapped box of hotel chocolates, and the deluxe photo package, which also included a personalized video.

He'd gotten drunk and burned the photos after she left. But he'd kept the video, which he'd even had converted to DVD.

"Christ, she's a looker," he muttered now as he watched his runaway bride walking down that white satin runner toward him.

Not that he was one to brag, but Sal knew he wasn't bad looking. There'd even been women who'd told him he looked a bit like Stallone in his early Rocky days. But that had never stopped him from feeling like the Beast to Faith's Beauty.

Although she'd protested the cost, he'd insisted on buying her a dress in one of the pricey hotel lobby shops. The store, catering to spur-of-the-moment brides, carried a rack of cocktail dresses in traditional bride's white, but she'd decided against any of those, instead choosing a sexy, body-hugging, short silk number the color of autumn leaves that had brought out the gold flecks in her whiskey-hued eyes.

When she'd come out of the dressing room, Sal had felt as if he'd swallowed his tongue.

The oldest of eight kids, he'd grown up taking care of people. He'd never minded. Hell, he'd liked it. It made him feel big. Important, the way his younger brothers and sisters looked up to him.

It's why he'd become a cop in the first place. And, for a while, whether Faith wanted to admit it or not, she'd damn well liked being taken care of.

Until the trial. When things started sliding downhill.

"Forget about that!"

God, he needed a drink! Wasps were buzzing around in his brain and fiery needles were prickling beneath his skin.

"It was her fault, dammit."

Okay, maybe not entirely. Maybe the shrink was on the right track, about them both having had issues.

But shouldn't she have understood how

rough all that testimony had been on him? Why couldn't she have warned him? What man would like having to hear details about his wife's sordid past?

Images of her having down and dirty sex with all those faceless, nameless men had begun playing over and over in an endless loop in his mind. There'd been no escaping them.

They tormented those daytime hours when he was supposed to be working; kept him awake long into the night; and on those rare occasions he was able to sleep, his dreams were of sleazy, X-rated porn movies, all of them, goddammit, starring his wife.

No one down at the cop shop ever said anything. At least not to his face. They wouldn't have dared. But from the way conversation would immediately drop off whenever he entered the bull pen, he knew they were talking about her.

Laughing at him for ending up one of the most pitiful of stereotypes — the alkie cop who marries a hooker, for chrissakes! — their scorn gnawing away at his manhood.

Shit. He scrubbed a hand down his face.

He'd dragged his sorry ass all the way up here yesterday to Icepick, Wyoming, to settle things with Faith once and for all. Sitting here in the hotel room, watching a replay of the marriage she'd walked out on, wasn't doing the job.

The only thing left to do was just suck up the pain that was even making his teeth hurt and go find his goddamn bride.

33

"This is going to sound crazy," Faith said, "but all this silence is starting to get on my nerves."

She'd put on the robe again and was sitting cross-legged on the bed, watching as Will dressed to leave. Clothed, his body was impressive. Naked, it was downright magnificent.

His shoulders were broad, roped with muscle, and one was slashed with a raised, red scar she'd wanted to ask him about, but they hadn't spent a lot of time conversing.

Later, she decided.

His torso, which carried not an ounce of excess flesh and was ripped enough to do laundry on, narrowed down to lean cowboy hips. His legs were long, firm, and, like his arms, sinewy and muscled.

He was male physical perfection personified, and if she'd been an artist, she would have been salivating to immortalize him in marble. As it was, she was just salivating.

"It happens."

She felt a little twinge of loss as he pulled the jeans over the tight-fitting knit boxers. Even after all they'd shared, she had a sudden, almost overwhelming urge to get between Will Bridger and his Calvins.

"You can get so used to the wind blowing, it's difficult to adjust when it stops," he said. "Like the yelling." He plucked the khaki shirt from the floor. "People grow up having to shout over the wind; when it's not blowing, it takes everyone a while to realize they don't have to scream anymore."

"I noticed that."

Though what was drawing her attention at the moment was that dark arrowing of hair that disappeared beneath the briefs. Faith felt another pang when he buttoned the shirt.

"When I stopped at Earl's Exxon to fill up this morning, Earl Jenkins nearly screamed my ear off," she said. "I thought perhaps he'd started going deaf since the last time I was there last week. It was the same thing with Rayanne at the market.

"And last night Mike claimed he was even having to adjust the volume when callers phoned in. But I thought he was exaggerating."

"Nope. It's just one of the symptoms." He tucked in the shirt. Next those same fingers that had created such havoc on every inch of her body deftly refastened the metal buttons. "It's like everything suddenly gets exaggerated. People talk a lot louder, drink more. Laugh more. Fight more.

"Hayworth could probably do a study on it. Back when I was in high school, a sociology professor tracked birth rates for a three-year period and there was always a boom nine months after the wind stopped for a day or two."

"You're kidding."

"Nope. I don't remember all the socio-scientific details, but the gist of the study was that any abrupt change in weather can cause a loss of inhibitions. He likened it to those crazy hurricane parties you see people havin' down in Florida. People rip off their clothes and fuck like minks."

He grinned. "Needless to say, at sixteen I found that idea real appealing."

"I can imagine," Faith said drily. "So, is that what this" — she smoothed a hand over rumpled white sheets that still carried the redolent scent of their lovemaking — "was all about? Wind-cessation sex?"

"Hell no." His square jaw angled; a flash of hot annoyance darkened his eyes so it was impossible to tell where the iris left off and the pupil began. "You can't really think that?"

"No." She scooped a hand through her hair. "I was being overly defensive." She managed a faint, self-deprecating smile. "Maybe this wind thing is getting to me, too. Making me exaggerate stories in my mind. Especially since, if Selma down at The Wild Hair is to be believed —"

"Faith." He crossed the few feet to the bed, sat down, and put his arm around her shoulder. "I left Hazard when I was a few weeks from turning eighteen. I'm not saying that I didn't do my share of teenage fooling around. But Selma isn't even remotely qualified to comment on any women I may have tumbled after leaving town.

"In fact, except for one admittedly memorable Halloween party when I made it to first base with her, that's the only firsthand knowledge she could possibly have concerning my sex life."

"Unfortunately, that doesn't stop her from speculating," Faith said. "And sharing those speculations with anyone who'll listen."

Faith had never considered herself a jealous woman. Until now. She also knew that if she worried about every woman Will might have had sex with, whatever relationship they might be able to forge would be doomed from the start.

"No. It doesn't." He shook his head. "But as you've undoubtedly figured out, given the fact that among the morning coffee club at The Branding Iron, your sex life ranks right up there with beef prices and the weather —"

"My lack of sex life, you mean."

"Obviously you were saving it up for a man who knew what to do with it."

Faith didn't take offense at his male arrogance, because if she was to be perfectly honest, it was one of the things that had attracted her to him.

"My point is," he continued, "gossip is the coin of the realm in a small town. Selma's mother was self-appointed queen of that realm while I was growing up here. From what I've heard, Selma's inherited her tiara."

"That's putting it mildly. If the woman had been around in Wyoming's pioneer days, the Pony Express wouldn't have had to hire all those orphans to deliver the mail."

He smiled, with his lips and his eyes. "She's always needed excitement. If there isn't any readily available, she'll try to stir something up."

He pressed a snowflake-light kiss against

the top of her head. Her temple. "Has she mentioned the time aliens landed on top of Devils Tower?"

"I don't believe it's come up." Or if it had, she'd missed it. Except when she was talking about Will, Faith tended to tune the chatty hairdresser out. Fortunately, Selma seemed to prefer her conversations to be one-sided, so responses weren't often necessary.

"Isn't that the mountain Richard Dreyfuss's character carved out of mashed potatoes in *Close Encounters of the Third Kind*?"

"The very one. Some people, like Selma, obviously have a problem determining between fiction and real life." There was amusement in his tone. "By the time she finished embellishing the tale, a great many people were convinced we'd been invaded by pod people, which caused a run on Reynolds Wrap at the mercantile."

"Aluminum foil?" Faith eased back so she could look up at him.

"Obviously you've never covered an alien invasion during your reporting days." He brushed his lips against hers. "Otherwise you'd know aluminum-foil hats block alien mind-control rays."

"Live and learn." Her hands slipped

around his waist. She could feel her body softening, fitting itself to his solid strength. "I'll keep that in mind if the aliens ever return."

"Despite what the *National Enquirer* put on the front page, after they picked up the story from the *Hazard Herald,* they were never here in the first place."

He kissed her again. No more than a feathery brush of his mouth against hers, but it was still enough to cloud her mind. "She made it all up?"

"Not exactly all. Seems the northern lights reflected off a weather balloon sent up from Warren Air Force Base. Of course, there are still skeptics — like Selma and those guys who live alone out in their one-room cabins, sharing conspiracy theories about Area 51, who insist on believing the alien story."

He stroked her cheek with his knuckles, then curled his fingers around the back of her neck.

"Getting back to your question about what happened earlier, I wanted you the instant I laid eyes on you back in Savannah. Hell, you've got to believe that I'd want you, wind or no wind, rain or shine, snow, sleet, whatever the weather."

"I do." She smoothed her hands up his back, felt sinew and muscle beneath the stiffly starched khaki. "Believe you want me." Which was a major leap for her. Despite her name, faith had never come easily for her.

"Good. But dammit, as complicated as things already were back then by the second time we'd gone out, I knew it was becoming a lot more than that. Since we didn't have time to explore it further, I don't know what, exactly." His tone took on an edge of frustration.

Faith suspected it wasn't often Will Bridger was at a loss. She also suspected he didn't like it very much. "But, like I said, I figure since fate seems to have landed us both back here together, it's time we stopped playing games and found out."

She drew in a breath. Let it out. The moment she'd tried to avoid had finally arrived and she wasn't any more ready for it than she'd been three years ago.

"You're right about us needing to talk." Where to begin?

"Yeah. I know. Because there's things about me, things that happened down in Savannah, you deserve to know."

"You're not the only one with a past."

And wasn't that the understatement of the century. Any man would probably have trouble accepting what had been done to her. And worse, what she'd done to herself to survive during her teenage years on the mean streets.

Surely a cop would have a harder time than most men?

"Not unexpected, since neither of us are sixteen-year-old virgins."

Here's your opening. Just slip in the news that you lost your virginity at twelve.

He traced a fingertip around her lips, which, instead of forming the words reverberating in her mind, merely parted at the light caress. "But there's nothing that you could've done that's going to make me feel any differently.

"I'm going to get Erin Gallagher's killer," he promised. "Then I want to go away somewhere with you. Away from all this snow and ice. Some place warm and sunny. Tropical. We'll feed each other ripe fruit —"

"Passion fruit." The idea sounded like heaven. If he'd still be speaking to her after he heard the truth about her less than pristine past.

"You bet. And we'll lie in the sun, and I'll rub coconut oil all over your body, then —"

He cursed without heat as his cell phone rang. Given that he epitomized the Lone Ranger, she was not surprised he'd chosen the *William Tell* Overture.

"Bridger." Watching him carefully, Faith detected the faint tensing. "Okay, I'll be right there."

He closed the phone and turned to Faith. "That was Sam. The autopsy report was just faxed over from Jackson."

"Will you let me know what it says?"

"I can't keep giving you exclusives, Faith. Not without compromising the investigation, now that we've had sex."

She opened her mouth to point out he hadn't minded mixing sex and work three years ago. Then reminded herself it wasn't really fair to continue to hold that against him. Especially since she hadn't exactly been a bastion of truth herself.

"I wouldn't expect you to."

"Okay, then." He bent down and brushed his lips against hers. "I'll fill you in as soon as I can. Meanwhile, keep thinking warm thoughts."

As the kiss deepened, Faith knew she'd have no problem with that request.

34

Where the hell was he? What was the point in paying people to always be available if they felt free to just take off whenever they pleased?

Susan glared out the window, through the thick screen of tall pine trees, toward the lodge. Where she was now wishing she'd just stayed, instead of insisting on this chalet. The log-sided, three-bedroom rental with the vaulted wooden ceiling, gourmet kitchen with granite countertops, hot tub, game room, and wireless internet was way more space than she needed, but it was important for a woman in her position to keep up appearances.

It was already growing dark. Deep purple shadows were spreading across the snow, and the sky was so low she imagined she could reach up and touch it. Despite the fire blazing in the two-story stone fireplace, Susan could tell the temperature outside was plummeting.

She shivered against the bone-numbing chill that was creeping into the cabin on silent cat feet. She'd always disliked winter, which was ironic, given that she'd chosen to leave Southern California — and her marriage — to live most of her adult life first in the mountains of Utah, then Colorado.

But Erin needed to be where the coaches were. And where the skating press was more likely to gather. So, she'd put up with the snow and the ice and the cold.

A mother, after all, had to make sacrifices.

Now Erin was dead. And Susan's life as she knew it was over.

And that damn Chad, who'd said he was just running over to the lodge gift shop for cigarettes, still hadn't come back to mix her martinis.

He hadn't taken the car. So he couldn't have gone far. She'd bet her new Armani jacket the bastard was in one of the bars with some ski bunny.

Or that bimbo cop.

Susan had seen the way he'd been looking at her. Like a cocaine addict looking at a line of white powder. Bad enough that he might be fucking her at this very moment. Worse yet might be what he was telling her.

Pulling on her mink jacket and boots, she

stomped out of the chalet, determined to remind him who, exactly, was paying for those little bags of coke that kept disappearing up his nose.

Faith had been living alone since she was sixteen years old. Never had empty rooms seemed lonely.

Until now.

When she'd first come to Hazard and started working at KWIND, the change in hours had played havoc with her inner clock. But after a few weeks she'd become adjusted to working the midnight shift and hadn't had any trouble sleeping during the day.

Until now.

Even after having been awake for over twenty-four hours, she tossed and turned, her mind whirling, scenes flashing like strobe lights in her mind: the brightly lit crime scene at the lake; Josh, literally sick with the horror of the innocent girl's murder; Sal showing up in Hazard — and where the hell was he, anyway? — and most vivid of all, the past hour with Will, which would, whatever happened between them, always remain one of the most amazing experiences of her life. Even better than when they'd been together in Savannah.

She hoped there would be more. Whom was she kidding? She hoped there'd be a lot more.

The problem was, although he was certainly willing to bend the rules during his sex-trafficking investigation, she suspected Will Bridger undoubtedly lived in a cop world of good guys and bad guys. Black and white.

How would he ever deal with all the shades of gray she'd accumulated in her life? Not to mention that she'd lied to him.

Oh, she hadn't out and out lied. She'd never said, "Oh, by the way, I was never a prostitute." And she'd never told him that she wasn't married.

But she suspected he wouldn't see it that way. And neither would she if she were him.

The thing to do, she decided, as she gave up on trying to get any sleep and climbed out of bed, was to go to the inn and track down Sal, before he found her.

She'd clear the air, apologize profusely, grovel as much as it took to send him on his way back to the desert.

Then, hopefully when she had the long-overdue conversation with Will, she'd be able to honestly assure him that she was on her way to being free.

She could only pray it would be that easy.

But just in case it wasn't, she grabbed the red bag with the revolver as she left the house.

Just in case.

35

"Well," Will said to Jack Dawson, whom Sam had also called to the office, "it's official. Erin Gallagher's throat was slit."

"See," Jack said drily, "I was right. You were definitely better off handing the case over to the pros."

"It's a wise man who knows his limitations," Will murmured as he read through the pages Heather Jackson had faxed over.

A sharp instrument had been used from left to right, cutting both jugulars, her larynx, and the muscles on both sides of her neck.

"The guy knew what he was doing," Jack repeated what he'd said at the scene. "And to cut the muscles without having to saw away at them definitely shows strength."

"Which rules out a woman," Sam said.

"I never rule anyone out," Will responded. "But it definitely lessens the odds. There was blood in her lungs."

"Aspirated when she bled into her windpipe," Jack diagnosed.

"Which means," Desiree, who'd come in from patrolling out by Silver Lake when she'd heard the report had come in, said, "she was alive and breathing at the time her throat was cut."

"That's Heather's conclusion. She also writes that by the way the larynx was cut, and the way the windpipe was slashed, the girl's head must have been pulled back."

"Meaning that her killer came to her from behind. Which is undoubtedly why there weren't any defensive marks," Sam said.

Will nodded. "Yeah, that'd be my guess, too." He turned back to the report. "Christ, this says she had the bone density of a seventy-year-old woman. That's gotta be a mistake."

"Not necessarily," Jack said. "I see it a lot in orthopedics, mostly from the superathletic girls who are literally starving to death. Which, in turn, starves their bones."

"Hayworth said female athletes are prone to eating disorders," Will mused as he continued reading through the report. "Which doesn't exactly gel with the fact that she'd eaten pizza before being killed."

"Which your son already testified to," Sam said.

"Everyone we've talked with said she was starting to enjoy discovering a real life," Desiree said. "That would include eating like a normal person."

"Yeah, I suppose it would." Will frowned. "Her tox screen came back with trace amounts of MDMA."

It was Desiree's turn to frown. "Ecstasy."

"I hate to ask this," Sam said carefully, "but do you think she could have gotten the drug from Josh?"

Will plowed a hand through his hair. "Hell, I don't know. Anything's possible. He's done drugs before, but I thought we were beginning to move past that. And Hazard doesn't exactly have a huge rave scene."

"True. But small towns aren't immune from drugs."

And didn't Will know that?

"I'm still waiting to get his screen back."

"Which won't be definitive proof of his innocence."

"No." If Josh weren't his own son, Will knew he'd be as cynical as Sam sounded. The kid could be as clean as a hound's tooth and still have supplied her with it. Or at least watched her do it.

"I heard a speech on MDMA at a medical convention a few years ago," Jack offered. "It's supposed to open up the capacity for feeling loving, and affectionate, and trusting. Although it's being sold on the street, a lot of therapists continue to prescribe it."

"Well, that sure as hell should let Josh off the hook," Will muttered. "Since loving, affectionate, and trusting sure as hell doesn't exactly describe my son."

"Not outwardly," Desiree said. "But if you two weren't at such loggerheads, you'd see that deep down inside that rock-hard shell he's built around himself is a pretty sensitive boy."

"Yeah. That's what Faith Prescott keeps telling me."

Despite the seriousness of their conversation, Jack grinned. "You should listen to the lady. Not only is she smart, she's got great legs."

"Not to mention a very fine ass," Sam said.

"Mention her ass again and I'll have to shoot you," Will said mildly. Returning to the report, he missed the knowing look that flashed between the three other people in the room.

"There was pubic hair on her groin area."

"Not surprising, since Josh also admitted having sex with her."

"Yeah, but the samples came from two different people."

Jack blew out a low whistle. "You don't think —"

"That there was another person with them?" Will shook his head. "I seriously doubt that. Josh was sweating bullets while Sam was questioning him."

"There were a couple times I thought he was going to pass out on me," Sam agreed. "If he'd been involved in a three-way, I think it would've spilled out."

"Definitely," Will said.

"And if there'd been someone else there with her and Josh, she'd have been less likely to have gone out to the lake alone," Desiree said.

"Unless she went out there to meet someone. Which would also explain the lack of defensive wounds," Jack surmised.

"That doesn't work if Josh is telling the truth about her wanting him to go out there with her. Which his showing up on the scene later confirms."

"Not if he was jealous," Will said, playing devil's advocate. "Maybe he realized she was going straight from him to another guy and drove out there to catch her."

"Jesus, Will." Jack's brow furrowed. "Don't you trust anyone?"

"I may have left the big city, but I'm still a cop. With a murder to solve. So, the answer is no. . . .

"There's no sign of either pre-or postmortem rape, so, although I'm not ruling anything out, I suspect she had sex before she picked up Josh at the gas station."

"Girl had a busy night," Jack said.

"Seems so." Yet another case, Will thought, of people going to extremes when the damn wind stopped. Unfortunately, Erin Gallagher's recklessness had gotten her killed.

"We're going to have to comb the town. There must be someone who saw her before she and Josh had sex."

Will turned to Desiree. "And check with Debroux's pharmacy to see if they've filled any prescriptions for MDMA lately."

"Will do." She stood up. Pulled her parka off the wall hook. "It wasn't Josh, Will."

"Hell, no." Will would bet his badge, his career, hell, his life if need be, on that. "Which is why we have to find the guy. Before he decides to slice and dice again."

They were outside when Sam came over to him. "We need to talk," the deputy said.

"Sure," Will said. "But can it wait, because —"

Damn. The phone rang again. He'd gotten more cell phone calls in the past sixteen hours than he had in the past six months.

"Hold that thought," he said as Desiree drove off in the direction of the drugstore.

It was his dispatcher, Earlene Spoon-hunter, calling from the office upstairs. Her message was short and brief. And unwanted.

"Goddammit," Will ground out. "Tell them I'll be right there." He slammed the phone shut. Closed his eyes. Why was it that murder, which had been almost common-place when he'd been working vice, now seemed even more evil than it had in the city?

Because, he answered his own rhetorical question, small towns were supposed to be the last bastion of civility in America.

"We've got ourselves another body." Will blew out a harsh, frustrated breath. "A woman, out at the lodge."

"Oh, Christ, Will. Don't tell me —"

"Her throat was slit."

36

Only a few days after the start of winter, the sun set early. Which was why darkness had already fallen when Will pulled up outside the Red Wolf Lodge.

"Hey, Sheriff," the man standing in the spreading yellow glow of the mercury-vapor lamp outside the main entrance greeted Will as he climbed out of the Cherokee. Falling snowflakes sparkled like crystal in the light. "Talk about your small worlds. Or, I guess you could say, your small towns. Good to see you again."

"Mr. Sasone." Will nodded at the burly man he'd driven to the hospital. "How's the arm?"

"Hell, a little broken elbow can't keep a good cop down."

"You're a cop?" That little piece of information hadn't come up on the drive to the hospital last night. Of course that could have been because the man had cursed nonstop all the way into town.

"Was. I'm retired. Been working for myself as a bounty hunter these days."

"Is that what brings you to Hazard?" The last thing he needed was some armed and dangerous former cop running around loose in his town.

"Nah." Shoulders as wide as an ax handle shrugged. "I just figured I'd come here, do some skiing, maybe some ice fishing. Not a lot of either one of those things in the desert," he said with forced joviality. "Course that damn accident last night pretty much put the kibosh on that."

The guy was lying through his teeth. There was a story there. Will didn't know what it was. Didn't care unless it pertained to his murders.

"Well, you called in a possible crime, Mr. Sasone?"

"Not *possible.* Unless it's legal to go slashing women's throats in Wyoming."

"No."

"Didn't think so."

Sasone seemed to be enjoying himself. Will was not. "And you found the body where?"

"Over in the trees." He gestured toward a small stand of ponderosa pine beyond the circle of light. "I'll show you."

"Why don't you stay here —"

"I may look like a jackass to you, Bridger." The overly friendly tone turned hard. Familiar. Will recognized it, having used it on more than one occasion himself. It was the no-nonsense, take-no-prisoners voice of command. "But I was, until eighteen months ago, the goddamn best detective in the city of Las Vegas. I know enough not to compromise a crime scene."

Now that Will believed.

Will pulled the Maglite from his utility belt and followed Sasone into the trees, both men treading in the former cop's original footprints.

"There she is."

Her amber eyes stared unseeingly up at the falling snow. The mink coat that had looked so spiffy only a few hours earlier was wet and matted with blood. The meticulously made-up face was bleached to the color of ashes, and a bloody line, looking like a grotesque, scarlet grin, curved beneath her chin.

"It's Susan Gallagher."

A dark brow climbed the former detective's brow. "The dead skater's mother?"

"Yeah." Will crouched down and used the tip of his pen to lift the laminated piece of plastic from around her neck. Another damn poem. What the hell was going on here?

"Fuck!"

Will glanced up. Sasone looked as though he were about to have a stroke. "What?"

"The girl's name kept niggling at me, but with all the drugs they pumped into me, I couldn't get a handle on it. But that Russian who sat next to me on the plane was her coach."

"Erin Gallagher's coach is in Hazard?"

"Yep. In fact he's staying here at the lodge. I saw him early last night in the dining room." Sasone dragged a huge bear paw of a hand down his face. "Christ. Guess who his waitress was."

Will didn't have to guess. Remembering what Mike had said about the former skater complaining about tips, Will knew.

"Erin Gallagher."

It was, Faith thought, as she approached the lodge, déjà vu all over again. The parking lot, and the small stand of trees between the lodge and a semicircular grouping of log-sided chalets, were lit up like the middle of the day.

The flashing lights atop three sheriff department SUVs and two ambulances parked outside the lodge added surrealistic color, causing the falling snowflakes to resemble red and blue butterflies.

Unlike last night, the press, who'd come to Hazard to cover Erin Gallagher's death, were in full force, the TV folks setting up huge klieg lights that rivaled the brightness of the Vegas Strip, while the flashes from the still photographers' cameras winked like manic fireflies.

Faith recognized Will's black Jeep Cherokee immediately. She debated trying to join the other reporters clamoring for attention, but decided, since there was no way she was going to find out anything the others wouldn't know, she'd stick to her original plan of dealing with Sal. Hopefully Will would be so occupied with this latest crime scene that he wouldn't notice her slipping into the lodge.

Her boots crunched on the snow as she approached the main entrance, only to find her way blocked by police tape guarded by Hazard's very own Dudley Do-Right, Trace Honeycutt.

"I'm sorry, Ms. Prescott," he said, as she started to duck beneath the tape. "But I'm not allowed to let anyone past. Sheriff Bridger's orders."

"I understand."

She didn't like it, but she did honestly

understand Will's reasoning. That, however, wasn't going to stop her. If anything, the fact that her husband and the man she'd just made love with were both in the same location made her even more determined to get to Sal.

Nearby, three fire department paramedics were lifting a stretcher into the back of one of the red-andwhite ambulances. The driver of the other was standing beside his vehicle, smoking a cigarette, which suggested his services weren't going to be needed anytime soon.

"Would you mind doing me a favor, Deputy Honeycutt?"

Her voice dropped into its lowest registers. It was her husky, black velvet *Talking After Midnight* tone. The one Will said inspired sexual fantasies in men all over the high-mountain region. She could only hope it worked on this man.

His Adam's apple bobbed visibly. Bingo. "What favor would that be, Ms. Prescott?" His voice cracked like that of an adolescent asking a girl to the prom.

"Could you go get Sheriff Bridger for me?" She leaned forward, across the tape. "It's imperative that I speak with him."

"I'm sorry, ma'am, I'm not supposed to leave my post."

"Of course you're not. But believe me, he'll want to hear what I have to tell him."

If Sal didn't kill her, Will would for what she was about to do. Hopefully, he wouldn't also kill his deputy. Even as she told herself that it was important for the young man to learn the importance of following orders, she felt like the worst person on earth as his blue eyes darted toward the shaggy, dark trees.

"You'll have to stay here," he said hesitantly.

"I promise not to move a step," she lied.

"Well then, I guess, if you've information about the murder . . ."

So there had been another murder. Faith's blood, which was already chilled, turned even icier than the air as two men carried a stretcher bearing a black body bag out of the trees.

She was debating just giving up this fool's errand when the deputy suddenly turned and walked away, headed in the direction he'd just looked.

It was now or never. Taking a deep breath, Faith ducked beneath the tape.

"Hey, Faith baby!"

She froze at the all-too-familiar voice. Her heart in her throat, she turned slowly toward the tall, burly man who, if size was all that mattered, could easily have played linebacker on any professional football team in the country.

"Hello, Sal. This is a surprise."

"Small world, huh, baby?"

"Apparently."

Definitely not as large as she'd hoped when she'd escaped Las Vegas. She clutched the bag to her side and surreptitiously unzipped it. She couldn't believe Sal would try anything with all these cops on the scene. Then again, she'd never thought he'd hold a gun to her head and threaten to kill her.

"I planned on catching up with you last night, after I called you at the station, but I had myself a little accident. Ran my rental car into a tree when some idiot jackass on a snowmobile ran across the road in front of me.

"And, no, except for a busted elbow, I wasn't seriously injured, thank you very much for asking. They wanted to keep me overnight at the hospital, make sure I didn't drop dead after walking out of the ER, but, hey, didn't I always say you can't keep a good man down?"

"That's what you always said." Her hammering heart sank as she viewed the other man headed toward them.

"Hello, Faith." She heard the question in Will's voice. Hoped he'd believe she was here as a reporter.

"Sheriff." Her mind spun as she tried to remember whether there were earthquakes in Wyoming. Because she certainly wouldn't mind one opening up beneath her feet right now.

"Deputy Honeycutt said you had something important to tell me?"

"I believe he must have been mistaken."

"I think your deputy must've got himself snookered," Sal volunteered. "I've seen this little lady sweet-talk her way past more than one police line back in Vegas."

"Vegas." Will rolled the word around, as if trying it out on his tongue. "I take it you two know each other." His words were directed toward Sal, but his eyes were dark and hard on hers.

"You could say that," Sal said. He winked at Faith. "This pretty little gal is my wife."

37

"Well," Sal said, five minutes later, "this reunion started out with a bang."

They were seated across from one another at a corner table of the lodge bar.

He'd invited her back to his room to talk, but while Faith might have gotten reckless the past twenty-four hours (which she'd decided to blame on the damn lack of wind), she hadn't turned stupid overnight.

Telling herself yet again that he'd never try anything with so many cops here at the lodge, there was still no way she was willing to be alone with him. Which was why she was holding her bag on her lap, her right hand just inside it.

"What are you doing here, Sal?"

"I don't suppose you'd buy that I've missed my wife?"

He didn't seem nearly as frightening as she remembered. Maybe that was because she'd blown up the memory in her mind, like a child creating a bogeyman who lived beneath the bed. Of course in the case of Faith's childhood, the bogeymen had been all too real.

Or, she thought, maybe because that aura of violence that had surrounded him like a noxious cloud was gone, leaving behind the single-minded cop who'd vowed to protect her.

"I don't know why you would've missed me. Excuse me if I don't understand all the nuances of marriage, but it seems to me that if a man hits a woman, holds a gun to her head, and threatens to kill her, he's not all that fond of her."

He had the grace to flush a deep, dark red at that. "You deserve to take your best shot," he said. "Believe me, baby, there's nothing you can say to me that I haven't already said to myself a million times over."

Demonstrating lousy timing, a waitress in a short denim skirt, red-and-white-checked blouse, and white-fringed cowgirl boots stopped by the table.

"Can I get you something?" she asked with a blindingly white flash of cover-girl teeth. The smile, Faith noticed, was directed straight at Sal.

"Coffee, please. With cream." Her nerves were starting to settle, but unable to trust him completely, there was no way she was going to risk alcohol slowing down her reflexes.

"I'll have coffee, too," Sal ordered. "But make mine black." The smile he gave the waitress reminded Faith of the way he'd once smiled at her. Before things had gotten ugly.

"I've been sober for six months," he said after the woman had taken their orders over to the bartender.

"I'm glad to hear that." She really was. Her fingers loosened their hold, just a little, on the bag.

"I wanted to talk with you sooner, but I needed to make sure I was really going to stay on the wagon. I know six months might not seem all that much —"

"But it's a start," she said. "You're a strong man, Sal. One of the strongest I know. I can't believe you can't do anything you put your mind to." He'd certainly found her.

"Yeah, that's what I keep telling myself. I've been doing a twelve-step program."

"I hear they can be very effective."

"Yeah. Of course everyone, including me, smokes like fuckin' chimneys at the meetings, but I figure I can tackle that down the road."

“One thing at a time,” she agreed, glancing out the window.

The ambulances were leaving. One with siren and lights flashing, the other, she guessed, headed to the Jackson morgue. She’d been stunned when, while they’d all been standing together outside, Sal had informed her that Erin Gallagher’s mother had been killed and Erin’s coach had been found unconscious in his room.

“Course, not getting drunk or stoned has left me with a lot of spare time.”

“I can see how that could be a problem.”

Two of the police vehicles had driven away as well, which left the black Cherokee. Faith figured Will had probably been forced to stay behind to give a statement to all the reporters who’d taken over the parking lot.

She wished she could care what Will was saying, but after all that had happened in the last twenty-four hours, her desire to get back into hard news didn’t seem nearly as important as the way Will had looked at her when he’d learned she was married.

“Which is why I decided to take up a life of crime,” Sal said. “Nothing like becoming a serial killer to jazz up a guy’s life.”

“Mmm.”

Would Will come looking for her? From the black ice in his eyes and the chill in his voice when he'd informed her he had a crime scene to get back to, she suspected not.

Sal's words belatedly sank in.

"What did you say?" Surely not what she thought she'd heard.

"Hey!" He held up his hands. "Just kidding about that serial killer thing."

"It's not exactly a joking matter."

"No." He frowned. "It's not. But your sheriff's probably up to handling it. Given his background."

"How did you know about Will's background?"

"I looked him up after I realized I was coming here. Just to get a feel for who all the players were in case you tried to get me arrested. That's how I found you. I was checking out radio broadcasts online, and damned if your sexy voice didn't come up number one hundred and twelve."

She'd worried about that, when the station had started simulcasting on the internet last month, but had then decided the odds were against Sal ever hearing her.

"So, I guess you neglected to tell him about me."

"Tell who?" Faith hedged. She was never so relieved to see anyone in her life as she was the waitress who'd arrived with their coffees. She poured in cream from the small stainless steel pitcher, added sugar, and took a drink of hers as the young woman, seeming to sense a serious discussion taking place, left them alone again.

"Faith, baby." Sal clucked his tongue. "Did you forget that I used to have the best confession rate on the force?" He reached across the table, then frowned when she flinched.

He leaned back and studied her silently. His expression was not in any way threatening, but it was steady and had her understanding how he'd gotten all those criminals to confess.

"You're not going to come back to Nevada with me, are you?"

He'd never been anything but direct. There'd been a time when she'd liked that about him. Which is why she knew she owed it to him to be equally forthright.

"No."

Faith had spent the past eighteen months afraid Sal would catch up with her. Now that he had, she was surprised it was proving so emotionally painful.

"I sorta figured that." He sighed heavily. His broad shoulders sagged. "I guess I really fucked things up."

"It wasn't just you." Her eyes were burning behind her lids. "I shouldn't have ever let things get so out of hand. It was just that no one had ever taken such good care of me. Never."

"I liked taking care of you. And, if I hadn't been so head over heels, I would've realized that you'd confused gratitude with love."

She bit her lip. Was about to lie. Then reminded herself that it was time — past time — for honesty. "I wasn't confused."

"But you didn't love me."

This was the hardest conversation she'd ever had. Yet. She glanced out the window again, hoping that Will would even give her an opportunity to try to explain. "No." It was barely a whisper.

"I figured as much. To tell the truth, I think I knew it all along. But I wanted you so damn bad, I wanted to rush you into that chapel before you wised up. And before I had to face reality."

She tried a smile, which wobbled slightly. "That's very insightful."

"This anger-management therapist I'm going to suggested it."

"You're seeing a therapist?" That idea actually did make her smile.

"Hell, it wasn't my idea."

Faith was relieved to see a bit of the old Sal bluster. While clean and sober was a good thing, she would've hated to see this man emotionally castrated. "The police union worked out a deal with the department. If I get counseling, and work my way through all the steps and stay sober for six months, I can go back on the job."

"I'm glad."

"Yeah. Me, too." He drew in a deep breath. Blew it out. "You're numbers eight and nine."

"What?"

"Step number eight is to make a list of everyone I've harmed," he explained. "Nine is to make amends."

"That's what you're doing here?"

"Yeah. I know I can't make things up to you for what happened, a lot of which I can't even remember, if you want to know the absolute truth, but at least I can let you know how damn bad I feel about having hurt you."

He eyed her curiously over the rim of the thick, white mug emblazoned with the red wolf logo. "What did you think?"

She took another drink of her coffee. It seemed foolish now. Almost embarrassing.

"Shit." He dragged a hand across the top of his short, stiff brown hair. "You thought I was going to hurt you?"

"You said you would," she reminded him.

"Actually, you said you were going to shoot me if you ever so much as caught me talking to another man."

"I was drunk out of my friggin' mind."

"You scared me, Sal. I trusted you, and you —"

"I turned out to be no better than any of those bastards who used to beat up on your mother."

"You weren't like them." He'd had problems. But this much she wanted to make clear. "I should have told you," she repeated what she'd said earlier. "I would have, if I'd had any idea my past would come out in the trial."

"Blame the victim," he said grimly. "That's what those scumbag defense attorneys always do. If I'd known about your juvenile record, I could've protected you."

Faith knew he would have tried. "Where the hell were you when I was twelve years old?"

He did the math. "In a black-and-white keeping the streets of Vegas safe from crime."

She smiled at the idea of a young, idealistic Sal Sasone. He had probably looked great in uniform. "I'll just bet you did, too."

"I sure as hell tried."

He took another drink of coffee and

glanced out the window as the TV lights turned off, casting the outdoors back into night. A pair of red taillights disappeared down the long, circular driveway.

"So, if you didn't tell the sheriff about me, can I suppose you haven't exactly filled him in on past events in your life?"

"No. I was going to. But things got complicated."

"Yeah. He told me about the poet slasher."

"Shhh." She leaned forward. "He doesn't want that to get out."

"It's not like I'm going to call a press conference, Faith."

No. As low as Will's opinion of the press was, Sal's had always been lower. He'd made an exception in her case. Just as she'd made one in his.

"A cop and a former hooker turned reporter," she murmured. "Who'd have thunk it?"

"Dammit, I hate it when you call yourself that. You were just a kid, Faith."

More of the old Sal she remembered, the cop who'd tracked down her stalker and saved her from ending up dead in some horrid basement cage her crazed stalker had built for her, had returned.

"An abused kid whose mother, may the bitch rot in hell, sold you for a goddamn fix," he continued, his voice rough with anger on her behalf, "and even when social services finally got around to taking you out of that piss-poor excuse for a home, without anyone watching out for you, taking care of you like any kid deserves to be taken care of, you fell through the damn cracks of the system!"

Realizing he'd raised his voice, he looked around, then leaned across the table until their faces were inches apart.

"You did what you did to survive," he said through gritted teeth. "You think I didn't see stories like that every day on the street? You think I couldn't understand?"

When her eyes began to fill, she dragged her gaze toward the stone fireplace where a couple clad in après-ski clothes seemed to be enthralled with each other.

Faith felt a little twinge of something she reluctantly recognized as envy. Although she'd been married, she'd never had anything resembling the romantic relationship that couple seemed to share.

She'd hoped she might be on the brink of one with Will. But then she'd screwed it up.

"I was ashamed," she said, her voice barely more than a whisper.

"Well, yeah. That makes two of us, because I'm goddamn ashamed of the way I reacted.

Christ, I'd never hit a woman before in my life. I've always thought the guys who mistreated women were lower than scum."

"I should have told you. Warned you, so you wouldn't have to find out so publicly."

If only she'd had an inkling of what would happen, she could have prepared both of them. As it was, the wealthy stalker's dream team of defense lawyers had somehow unearthed her supposedly sealed juvenile court records.

"That would've probably been a good thing to do," he agreed. "And maybe I should've acted like an adult when I did find out. Blaming you the way I did was worse than what that damn lawyer did. Because you deserved a whole lot better from your husband. So, maybe we're even. And maybe you ought to pay a visit to my therapist."

"Actually, I just happen to know one."

She'd toyed with the idea of talking with Drew Hayworth on a professional basis. Seeing the difference therapy had made in Sal, perhaps she might try it.

"Can't hurt," he said.

"The same old Sal." She shook her head. "Sitting here now, I can't remember why I was so afraid of you."

"Because it wasn't me. It was somebody

else. I'm not an easy guy to get along with on my best day," he admitted, which was definitely an understatement. "But that alien using my name, wearing my clothes and driving my car, and living in my house who showed up during the trial, hell, he's lucky I didn't shoot him and put him out of his misery."

Faith had actually been afraid of that. Of the two of them ending up in the headlines as a cop murder/suicide.

"I'm glad you didn't," she said truthfully. "But I'm also glad that alien Sal is gone."

"Dead and buried," he assured her. He blew out a long, obviously relieved breath. "So, we're square on this?"

"Of course." She zipped the bag shut. "I suppose the easiest thing to do would be for you to file for divorce in Vegas?"

"Makes sense. Given that you're not even going by your legal name here in Wyoming."

"You knew?"

"From day one. That guy you bought the phony IDs from? He just happens to be one of my snitches."

"I should have known better than to try to put anything over on you."

"Yeah. You should've." He polished off his coffee. "So, you want me to talk to Matt Dillon for you? Straighten things out?"

The amazing thing was, the man meant it. Sal was still a control freak. He probably always would be. But at least his efforts would always be for a good cause.

"Thanks," she said. "But this is something I need to do for myself." She covered her hand with his. "Thank you."

"For what?"

"For protecting me from that stalker who would have eventually killed me. For loving me enough to marry me." She felt her eyes growing moist. "And for understanding that it just wouldn't have worked out between us. Even without your drinking problem."

"You know what they say. If you love someone, let them go." He forced a smile that didn't reach his dark eyes. "You gonna be okay?"

"Absolutely."

He gave her another of those long probing looks. "Yeah. I think you will. Finally."

Faith knew Sal hadn't been the only one with issues. She'd been running from her past all of her life, from town to town, station to station, never stopping anywhere long enough to catch a breath. To examine her life. To acknowledge all she'd overcome. All she'd managed to accomplish. And, equally important, what she wanted.

And what she wanted, what she'd been

wanting since they'd first met at that campaign cocktail party at the Pirate's House in Savannah, was Will Bridger.

"Some of us are late bloomers," she said, thinking back on her conversation with Will, and feeling a deep pang of sadness that Erin's life had so tragically been cut short before she'd had a chance to create a new life for herself.

"Yeah." His gaze, as it swept over her face, was warm with masculine appreciation. He lifted his mug in a toast. "You bloomed real good, sweetheart."

This time her smile was real and came from that hidden, locked-away place in her heart as she felt the last of those chains she'd forged link by link during childhood falling away.

"You know, for the first time in my life, I believe I did."

38

"The guy's got it wrong," Desiree announced, looking up from her laptop. "It's not 'tusk and claw.' It's 'tush and claw.' "

"Well, that sure as hell doesn't sound all that scary," Trace Honeycutt offered.

"Ah, but I checked an online dictionary and *tush*'s old meaning is 'tusk,' so either our slasher learned the poem wrong, or he purposely changed it to sound more threatening."

"You'd think slashing a woman's throat would be bad enough," Sam said, pouring another cup of toxic waste from the carafe. It was looking to be another long night. "Without having to tweak some Kipling poetry. Sounds like he's using the *Jungle Book* as a murder manual."

"I read that book," Honeycutt remembered. "In Cub Scouts."

"That's where I learned it," Sam said. "It was required reading in my pack on the rez."

"Yeah, I think they gave the book to me, too."

Will forced his mind onto the conversation when what he really wanted to do was go confront Faith about the little personal-history item she'd forgotten to share with him. Like the fact that she had a goddamn husband.

"It was all about how Mowgli, the man cub, came to live with the wolves and had to get accepted into the pack," Will said.

"Yeah. Akela, the leader, called two people to stand for him," Sam remembered.

"Baloo, the bear, and Bagheera the panther," Honeycutt recalled. "God." He bit into a stale donut that had somehow survived since morning. "I remember getting goose bumps when all the wolves shouted, 'Let him join!' "

Will remembered having his own thrill of being accepted into the Cub Scout pack during the nighttime, fireside ceremony. Belonging had been a big deal when you were seven years old. It was only later, after his mother, then Matt, died that he'd gone off and become a lone wolf.

"I hated *Jungle Book,*" Desiree scoffed. "All those stupid animals going on and on about rules. And the scout uniforms were creepy. Reminded me of little Hitler Youths."

"I'll bet you were a Girl Scout," Honeycutt challenged.

"You'd lose." She put a hand on a hip and fluffed her hair with the other. "Even as a child, I was an original. Why would I have wanted to join a group where everyone has to fit in?"

"It's a guy thing," Sam said. "We're brought up to want to be part of a team. To honor the law. Just like cops are," he tacked on pointedly.

"Touché." She lifted her blue can of diet Pepsi. "Obviously there are teams and there are teams. Besides, our mighty pack leader recognizes and appreciates individuality."

"That's the thing," Will mused out loud. "If this guy ever was a Scout, and he's using the book as any sort of reference guide, he wasn't paying attention. Because the whole thing is about the importance of being part of the pack."

" 'The strength of the pack is the wolf,' " Sam agreed. " 'And the strength of the wolf is the pack.' That's the entire symbolism of Kipling's story."

"And wasn't there something in there about not killing men?" Honeycutt asked.

" 'Ye may kill for yourselves, and your mates and your cubs, as they need, and ye can,' " Sam quoted. " 'But kill not for the pleasure of killing and seven times never kill Man.' "

"That's really good," Desiree said. "Not the quote, which I still think is stupid. But the fact that you can remember it after all these years."

"Maybe the pack thing stayed in my mind more," Sam suggested. "Given that it fits in with the fact that I'm already part of a tribe."

"That's probably it," Honeycutt agreed. "So, do you think this guy might be from the rez?"

"Did you hotshots ever consider that perhaps this guy has never read the damn book?" Desiree asked. "That he just went online and Googled up poems about murder."

"Good point," Will said. And one that Faith had already thought of. "But serial killers tend to be people who fit into the community."

"Like the BTK guy." Honeycutt nodded. "And Bundy."

"Of course we don't know we're dealing with a serial killer," Sam said. "Could be just someone who's got a grudge against the girl and her mother."

"Quite a coincidence the first two murders the town's had in decades are both in the same family," Desiree agreed. "Both outsiders."

"Yeah." Once again Will considered how much he hated coincidence. "From the emails that went back and forth between Susan Gallagher and Fyodor Radikorsky, on the woman's computer, it was obvious they were here to drag the girl back into skating."

"You think the Russian killed her?" Honeycutt asked.

"Doubtful, since we found him lying on the floor of his room in shock." He'd been diagnosed with a kidney laceration and was currently in surgery to repair a torn urethra. "He's blaming the Gallagher woman."

"Lucky thing for the Russian that Sasone put those pieces together," Desiree said.

"Yeah," Will agreed even as he considered Salvatore Sasone's arrival in Hazard to be one of the unluckier things that had ever happened to him.

"Think the coach was the other guy?" Honeycutt asked. "The one whose pubic hairs were found on the Gallagher girl?"

"I had Jack get a sample before they prepped the guy for surgery. Right now, all we can do is wait for the lab results."

"I heard Faith Prescott reading that message you wanted broadcast," Desiree said.

"Asking people to call in if they'd seen her with anyone the day she died."

"That's something." He wondered if Erin Gallagher's death would get Faith the news slot she'd professed to want so badly. Wondered if it would boost her out of Hazard into a larger market.

And why the hell should he care?

Because, dammit, he did.

He scrubbed his hands down his face.

"Will," Desiree said. "You look like you've been rode hard and put away wet."

"Now there's a coincidence. Since I feel the same way."

"Go home. You're working on your second day without sleep. You need some rest so you can think clearly."

"You have a problem with how I'm working this case?" he shot back.

"No. I have a problem with you running yourself into the ground. In case you haven't noticed, Lone Ranger, this isn't a one-man operation. So, why don't you take some of that male-bonding law-of-the-pack stuff to heart and go home. Get some rest."

She wrinkled her nose. "Take a shower. Get something in your system besides caffeine and sugar. Then come back to work. Meanwhile, we can hold down the fort."

"She's right, Sheriff," Honeycutt said. "If

nothing else, you looked like shit on that TV report from the lodge."

Will figured he must look bad if even his deputy was daring to say a critical word about his leadership.

"Two hours," he said. "Meanwhile, if anything at all comes up, I expect you to call me."

"Yessir." This time Honeycutt actually did salute, making it official. Will was now older than dirt.

"This honorable wolf pack member promises to notify the great leader Akela of any incident relevant to the pack goal of tracking down the Man killer," Desiree said with a low bow.

Will shot her his middle finger.

Sam, he noticed, said nothing, but he knew he could count on the senior deputy.

The temperature had dropped precipitously since the impromptu news conference at the lodge. At least into the negative digits. Which had, fortuitously, driven the vultures back into the cozy, secure warmth of their dens. Given that because of the Ride the Divide race there wasn't a vacant room to be had in town, he could only hope they'd had to return to Jackson, at least for the night.

His Cherokee beeped as he hit the remote.

Will had just reached for the door when a hand landed on his shoulder.

39

"Let me get this straight." Drew Hayworth leaned forward, his hands clasped loosely between his knees. "You're married."

"Yes. But my husband is filing for a divorce." Faith wondered if her excuse sounded as lame to him as it did to her.

"Yet you had no way of knowing that was in the cards when you slept with Will Bridger." Well, that certainly answered her question.

"No."

"And it was more than just a one-night hookup?"

"It was for me." She felt the flush rise in her face. "As I said, we'd known each other before, but it hadn't worked out. But when we were together, it just felt so right. I'm not entirely sure if it was the same way for him. . . .

"Wait." She held up her hand. "Okay. That's not entirely true. He said that what he felt for me was different."

"If that's the case, you probably should have expected him to be pissed off when he found out there was a husband out there."

" 'An impediment,' " Faith murmured.

He lifted a blond brow, inviting elaboration.

"It's from *Jane Eyre.* Right before the clergyman invites Mr. Rochester to pledge his vows, he asks the congregation if anyone knows of any reason why this couple should not, in the eyes of God, be wed. That's when the stranger declares that the marriage cannot go on. That there's an existence of an impediment."

"That impediment being a mad wife in the attic."

"Technically, it was the third floor. But I suppose it's the same thing."

"I may not know one Brontë sister from the other, but didn't Jane walk away from the situation?"

"Yes. She left Thornfield Hall. Oh, she loved Mr. Rochester, of course. Despite his situation. But as she explained to him, principles and laws were not just for times when there weren't any temptations."

"And Sheriff Bridger is nothing if not a man of laws and principles."

"Tell me about it," she muttered.

"So, you should have expected him to respond the way he did."

"In the beginning, I didn't expect to have to say anything. Because I had no intention of getting involved with him."

"Because you weren't attracted? Or because of the impediment?"

"I'm married. I didn't believe I could do anything about that, at least not at the time."

"Because you were afraid of your husband."

"Yes." She folded her hands and spoke firmly. Surely.

"And now you're not."

"Sal's changed."

"Enough to make the marriage work?"

"No. Because I never loved him."

"That's got to be a tough thing to admit."

She laughed, but the ragged sound held little humor. "It's sure as hell not easy."

"You wouldn't be the first person to get married for the wrong reason," Hayworth said. "Undoubtedly you won't be the last." He stood up and crossed over to the couch, then held out both his hands. "You look wiped out. Why don't you go home and get some rest. Things will look better in the morning. They always do."

"I won't get any sleep, worrying about what he's thinking. The more we avoid the subject, the worse it's going to get. I've already waited too long."

"Which is why a day or two more isn't going to make a difference," he pointed out mildly. "You're dealing with a damaged romance, Faith. The sheriff's dealing with two murders which took place over a twenty-four-hour period. And a son who may or may not be a suspect."

"He's not." Faith remained unmoved on that. "But you're right. I suppose it would be selfish to expect him to stop everything so I can grovel."

He smiled at that. Took hold of her hands and eased her to her feet.

"I strongly doubt he's going to make you grovel, Faith. I've watched him since he's come back to town. He's fair-minded. He'll give you a chance to state your case. And if things have progressed, as you say they have, he'll forgive you and move on."

Faith certainly hoped so.

"There is one more thing to consider," he said, as she shrugged into her parka.

"What's that?"

"His pride may be hurt."

"Because I didn't trust him enough to tell him the truth."

"He's the sheriff, Faith. His sworn duty is to serve and protect. By keeping your secret, you prevented him from doing either one of those things. You wounded his ego."

"Ah, the famously delicate male ego. The 'Me Tarzan, you Jane' syndrome."

He laughed. "You just happened to have hit upon the one stereotype that's unfortunately true. You can't blame a man for wanting to protect the weaker sex. Even," he said quickly, "when that weakness has been proven time and time again to be a fallacy."

He toyed with one of the beaded pipe holders hanging on the pretty Christmas tree. "That's one of the things I appreciate most about the Native American tribes. Even the ones who aren't strictly matriarchal still share power with their female members. That's something we males of European descent could learn to do better."

"Well, I'm not going to argue with that." She tugged on her gloves. "Desiree and I have talked about her being a police officer. She's seen a lot of prejudice over her years."

"I can imagine."

"But she insists Will doesn't have a prejudiced bone in his body."

"Well, then." Hayworth shared another smile. "He sounds just about perfect, so my advice, given only because you asked, is that as soon as he has his killer behind bars, you tell him what you've told me, about your childhood, and how you've survived it, and I'll bet, rather than be pissed off at you anymore, he'll admire what you've made of your life."

"I hope so."

"I've not a single doubt." He ruffled her hair. "Though I have to say, there will be a lot of men in Hazard down at The Watering Hole crying in their beer when you get taken off the market."

"Off the market." She punched him lightly in the arm. "Talk about your chauvinist statements!"

"Hey," he said on a laugh. "You can't blame me for the attitudes of these Wyoming cowboys." He put a hand on her back as he walked her to the door. "Go home. Get some rest. Hopefully by tomorrow the sheriff will have arrested the killer, and everyone can get on with their lives."

"I'd love to go home. However I still have a program to do."

"No need. Let me fill in for you."

It sounded so tempting. "Are you sure?"

"Sure. Besides, I get a lot more interesting callers when I'm on at night."

"The crackpots, you mean."

"A good therapist never uses that term," he said easily. "Although, I have to admit, some of your callers do appear to live out on the far fringes of normality."

Since Faith could not argue that point, they shared a laugh. As she drove away from the college, she felt a great deal better.

So much so, she decided that although Drew had advised against it, she was going to drop by the Sheriff's Department and ask Will to at least give her an opportunity to explain, once he'd wrapped up his case.

40

Will spun around, his hand instinctively going to his sidearm.

"Christ, Desiree," he said on an exasperated breath. "You should know better than to sneak up on someone that way! I could've shot you."

"Which would've been the least of our problems. We need to talk."

Will knew that she hadn't approved of the way he'd driven away from the lodge crime scene without checking on Faith.

"Look, if this is about Faith —"

"No. I just got a call from someone about the Gallagher girl. A potential witness the night she died."

Her face was as grim as he'd ever seen it. "And that's not a good thing why?"

"It's Sam."

Puzzled, Will glanced up at the office window. "Sam called?"

"No." She dragged a hand through her

dark curls. "Sam's our new suspect."

"I was with her." They were alone in Will's office. No way was he going to put Sam in the box. The deputy closed his eyes for a brief, painful moment. "The night she died."

"What do you mean you were with her? Christ," Will said, as the answer hit like a bullet between his eyes. "Are you saying you had sex with her?"

"No. She was just a kid, Will. There was no way I had any sexual feelings toward her." Sam let out a long, tired sigh. "She had this thing. About older men. Like that complex about girls and their fathers."

"The Electra complex?"

"Yeah. That's what Dr. Hayworth called it when I talked to him about it."

"You discussed Erin Gallagher with Hayworth?"

"I didn't know what else to do," Sam exploded uncharacteristically. "She worked for him. He's a shrink. I figured maybe he'd have a handle on what I should do.

"Will, the girl wouldn't leave me alone. Every time I turned around, there she was. Smiling. Flirting. It was like she'd decided to go hunting and I was in her crosshairs and she wouldn't give up until she bagged me."

And there were a lot of women, Will thought, who'd consider Sam a trophy animal.

"What did Hayworth suggest you do?"

"At first he suggested avoiding her. But that only made things worse. Then he suggested talking it out. He's big on talk," Sam said drily.

"I take it that didn't work."

"I guess the fuck it didn't. Considering I came home that night and found her naked in my bed."

Could his night get any worse? The woman he was actually contemplating a future with turned out to have a husband, and the man who'd become the closest thing Will had to a friend since returning to Hazard had managed to put himself smack in the middle of a high-profile murder investigation.

"Tell me you didn't fuck her."

"That's exactly what I'm trying to do." Sam was obviously offended, but Will was too exhausted and too pissed off to care. "She said she'd made a big mistake and needed to move past it."

"Move past it by having sex with you?"

"Apparently."

"What kind of mistake?"

"I didn't have any idea at the time. But given that her coach was in town, and from what she'd told me about him —"

"This wasn't the first time you were together?"

"I pulled her over for drunk driving when she first came to town."

"I don't remember a ticket."

"That's because I didn't issue her one. I figured everyone deserves a chance, and besides, any other college kid can have a few too many beers at a kegger and get away with it. The minute Erin Gallagher's name showed up on a police blotter, the press would be crawling all over the story."

Will couldn't argue with that.

"So, I confiscated her keys, to keep her from having a wreck, then drove her home to her apartment. When she had trouble standing up, I helped her upstairs to her apartment, put her into bed — fully dressed," he added, in case Will might think the worst, "then left.

"The next day she tracked me down in The Branding Iron, looking for her keys. I bought her breakfast. We talked. Not about anything personal. Just school, Indian stuff. She seemed really interested in the Shoshone culture."

"I'll bet."

"I may just be a rural county deputy, but I believe I just detected a bit of sarcasm."

"Ever think you were the flavor of the month?"

"Of course. Which was one reason I never gave in to her feminine wiles. Another one was, I was nearly old enough to be her father."

"That may have been the point."

Sam shrugged. "That's pretty much what Hayworth said. She didn't exactly confirm it, but she'd been at the lodge that afternoon, and from what you said about the different pubic hairs found on her body, I'd bet the mistake she was trying to forget with me was fucking that Russian coach."

Will ran the matrix through his mind. "Makes sense," he agreed. "So, how come you didn't tell me earlier? Like in the beginning."

"Because I was hoping it was a slam dunk. That the big-city detective —"

"Which would be me."

"Which would be you," Sam agreed, "would be able to nab the bad guy and put him behind bars before anything got out."

"So much for that idea."

"I did try to talk with you earlier," Sam reminded him. "Then you got that call about the Gallagher woman being killed and we had to go out to the lodge."

Will cursed. "You realize I'm going to have to take an official statement on this?"

"Yeah. But there's another problem."

"Of course there is." Will cast a quick, frustrated glance upward, wondering what the hell he'd done to deserve all this.

"The reason I didn't mention anything about Erin stopping by is that I knew it would trigger an investigation into where I was later that night."

"Okay. So, where were you?"

Will figured the only thing that could have his deputy looking so uncomfortable would be if he'd been spending his paycheck at the so-called massage parlor outside the county line.

"On the rez."

"Okay. Alone?"

"No."

Sam was, like most Native Americans, not all that loquacious on a good day. Which this was not.

"Want to tell me who you were with?"

"No. But obviously now that the shit's hit the fan, I'm going to have to." Sam sucked in a breath. "Leon Ducett."

"The kid from the college? Who works at KWIND?"

"The 'kid' is twenty-three years old," Sam

said with uncharacteristic defensiveness.

"Okay. But this is the same guy who wasn't available to work the news? Because he was supposedly spending the night with his girlfriend?"

"Yeah. And before you ask the next question, about why we kept our mouths shut for the past twenty-four hours, maybe you ought to ask yourself how eager you'd be to come out of the closet if you were a Native American homosexual in northwest Wyoming. The state where two heterosexual men brutally beat a gay college student, lashed him to a fence, and left him to die out on the remote prairie."

"That case changed a lot of minds," Will argued. "And look at all the people who went to that gay cowboy movie. Attitudes are changing. Maybe not as fast as we'd like, but they *are* changing."

Sam tilted his head. His eyes were typically expressionless, but Will could feel the skepticism radiating from him. "And you'd be willing to let someone you loved risk that?"

When Will's mind immediately turned to Faith, he knew that, however angry at her he was, it didn't change the way he felt, deep down. That she had a husband complicated things. Fortunately, he'd always thrived on complication.

"I don't know," he said honestly. "But the fact remains that a deputy of the Hazard Sheriff's Department may have information regarding a double homicide. We may be friends, but I can't overlook that."

"I didn't expect you to. I just wanted to give you a heads-up."

"I appreciate that," Will said, feeling more exhausted than he'd ever before felt in his life. "I'm going to need you to fill out a statement."

"Yeah, I'm already on that."

"No." Will hated what he was about to say. But knew he had no choice. "Tell Desiree what you told me. Have her put it in an official report. If you want to lawyer up —"

"I don't need a damn lawyer."

Since they both belonged to a group of people who'd routinely been screwed over by attorneys who'd eagerly take their money, promising to help them gain access to the white government who'd screwed them in the first place, Will understood.

"I'll instruct Desiree to hold off filing the report for another twenty-four hours."

"That could get you in a world of hurt with the AG's office and the DCI if things go south."

Right now, Will didn't give a flying fuck

what the suits in the Department of Criminal Investigation might think. Sam was his deputy. Hazard was his town. And he damn well intended to handle things his way.

"We'll jump off that bridge when we come to it," he said. "Meanwhile, let's get your statement on the record."

Clouds had been rolling in from the west all day. A storm warning had been issued for western Wyoming, and after a flurry of shopping, residents seemed to have hunkered down for the duration.

As he drove through the dark and empty streets, listening to Drew Hayworth advising parents to monitor their children's computer use to protect them from sexual predators, Will couldn't help thinking of his own child.

He still knew, all the way to the marrow of his bones, that Josh had nothing to do with Erin Gallagher's death. But how the hell was it going to look when the two individuals who were the last to see her, to be with her, were the sheriff's son and the deputy who'd interrogated him?

41

The man raised by wolves was disappointed. He'd tried a new murder technique, but it hadn't been the same. Oh, it had done the job, all right. Hadn't he left his prey lying in a lovely pool of blood? The problem was, he'd had, by necessity, been too far away, which had left the killing feeling too remote.

Although he had no intention of ever getting caught, the man raised by wolves had begun to feel that something was missing. He wasn't receiving the pleasure he usually did from taking a life.

Strangely, even slashing pretty Erin Gallagher's throat hadn't been nearly as exciting as he'd hoped. In fact, it had been the first time since he'd killed Snowball, the unlucky kitten, that he'd been able to wait until he returned home from the hunt to satisfy the throbbing erection that had always come with killing.

Of course, the stone-cold bitch of a

mother didn't count. That kill had been for utility, and a well-deserved punishment, after all. Not for enjoyment.

He had hopes for this new murder. But it hadn't lifted his spirits. Hadn't made his blood sing.

He was so . . . well, fucking bored.

What he needed was something to jump-start the pleasure again. Something big. Even outrageous. Something that would have people talking for months. Perhaps even years.

Something the good citizens of Hazard could be afraid of even while they were in the supposed safety of their own homes.

This need to escalate wasn't surprising. He had been upping the ante for years. Which was why, in the early years, as he'd practiced his technique, he'd remained so far below the radar no one had ever noticed a serial killer was living among them.

And hadn't Ted Bundy spoken eloquently to the problem of desensitization?

Bundy — who certainly belonged in the pantheon of killers — had stated that each time he'd killed someone, he'd suffered an enormous amount of guilt, horror, and pain. But then, that would wear off and the impulse to kill again would return. Even stronger than ever.

That's obviously what was happening here. While his bloodthirst increased exponentially with each hunt, the joy he'd experience was diminishing in an equal percentage.

Perhaps there was some merit to that three-cornered-stone image. Perhaps he had a killing stone in his breast that had, after all these years, begun to wear smooth.

No. That was negative thinking, something he would not allow.

The problem, as he was beginning to see it, was that there was no point in being the world's most deadly hunter of Man if no one ever knew about it. If you couldn't enjoy the process. Bask in the terror of the victim.

Play with the kill. Like a clever cat playing with a plump mouse before ripping it to pieces, then devouring it.

The man who was once the boy raised by wolves smiled.

He knew just how to reclaim his bliss.

42

Faith vacillated after arriving at the Sheriff's Department and being told by Trace Honeycutt that Will had gone home for a couple hours. If he was in bad enough shape to actually give in to pressure to take a break, he undoubtedly wouldn't be all that eager to have her showing up at the Bridger ranch.

On the other hand, his father and son were still out of town, and how many chances could they get in a town this small to actually talk in private? Besides, maybe if he was as tired as she suspected he must be — as she herself was — then perhaps he'd be less likely to go on the attack when she tried to explain her case.

She came to the Y at the edge of town. To the right was the road to her house. The left fork led to the ranch.

"In for a penny," she decided as she turned left.

Had the SUV not been parked outside the

house, Faith would have thought no one was home. There wasn't a light on in any of the tall windows.

She pulled up beside the Cherokee, waded through the snow, and rang the bell.

Nothing.

She tried again, hearing it chime inside.

Still nothing.

She tried knocking, but her gloved hand made even less noise, so she pulled them off and tried her bare knuckles.

Still nothing.

Unwilling to give up now, she pressed down on the heavy-handled set latch. And pushed.

The door opened on a loud, horror-movie squeak. That the dead bolt hadn't been fastened showed just how exhausted he must be, since she suspected he might be one of the few people, other than herself, in Hazard who locked their doors.

"Will?" Her voice echoed. But there was no answer.

"Will?" She ran her hand along the wall by the inside of the door, found the light switch, and flicked it up.

Blinding-bright light flooded down from a chandelier that appeared to have been created from elk antlers.

"It's Faith."

Not wanting to drip melting snow all over what appeared to be antique Indian woven rugs, she unzipped her boots, left them by the door, crossed the long room, and headed down the hall she suspected led to the bedrooms.

The first room, with its clutter of teenage life lit by the glow of a computer monitor featuring a sunny-beach-scene screen saver, and posters of Destiny's Child and Black Eyed Peas on the wall, was obviously Josh's.

The one next door, which was as tidy and Spartan as a monk's cell — save for the Stetson hanging on the wall beside a framed photograph of a beautiful young woman, dressed in a short white dress and veil — obviously belonged to Will's father. The woman's long black hair, parted in the middle, fell over her shoulders. Her dark eyes, the rich ebony color of her son's, radiated love as her groom, wearing a dark, Western-cut suit and looking like a 1960s version of Will, slipped a gold band on her finger.

Faith heard Will as soon as she opened the third door, across the hall from the others. His breathing was deep and steady.

Outside, the clouds were starting to move down from Canada and Montana, but there was still enough moonlight slanting in the window for Faith to see him, sprawled on the bed, a towel wrapped around his waist.

Obviously he'd taken a shower, then crashed.

The sight of a near naked Will Bridger was vastly appealing.

Given that she'd been awake for nearly two days, straight, the bed was even more so.

And she was suddenly so incredibly, bone-weary exhausted.

Of course, if sleep was all she wanted, there were two other unoccupied beds.

What she wanted was sleep.

Then Will.

In that order.

She pulled off her sweater and slacks and laid them over the arm of a wing-back chair covered in a black-and-brown-striped fabric that matched the comforter he'd managed to toss back before falling into bed.

Her bra and navy blue silk long johns were next to go. Then she slipped beneath the sheets. The minute her head hit the pillow, Faith fell asleep.

He was dreaming of her. As he had too many nights to attempt to count.

They were lying on some beach beside a turquoise lagoon. On Kauai, perhaps. Or

Tahiti. It didn't matter which. All that mattered was that they were together. And alone.

He took a bottle of oil, poured it into his hands, and began rubbing it over smooth skin tanned to a golden brown by the benevolent tropical sun that was beaming down from an impossibly blue sky.

She was boneless, pliant beneath his caressing hands as he touched. Stroked. Aroused. Her flesh was hot and slick and warm. And his.

All his.

Drifting on the soft fantasy of the dream, he pressed a kiss against the fragrant hollow at the base of her throat and imagined he could taste her sudden increase in pulse beat.

Time slowed. Then stilled. There was no yesterday, and tomorrow was a lifetime away. There was only his exquisite, stolen moment in time.

Savoring every shimmering sigh, every humming moan, he planted kisses down her throat, over her shoulders, then lower. He cupped a hand beneath one smooth breast, stroked his tongue across the heated flesh.

When he took the tight, dusky nipple between his lips and tugged, her eyes flew open.

"You came." Fully awake now, he stroked his hand down her side, from her breast to her hip.

"How could I not?" she asked.

Her eyes were a soft and gleaming gold. As he gazed down into them, the thought that had been playing around the edges of Will's mind for so many months struck home.

Mine.

He tangled his free hand in her hair, dragging her head back. "Once we do this, there's no going back. With so much in flux, I don't know what's going to happen in the short term. But I do know that if you stay, you'll belong to me." His jaw tightened as he thought about her husband. "Only me."

Her breath hitched. "And you to me."

Something in his heart turned over. "Only you."

Those remarkable eyes he knew would still have the power to make him hard as a pike when he was ninety brightened with a bright, moist sheen.

With his eyes still on hers, Will slid into her, as smoothly as if they'd been created solely for each other.

Outside the ranch house, the moon continued its nightly ride across the midnight sky. Snow fell, faster now, shawling over the ground, draping the dark green trees in thick coats of winter white.

Somewhere atop a hill, a coyote howled. Out on the lonely highway, racing toward the Dakotas with a load of caskets from Boise, a long-haul trucker tuned into *Talking After Midnight,* then cursed when he discovered the voice coming from his overhead speakers wasn't sexy Faith Prescott's at all, but that of some shrink who was yammering about communication in a marriage.

Back in Hazard, Deputy Trace Honeycutt drove through the dark and empty streets, on the lookout for bad guys, while upstairs, on the second floor of the century-old courthouse, Deputy Desiree Douchet took the statement of a man she'd come to respect.

Inside a sprawling log ranch house on the edge of town, caught up in the beauty of the night, and in each other, Faith Fletcher and Will Bridger slipped effortlessly, sumptuously into love.

43

"We moved a lot," Faith said, as she lay in Will's arms in the wide bed he'd told her had been created from pine logs harvested on the ranch. "Every time social services got a whiff of what was going on, we'd take off in the night. I got really good at packing fast and traveling light."

She'd thought, while driving out here, that telling Will about her less than pristine past would be the most difficult thing she'd ever done. But amazingly, he'd been even more accepting than Drew Hayworth had predicted. And certainly he'd behaved worlds differently from Sal. Of course he wasn't hearing it in a public forum.

"I thought, after she died, that I'd be free. But the foster care system in this country is a joke. And it was like I had this invisible sign around my neck. One that read *whore,* that only guys could see, because three of the first four homes I was sent to, the men would decide I was their own state-supplied sex slave."

"One more reason that case in Savannah would've been so hard for you to get involved in," he murmured.

"I suppose. But by the time I'd landed in care, my mother had been whoring me for a year, and I'd gotten desensitized to sex. It was when one guy beat me up so badly he broke four ribs and my wrist — when I tried to fight back — that I just walked away.

"I didn't know how to get phony papers back then, and no one wanted to hire a fifteen-year-old dropout, so I just started doing the only thing I knew how to do. But instead of having to turn all the money over to my mother, I got to keep it."

She sighed. "It sounds so ugly when you hear it out loud."

"You were a kid," he said, echoing what Sal had said in the bar of the lodge. "You were damn lucky you didn't get killed."

"I realize that." She shrugged. "I knew it at the time."

"But you didn't care."

She looked up at him. "How did you know?"

"I'm a cop. You think I haven't seen this sort of thing before?"

He drew her close. Pressed a kiss against

her love-tousled hair.

"I should have told you about being married." She trailed a finger down the arrowing of silky dark hair that she loved to feel against her breasts.

"Yeah, you should've trusted me enough to protect you against anyone who'd want to hurt you, Faith."

"I'd already gone the route of being with a man to protect me. And that didn't turn out real well.

"I was planning on telling you about my past that last night in Savannah. Because I wanted you to know how different things were with you." She looked up at him, wanting him to understand. "From that first time, I'd always separated sex from emotions. But from the minute I met you, they got all tangled up. At first it was terrifying to feel so out of control. Then it was wonderful."

"Then it was horrible," he said. His lips nuzzled her neck. "Which was my fault."

"Maybe we both could have done things a bit differently," she said, combing her fingers through his hair. "But it's important for you to know that I've never felt the way I feel with you with any other man."

"That's right. I seem to remember, that first time, back in your bedroom in Georgia, when you warned me you'd never been able to come."

"That was the truth."

"Not that night."

"You don't have to sound so smug."

"Sorry." He rolled over, taking her with him, hooking his bare leg over her hip, essentially anchoring her to the bed. "It's just that, correct me if I'm mistaken, but I remember losing count that night. And tonight, although I'll admit to being distracted, I believe I counted three."

"Four." Humor replaced the shadows in her eyes. "Although, they could have been aberrations."

"Could've been, I suppose." He grinned and nuzzled her breasts. "Perhaps, in the interest of scientific experiment, we ought to try it again."

"I suppose we could," she allowed as, amazingly, her thoughts began to scatter and her body warmed from the inside out, as if he'd somehow lit a candle inside her. "But since we're being honest with each other, in the interest of full disclosure I should warn you that I've never had a very strong libido."

"Really?" He sounded fascinated. At least she thought perhaps that was the case. It was hard to read his tone when he had that wickedly clever mouth buried between her breasts.

"Really." She struggled to concentrate on her breathing. "I think it has something to do with low hormone levels."

"Well then." His tongue had begun tracing wet circles around a nipple. "Maybe we should see if we can do something to spike them."

When he took that hardened tip between his lips and sucked hard, Faith discovered there was a direct connection between her nipple and that still warm, still pulsating place between her legs.

"I think that may have done it," she managed as he took her slowly, exquisitely, back into the mists.

"I don't want to go back to work."

"I don't want you to go back to work," Faith said. "But you have to. If for no other reason than to prove neither Josh nor Sam Charbonneaux had anything to do with Erin's death." He'd told her about his deputy's situation earlier.

"Yeah. Christ, what a mess."

"It'll be okay." She lifted her lips to his. "You'll make it okay."

"I used to believe I could," he admitted. "Make everything okay."

"Ah, the cop as superhero fantasy," she murmured with a half smile. "How did that work for you?"

"Lousy." He rubbed his chest in that gesture she'd seen before. "You know I got shot."

"I've heard something about a bust that went bad."

"Yeah. We were after this drug dealer, and, well, that's pretty much it. It went bad. He ended up being shipped back to Mexico in a pine box and I ended up in the hospital.

"The day after surgery, Josh showed up."

"He told me how his mother's lawyer dumped him on you."

"*Dumped* is, unfortunately, the word. Neither one of us had any idea the other existed, and I sure wasn't in the best condition to leap into playing single dad."

"That's understandable. Is that why you brought him back here? So things would move at a slower pace and you could get to know each other better?"

"No. Well, it was one reason. The real reason was I couldn't be a cop anymore."

"But you are a cop."

"Not like I was . . . Shit." He left the bed and began to pace. "I've got this heart thing."

Faith felt her own heart lurch. "What kind

of heart thing?"

"It bounces around when I get under a lot of stress. The doc said it wouldn't kill me or anything, but it's as annoying as hell."

"I can imagine."

"The doctor also suggested yoga."

As serious as this conversation was, Faith couldn't quite keep the smile from her lips. "Well, I'm sure you leaped at that suggestion."

"What the hell do you think?"

"Let me just take a wild guess." She paused. "I'd say no."

"Good guess." His fist closed at his side. "That's not all."

"All right."

"I lost my nerve."

Faith couldn't help herself. She laughed. "Will, I've watched you handle two murder scenes in as many days. You have nerves of steel."

"Look, you said you worked a police beat, right?"

"That's right. In Wichita."

"Ever know any vice cops?"

"Some. They're all cowboys." She remembered she just happened to be sitting in a bed in a ranch house. "And I mean that in a good way."

He shrugged his broad shoulders. Flexed

his fingers. "It wouldn't matter if you meant it the way most people do. Gray — he was my partner — and I were, well, I guess you could say we were two of the more unorthodox cops in the department. We pretty much wrote our own rules. Ran our own show. Both of us got off on the adrenaline buzz."

"Busting drug dealers and sex rings would probably be more exciting than dusting windowsills for burglars' fingerprints."

"Tell me about it. The thing is, we used to have this competition, who got to go up the stairs first, kick in the most doors. After three months of getting in each other's way, we finally decided to assign the job with a coin toss."

"That sounds fair," she decided.

"The first day I got back, after the shooting, Gray went ahead and gave me the lead position on a drug bust without doing the flip. He figured I deserved the honor."

"I'm not sure I wouldn't rather have balloons and a cake, but, hey, whatever works."

"I froze."

"I see." She did, and her heart went out to him. "I'm sure that's not so unusual. Obviously, you had something like post-traumatic stress, or —"

"That's not it. Well, maybe I did, somewhat. 'Cause I do have this damn glitchy heart. But the thing was, that right before I went to kick in the door, it dawned on me that if that Mexican drug dealer had aimed just an inch to the right, I could've died."

"That would get anyone's attention."

"You're still not getting it." He looked up at the ceiling either to seek patience or try to find the words to explain it. "But that's okay, because I wouldn't have either, if it hadn't happened to me. The thing is, what flashed through my mind was that if I died, Josh would be an orphan. He'd be all alone in the world. And that's when the goddamn heart thing started up."

"Oh. Wow." She shook her head. "Couldn't you have just switched to another job in the police department that was a bit less dangerous?"

"I could have. But I would've hated watching other guys go out on my cases. And while I'll admit to not being the most introspective guy on the planet, I figured out that if I hated my work, I'd pretty much hate my life, and what kind of father would that make me?"

"Don't ask me," Faith said. "I never had a father."

"Shit. I'm sorry."

"You had nothing to do with it. Besides, I moved past that part of my life a very long time ago. Though," she added on afterthought, "it is why I can identify a bit with what Josh is going through."

"It hasn't been easy on him," Will agreed. "From what I've been able to tell from the little he's been willing to share with me, he pretty much raised himself."

"So it seems. Which just goes to show what a good kid he is, deep down. Because he could be a lot worse than he is."

"You're not the first person to tell me that. But I decided that keeping him down in the city, even a smaller one, left to his own devices while I worked all night, wasn't the best thing. So I moved here. To keep him out of trouble."

"Well." She blew out a breath. "You know what they say about best-laid plans."

She held out a hand to him, about to see if she could tempt him back to bed, when they heard the front door open.

Although the article she'd been able to locate on him had mentioned his many commendations, Faith was surprised by how fast he'd grabbed the Glock from the bedside table.

Once a cop, always a cop.

"Dad?"

"Oh, my God. It's Josh," Faith said with a sinking heart.

"Guess I should have had Dad call when they were starting back." Will reached for his jeans. "Now I'm glad I never got around to oiling those door hinges."

"You can't let him know I'm here!"

"Faith. There's a forest green Explorer parked outside. I think that might just give the kid a clue that you're on the premises."

"Well, you'll just have to think of something!" She began quickly gathering up her scattered clothing. Where the hell were her underpants?

"Actually, I am." He rubbed his unshaven jaw as he watched her shimmying beneath the bed to retrieve her underwear. "I'm thinking that you have one fine ass. Maybe if we just ignore the kid, he'll go away."

"Will!" She raised up, banging her head on the bed rail. "This is not funny."

"It's not exactly a tragedy either." He reached down, held out a hand, lifted her back to her feet, and drew her close. "In case you've forgotten, my son has admitted to having had sex. That being the case, I don't think he's going to be shocked or appalled to discover his father with the sexiest woman in Hazard."

"Good try, Sheriff." She slapped a hand against his chest. "But flattery isn't going to get you anywhere in this case." She pulled away and yanked the underpants up her legs, not bothering to take the time to turn them rightside out.

"Go stall," she repeated. "I'll be out in just a couple minutes."

"Okay. I'll tell him you're getting dressed."

"Will!"

He lifted a hand. "Just kidding."

As he left the room — whistling! — Faith was tempted to throw the bedside lamp at his dark head.

44

"What's Ms. Prescott doing here?" Josh asked.

"She just came over to talk about some stuff."

"School stuff?" The defensive teenage tone was back. In spades. So much for hoping a day away could work miracles.

"Not exactly."

"It was about me, wasn't it?"

"We talked about you, some." Deciding it wasn't exactly a lie, Will resisted, just barely, shooting a glance down the hall. "How did things go with your grandfather?"

"Okay. We got the stock fed and found a couple breaks in the fence we got fixed."

"Good for you." Will's hearty voice sounded fake to his own ears.

"He's out in the barn. Checking the horses."

"Never has trusted me to make sure they get fed," Will said. When he'd been Josh's age, that had pissed him off. Now he just accepted it as his father's need to try to control his environment. Which had always been just as hard for a rancher as it was for a cop.

A little silence settled over them.

"I heard on the radio you haven't caught Erin's killer."

"Not yet. But I will."

"Good. Is it true about her mother?"

"I'm afraid so."

"From what she said, it's no great loss. But it's really weird."

"That's one word for it."

"You think they're connected? Or random?"

"At this point it'd just be conjecture. But my best guess is, yeah, there's a connection."

Another silence.

"So, where is she?" Josh asked.

"Right here."

Both father and son turned toward the living room doorway as Faith entered the room.

"Hello, Josh." Her voice was warm. Friendly. Having witnessed her earlier panic, Will was impressed by how quickly she'd managed to garner control. She was an even better actress than he'd thought.

"Hi. You weren't on the radio when we were driving home."

"Dr. Hayworth agreed to fill in for me."

"So you could come over here and talk to my dad?"

"That's right."

"And that's all you were doing, right? Talking?" There was an edge to the boy's tone Will didn't like.

"Josh —"

"I was talking to Faith," he said.

"Her name's Ms. Fletcher," Will corrected.

"Fletcher?" Josh looked from his father to Faith, then back to Will again.

"It's a long story."

"Yeah, I could tell from how much snow is packed up on the roof of your Explorer. Guess it takes a lot of time to tell a story when you have to keep stopping to fuck."

"Josh." Will's tone was a razor, slashing sharp. "That's no way to talk to a lady."

"Well, I can't see how that's any problem. Since if you ask me, rolling around in the sack with a guy who's supposed to be solving the murder of an innocent teenage girl isn't real ladylike behavior."

"Dammit, Josh —"

"No, Will." Faith reached out to touch Josh's arm. "I understand how you must feel, but —"

"The hell you do!" Hectic red flags waved in his cheeks as he turned back to Will. "That's the only reason you sent me away, isn't it? So you could screw her without me getting in the way."

"You're wrong about that, Son," Will said.

Faith cringed at the same I'm-in-control-so-you-will-listen-to-me tone he'd use to talk a perp into putting down his weapon. It might work out in the field. But not on a son.

Josh shot them both a look that was pure steel. Faith wondered if he realized how much his father's son he really was.

"Are you saying you haven't been fucking tonight?"

"Watch your language," Will warned.

"You don't understand," Faith said, reaching for him again.

"Now there's where you're wrong, Ms. Prescott. Or Fletcher. Or whatever the hell your name is!" He jerked away from her light touch. "I've had a lot of practice understanding about being in the way. Next time you decide to lie about having sex, *Dad*" — he heaped scorn on the word — "you might not want to go giving your girlfriend a fuckin' hickey!"

He stormed away, out into the snow, slamming the door behind him.

"Will!" Faith ran to the door, watching as Josh ran across the snowy field. "You have to stop him."

"He's not going to go far," Will assured her. "The keys to his truck are hanging on a hook in the kitchen. Dad's undoubtedly got the ones to his truck with him, and I've got the Jeep keys." Faith heard a jangling when he rattled his pocket. "He needs to be alone right now."

"That's the problem, Will. He's been alone too much."

"Well, there's nothing I can do about that, now can I?" he asked reasonably. "Meanwhile, the icy air will cool him down."

"I still don't think —"

"Faith." He drew her into his arms. Rubbed his broad hands up and down her back. "He'll get over it."

"Get over what?" Jim Bridger asked as he came into the house, stomping snow off his boots onto the mat just inside the door.

"It's one of those things where you had to be there," Will said.

As Jim Bridger's shrewd blue eyes took in the situation, Faith resisted, just barely, the urge to lift her hand to cover the love bite Will had given her.

"Gotta go unpack," Jim said. He touched

his fingers to the brim of his hat. "Nice to see you again, Ms. Prescott."

Will started to correct him. "It's —"

"It was good to see you, too, Mr. Bridger," Faith said, cutting off Will's planned correction.

He immediately nodded in silent agreement that perhaps there'd been enough honesty and openness for one evening.

45

The wind was back, roaring over the top of the Rockies like a freight train, barreling into the valley below, bringing with it the season's first blizzard.

As it rattled the windowpanes and pelted the glass with needlelike snow, Faith stood at the kitchen sink, peeling carrots for the beef stew, thinking what a difference two days could make.

The night the wind had suddenly stopped, she'd been a runaway wife who feared for her life, was living a lie, and was desperately attracted to a man she'd spent months trying to avoid because there was no way she could see how they could ever be together.

Now, although there were still some barriers to overcome — such as Will capturing the man who'd murdered Erin Gallagher and her mother — and Josh coming to terms with hers and Will's relationship, things were definitely looking up.

She'd always regret having inadvertently hurt Sal. The ironic thing was that she'd actually married him partly to make up for having disappointed him in the first place.

When he'd shown up at the hotel to tell her he'd captured her stalker, she'd been relieved. Grateful. So much so she'd even tried to make love with him. The only problem was that part of how she'd survived all those years was to separate sex from emotion. By holding back, she'd given Sal the impression that her lack of response had been his fault. That somehow he'd lacked the ability to satisfy her.

Which was partly why, when he'd proposed, she'd accepted.

Which, of course, she thought, as she poured herself a glass of the cabernet sauvignon she'd opened earlier so it could breathe, had turned out to be a huge mistake.

But she and Sal had moved past that. Amazingly, Faith thought they might actually someday be able to be friends.

And now she had Will. Who not only made her feel secure and happy, and cared for and independent all at the same time, but could make her fly.

"And that," she said, lifting her glass to her reflection in the night-darkened window, "is something to celebrate."

She wasn't sure where she and Will were going. But she did know that they were going there together. And that was all that mattered.

She heard the whine of a snowmobile engine and was momentarily blinded by the lights. A man wearing a black snowmobile suit climbed off the sled.

"I'll be right there," she called out as the doorbell rang. Wondering why Will hadn't driven the SUV, she pulled the white chef's apron over her head, checked her reflection in the glass again, and with her foolish heart skipping like a schoolgirl's with her first crush, went to open the front door. But not without pulling the curtain aside.

The male standing on her porch was a surprise. But not an unpleasant surprise.

She flung open the door. "Hey, Josh." Although she'd been expecting his father, her lips curved into a smile. "I'm so glad you're here." Half-afraid he'd change his mind, she took his arm and practically dragged him into the house. "Tell me you'll stay for supper!

"I'm making stew. It's my first try. Usually I just nuke some frozen dinner in the microwave, but Rayanne, down at the market, assured me stew is as easy as pie.

"Of course, the problem with that analogy is that I've no idea how to bake a pie, but . . ."

She stopped. Drew in a breath. "I'm babbling."

"Yeah. You seem to be." He'd taken off the thick jacket and insulated pants and hung them on the hooks beside the door. Stomped the snow off his boots.

He looked so like his father, with that hint of amusement dancing in his heavily hooded eyes. Oh, his might be blue, like his grandfather's, while his father's were that deep obsidian, but there was no mistaking the resemblance. Women were going to go crazy over this one, she thought.

"Just a little," he qualified.

"I'm nervous." She rubbed her suddenly moist hands on the front of her brown corduroy slacks.

"Yeah, me, too." His Adam's apple bobbed as he swallowed. He dragged his hand through his hair in a gesture she recognized all too well. "I owe you a huge apology. I acted like a jerk."

"You were upset. It's understandable. And you're right, your father didn't send you away solely to fix fences. He wanted to keep you away from the press until he had the murderer behind bars. Not because you were a suspect, but because he loves you. He might not have fully figured out how to say it, yet, but he does."

"I thought he wanted to get away from Savannah because he'd been shot. But my grandfather says he moved here for me."

"He did." She had a feeling it was the first time an adult had sacrificed anything for the teenager. "Come into the kitchen," she said. "I'll pour you some wine."

"I'm not twenty-one."

"Well, of course you're not." She reconsidered. "But you're very mature for your age. And it is just wine, after all. Not hard liquor. Children in Europe drink it with dinner."

"This is Wyoming," he pointed out. "And my dad's a cop." The grin was back. In his eyes and on his chiseled lips. Oh, yes, Faith thought. He was definitely his father's son. "Mr. Law and Order."

"Don't I know that." Her sigh ruffled her bangs. "Maybe I'd better get you a Coke."

"That sounds good. Especially since I'm not real big on wine. Now if you happened to have a beer —"

"Your father's a cop," she reminded him.

"Who undoubtedly drank beer himself back in the olden days when he was a kid."

"Why don't we stick with Coke for now and let him decide when he gets here?"

"Works for me," he said easily. He followed her into the kitchen. "This is a nice place, Faith. Uh, Ms. Prescott. I guess I mean, Ms. Fletcher."

He looked understandably confused. "I don't get it."

"It's a complicated story. And something we need to talk about." She took a bottle of Coke from the refrigerator, unscrewed the cap, poured it into a tall glass with ice, and handed it to him.

"Would you do me a favor?" she asked.

"Sure."

"Would you go down into the basement and get some wood for the stove, just in case the electricity goes out in the storm?

"I was meaning to, but I got home from town later than I planned, and this stew took more time than Rayanne told me it would." For a time she had been worried that she wouldn't get it finished before she had to leave for the KWIND studios.

"Okay." He put the glass on the counter and opened the kitchen door leading to the stairs.

Faith checked the detailed instructions the market owner had written down for her. "Okay. 'Peel three Idaho potatoes,' " she read aloud. "Piece of cake." Which she didn't know how to make, either.

She'd just finished chopping the third potato when she realized he'd been down in the basement a long time.

"Josh?" she called down to him. "Is everything all right?"

He appeared in the doorway, his face as white as milk. "I'm sorry, Ms. Prescott."

"It's Ms.—" She broke off the correction as she viewed the man standing behind him.

A frisson of icy fear skimmed up her spine when she viewed the gleaming silver blade pressed against Josh's throat.

46

Faith stared at the man standing behind Josh holding the deadly sharp knife. And suddenly understood exactly what it felt like to have a glitchy heart.

"Drew?" She couldn't believe it. How could a man who looked like the Sundance Kid be a cold-blooded murderer. "What are you doing?"

"What does it look like I'm doing?" he asked reasonably. "I'm hunting."

"Hunting?"

"Of course. That's what wolves do. They hunt."

"But you're not a wolf," she said, struggling desperately for a reasonable tone.

She tried, with her eyes, to signal Josh to remain calm and not do anything foolish that could get himself killed.

"It's obvious you've never heard of shapeshifters," Drew said. "There are quite a number of cultures who embrace the concept."

"And you do?"

"Let's just say I've been experimenting with the idea." His smile was cold. Deadly. Even remote. Why had she never noticed that before?

Because, she told herself, that's what serial killers do. They fit in. Hadn't she thought, herself, how amazing it was how quickly he'd blended into the day-to-day rhythm of Hazard life? And his office was like a Native American museum.

"It proved quite satisfying with Erin," he said conversationally. "Though unfortunately, humans don't possess as functional canines as a wolf or a bobcat."

"You're the one who killed her!"

Recklessly, Josh tried to turn on him. Expecting blood to come shooting from a knife wound in the teen's throat, Faith was relieved when Drew merely pinched Josh's neck with his four fingers and thumb, causing him to immediately lose consciousness and collapse to the wooden floor.

"How did you do that?"

"It's a simple nerve pinch," he said calmly. "Surely you've watched *Star Trek* at some point in your life."

"Of course I have. But that's fiction."

"So the writers would like you to believe. As I did, until I discovered a remote tribe in Kazakhstan who practice a similar technique. They were essentially nomads or farmers, but first and foremost they were excellent horsemen and were the first in the world to master arrow-shooting at full tilt. I'm proud to say I became quite accomplished at this feat."

"Congratulations," Faith said drily.

"You don't mean that."

"No. I don't."

"I didn't think you did. But it's quite the thrill, galloping across the mountains at night on the back of a steppe pony. Far more exhilarating than riding some damn noisy sled that stinks of gasoline."

He shook his head. Then returned to what Faith recognized as his lecture mode.

"The Saks set up their first state in Zhetysu, which is in southeast Kazakhstan. Their high priests served as their kings, protecting their language and their myths, and encouraging extremely well-developed animal art, which represents the struggle between predator and prey. Some of that gold and bronze art continues to be exhibited in the best museums of the world."

"Isn't that interesting."

He tilted his head. Studied her. "You're

stalling. Hoping against hope that Hazard's hunky hero sheriff will come riding in like the Lone Ranger, just in time to save the day."

"What makes you think anyone's coming?"

"Faith, Faith." He clicked his tongue. Wagged a finger at her. "Granted, the table's only set for two. But you've gotten another bowl and set of cutlery out, so, from appearances, you and Bridger were planning a romantic evening at home. Then his son showed up. So, now you're making the best of the situation by inviting him to join you."

"That's very good," she allowed.

"It wasn't exactly rocket science, darling. But I am, after all, a psychological anthropologist. I study behavior. And, of course, the meaning of it."

"And obviously you're very good at it."

He flashed a smile. "Flattery will get you a few more minutes. Only because I'd already decided to share my methods with you, because killing has lost a bit of its thrill without my prey understanding why, exactly, they're being killed."

"I assume it's because, basically, you don't like people very much."

He was right. She was stalling. But she wasn't just waiting for Will. She was reminded of the time, early in her career, when a mentally ill person had stormed the station, held her hostage, and required her to read a rambling, incoherent statement about the government trying to kill him by poisoning his water with uranium taken from nuclear bombs.

This was not that different. While she was struggling to carry on an outwardly casual conversation, her mind was scheming to come up with some way to get Josh and her out of this situation.

"Actually, I enjoy people," Drew said. "I enjoy watching them. Studying them."

"Manipulating them."

"Of course. Why else would I have gone through all that schooling? Even a high school dropout can take a life. Killing is easy. Just like dying is easy. It's the survivors who suffer."

Comprehension struck, like a blow to the head. "That's your trophy, isn't it? The people you kill aren't the real victims. It's the survivors. Who have to live with the pain of survivor guilt. You feed off that suffering."

Hadn't he even written what some in his field called the definitive study of survivor guilt?

He nodded. "That's very perceptive. And

here I thought I was going to have to spend far more time explaining. It probably would have been better for you to have played stupid."

He'd begun switching the blade from hand to hand. Faith couldn't take her eyes off it.

"Getting back to the nerve pinch, it's really quite exceptional. The elders of the tribe have allowed it to be used on their enemies, but it's too holy a process to be used for mere day-to-day killing, such as a crime of passion, which will be swiftly dealt with. It's also a popular hunting method.

"It's only too bad you'll never see a man drop a snow leopard with a spear, then kill him with a simple pinch."

Faith's gaze flashed to Josh, whom she'd believed to be merely unconscious. "You killed him?"

"Not yet," Drew assured her. "What would be the fun in that?" As if to demonstrate, he kicked the teen with his boot. Josh moaned, but didn't move.

"I lived among the Saks for three years, eating with them, sleeping with them, riding and hunting with them. And, of course, sleeping with their women. They have some very interesting sexual rituals. I've been thinking I might like to share some with you."

"I'd like that," she lied through her teeth.

He laughed again, appearing to enjoy himself. "No, you wouldn't." He winked. "But it really doesn't matter, does it? Because you don't have any say in the matter. I'm going to play with you, Faith. For a very long time. Then I'm going to let you go."

"Why don't I believe that?"

"I've no idea." His blue eyes widened. He was mocking her, but if that was the worst he'd end up doing, Faith wasn't about to complain. "I said I was going to let you go. I didn't say I was going to let you live.

"When I'm done playing, I'm going to let you escape. I'm even going to grant you a head start. Although, I'm afraid, given the storm raging outside, and the fact that you'll be naked, I doubt you'll be running for very long."

Out of the corner of her eye, Faith saw Josh's eyes blink open. Please, don't let him try anything foolish, she prayed.

"You were telling me about the nerve pinch," she said.

"Good try. Stall some more." He shook his head. "It won't make any difference.

Because your lover isn't going to make it here."

Shock waves reverberated through her. "You didn't kill him?"

"Of course not. He needs to stay alive. So he can mourn his lover. And" — Drew gave Josh another sharp kick — "his son." Josh moaned, this time, Faith thought, as he closed his eyes again, on cue. "But I did arrange for him to be delayed. Long enough for you and I to leave."

Which meant he was planning to kill Josh before taking her from the house. No way.

"If you hurt Will —"

He lifted a blond brow. "Is that a threat, Faith? Of course I wouldn't hurt him. I just provided him a new challenge to keep him busy."

"You didn't kill anyone else?"

"Good guess! Now, for the bonus round, can you tell me who's on the way to the morgue with a bullet wound in the brain?"

"How would I know?"

"Buzz. Sorry, you lose. The answer was, that intrepid lawman turned bounty hunter, Salvatore Sasone."

Her knees sagged. Faith grabbed hold of the edge of the stove to hold herself up. "You killed Sal? Why?"

"Because I knew how it would affect you.

And I was right. You're white as a bone, darling. The good news is that you won't have to grieve your lawfully wedded husband for all that long. But I'm going to enjoy it while you do.

"But you were asking about the nerve pinch . . . the tribal medicine man teaches that certain members, due to telepathic powers, are able to send a burst of psychic energy into another living being, overload its nervous system, thus rendering it unconscious. Since, with the exception of my shape-shifting ability, I've yet to develop any telepathic powers myself, I believe the pinch merely blocks nerve responses from reaching the brain."

He gestured down at Josh. "Voilà." Then rubbed his hands together in anticipation. "Well, as lovely as it's been chatting with you, Faith, I believe it's time we get on with the rest of this evening's entertainment."

He stroked the handle of the blade. Straddled Josh's prone body.

It was now or never. She hadn't been able to come up with a single way to keep Josh from being harmed. But there was a chance she'd be able to prevent him from being killed.

Just as Drew began to bend over, every atom of his attention riveted on the teen, like a wolf about to attack a lamb, Faith grabbed the pot of bubbling stew from the stove and threw it into his face.

He screamed like a wounded animal. Dropped the knife as he swabbed his scorched face with his hands.

At the same time, Josh jumped to his feet, the knife blade in his hand. A hand that was turning an ugly shade of red from the splash of stew.

"Go!"

Josh grabbed her hand with his uninjured one and they started running.

With their would-be murderer blocking the kitchen door, they were forced to run through the living room, dodging the boxes she still hadn't gotten around to unpacking.

The last one had been serving as a pseudo foyer table, and as they raced past it, she snatched up the red bag. They yanked their jackets from the coat hooks.

Then together, hand in hand, Faith and Josh ran out into the storm.

47

Will cursed as the Jeep started rapidly losing power. Seconds later, the power steering went out on him.

"Damn. Talk about a fucked-up holiday week."

As if Erin Gallagher and her mother being murdered, and a Russian coach in the hospital from a vicious attack, were not enough, Will would rather be covered in molasses and staked out on an anthill rather than have to break the news to Faith that her soon-to-be-ex husband had been shot in the head.

He knew, since the bounty hunter was only in Hazard because he'd tracked her here, that she'd blame herself. Which he totally understood because he'd do the same thing.

He'd have to figure out some way to dissuade her of the notion the attack was her fault.

But first he had to get to her place. Suspecting the problem, he climbed out of the Cherokee, opened the hood, and shone the Maglite into the engine. Just as he'd thought, the damn drive belt had broken. Just what he needed.

He waded through the drifting snow, around to the back of the SUV, where he kept his emergency toolbox.

The county had had the snowplows operating around the clock for days, since before the wind had stopped. But the Canadian clipper was bringing the snow in so thick and so fast, it was getting nearly impossible to keep the roads clear.

The sheriff of a rural county had to be prepared for any contingency, which is why the back of the SUV was packed with not only the toolbox, but wooden road barricades, tire chains, rolls of reflector and crime-scene tape, a portable defibrillator, which he'd learned to operate from Jack Dawson, orange safety cones, and flares.

He pushed aside two of the cones to get to the red metal box, opened it up, and stared down at the space where the long black belt was supposed to be.

The wind was howling as if all the lost souls of hell had landed in Hazard. He was all alone out on a road five miles from the nearest house. Which would be Faith's.

He trudged through the snow back to the engine and began to examine the belt more thoroughly, realizing his worst fear.

The long, serpentine belt that wove its way above and around just about every engine part, controlling so much of the Cherokee's operating system, hadn't broken. The black rubber had been cleanly sliced through.

But not all the way in the beginning, Will thought. Just enough to ensure he'd get far enough out of town to be stranded.

"Goddammit!" He yanked open the driver's door, grabbed the radio from the dash, only to discover that the coiled mike cord had been cut as well.

Okay. That's what God invented cell phones for, right? He ripped his off his belt and punched in the #HELP, the cell equivalent of 911.

"Sheriff's Department," the familiar voice answered.

"Earlene, this is Will."

"What's wrong, Sheriff?" She'd worked for his predecessor long enough to know that a cop wouldn't call into emergency just to chat.

"I need you to send out every unit we've got, right away, to Faith Prescott's house. I have reason to believe the killer is out there, and he's obviously armed and dangerous."

He waited for her to repeat the instructions as protocol required.

Nothing.

He checked the signal bars. Nothing.

Despite all those stories about people being able to make phone calls from the top of Mt. Everest, and the telephone commercials showing customers happily chatting to friends hundreds of miles away from out in the middle of the forest, the fact was that service was always iffy up in these mountains. And often, nearly impossible during a blizzard.

As he looked around at the near whiteout conditions, Will's damn glitchy heart began to go wild.

48

"Are you all right?" Faith shouted as she and Josh jumped down from the porch. Her words were ripped out of her mouth by the wind.

"I'll live," he said, sounding remarkably calm, so much more like his father than the sulky, tattooed, and pierced teen he'd been a mere two days ago.

The good news was, like so many sledders, he'd left the key in the ignition of the snowmobile.

"I wonder how badly you got him," he shouted, as he twisted the key and brought the engine to life.

They got their answer a second later when they heard the whine of a second sled start up from behind the house.

"Fuck!" Josh gunned the throttle. "Hang on!"

Climbing onto the sled behind him, she wrapped her arms around his chest.

The snow hit her face like sandpaper grit. Wondering how Josh could even see to be steering the sled, she shut her eyes tight. Then, deciding if they were about to crash into a tree and die, she wanted advance warning, she forced herself to open them again. Just in time to watch him turn into a grove of aspen.

"You're very good at this," she screamed in his ear as he wove his way through the winter-naked-limbed, white trees, which looked like ghosts bending in supplication to the wind.

"I surf. Or did," he shouted back. "It's not that different. Mostly a balance thing."

As the chain-saw roar of Drew Hayworth's sled screeched over the howling wind behind them, Faith was grateful for any edge they could get.

Her ungloved hands were already starting to turn numb. Her lips felt frozen on her face and her lashes were getting caked with snow. How long could they go on like this?

"There's a forest service road not far from here," Josh told her. She had to strain to hear him. "I doubt, with the storm, any plows would have gotten around to it."

"Wouldn't it be better if they had?"

"Plows make ridges. It's too easy to hit one and get thrown." He swerved around a snow-covered boulder. "Hold on."

What the hell did he think she was doing?

Nevertheless, she clung harder.

They were suddenly airborne. She shrieked, the way she might on a roller-coaster ride at an amusement park. But there was nothing even remotely amusing about this.

They landed like a stone, jarring every bone in her body, before sliding precariously so far that her right shoulder was nearly dragging in the snow. But miraculously — at least it seemed a miracle to her — they remained upright.

"All right!" Behaving like the teenager he still was, Josh pumped a fist into the air.

"Would you please just hold on with both hands?"

He turned his head to look back at her, his teeth flashing a bold grin in his ice-frosted face.

"Yes, Mother," he said, as he gunned the engine again.

Damned if he didn't seem to be enjoying himself. For, from what she'd been able to tell, one of the few times since he'd arrived in Hazard.

The enjoyment was to prove short-lived.

After weaving deftly around a second boulder, he topped a small hill and cursed.

"Jump!"

Not taking time to think about the peril, Faith did as instructed. An instant later, the sled plowed into a fallen, snow-covered Douglas fir. The thick tree was no less impressive lying on its side than it would have been towering into the sky.

"We are so fucked!" Josh shouted, slamming a bare hand against the trunk of the tree.

"Not yet." The bag she'd strapped across her body when she'd jumped aboard the snowmobile had not fallen off during their wild ride. "Get behind the tree."

She would have joined him, but the gigantic limbs, still wearing their dark green needles, would be in her way.

"Holy shit!" He goggled at the .45 she pulled out of the bag. "Do you actually know how to shoot that cannon?"

"Yes." Faith stood up in the position Sal had taught her. The memory made her heart clench and she wanted to cry at the idea of his having been killed because of her.

But as if she could hear him yelling at her to concentrate, she spread her legs, keeping her knees firm, but not quite locked, setting her trailing foot so that her natural point of aim would be on her target. "I do."

She took a deep breath, instructing the

rest of her body to relax, which was difficult when her stomach was turning somersaults, every nerve was jangling, and her heart was doing the jitterbug in her chest.

She held the heavy revolver in both hands and prepared herself for the kick of the recoil as Drew Hayworth came flying over the hillock on his wicked-looking, sleek black snowmobile.

49

Despite the way once again a woman had put a crimp in his plans, the man who'd been the boy raised by wolves was in near metaphysical exhilaration as he chased his prey over the white and drifted snow.

He'd been right. This was much better than the silent, quick kill. This was hunting on a grand scale. Akin to galloping a horse across the mountain steppes chasing a snow leopard.

Whenever he'd hunted with the tribe he believed to be the Saks, the leopard had always died. Always. The men had been exceptional hunters.

But the death had always seemed anticlimactic to the chase. And as magnificent as the white mountain cat was, both in life and in death, it couldn't live up to a human.

But, for the pleasure and profit together,
Allow me the hunting of Man —

The chase of the Human, the search for
the Soul
To its ruin — the hunting of Man.

It wouldn't be long now. His blood stirred and, despite the cold, warmed with sweet anticipation.

He'd planned to kill the boy quickly so he wouldn't be burdened by dragging them both away from the house.

But thanks to Faith's changing the rules of the game by trying to escape, he was going to be able to take his time and kill them both slowly. Painfully. Soon.

Double your pleasure, the hunter thought with a smile as the sled soared over the hill.

Double your fun.

It was then he saw her. Standing in front of him, the barrel of a revolver pointed straight at his chest.

Roaring with a warrior's rage, rather than turning away, the man who'd once been the boy raised by wolves pointed the sled directly at her.

Then gunned the accelerator.

50

Will had never thought he'd be grateful for the damn Ride the Divide race that had sledders racing all around Hazard night and day. Until a group came speeding toward him, their engines sounding like a hundred, no, a thousand, furious wasps.

"Sheriff's office," he shouted, holding up his badge just in case they hadn't noticed the big gold seal on the side of the Jeep's black doors.

Middle-aged and law-abiding, the entire pack immediately came skidding to a halt, sending up frothy white rooster tails of snow.

"I've got an emergency and need to commandeer one of your vehicles."

They exchanged confused looks.

"Like now," Will stressed, reminding himself that just shooting someone and taking the sled could well be considered overkill. "I'm in a hurry."

"Then this is the baby you want, Sheriff,"

one of the sledders said, climbing off a black-and-silver Bullet chassis with CMSA stickers plastered all over it. Her voice revealed what her heavily padded, yellow spaceman suit did not, that she was a woman. It also indicated Great Lakes roots. "I did one hundred and fifty-four miles an hour in a thousand feet on it back home in Clearwater, Minnesota."

Lake racing and powder were two entirely different things. But fast was fast.

"Thanks." Will pulled a helmet he kept in the backseat of the Jeep. "I'll get this back to you." Hopefully in one piece, but Will had been a cop long enough never to guarantee anything. "Where are you staying?"

"The Red Wolf Lodge. Alone," she tacked on in an obvious feminine ploy that caused more than one of the other sledders to chuckle.

"Well, like I said, thanks."

He strapped his rifle onto his back, swung his leg over the seat, and roared off.

"He's going to freaking kill you!" Josh yelled at Faith from behind the tree.

"Not if I kill the bastard first," she shouted back.

"Christ, if we get out of this, remind me to warn my dad never to piss you off."

"*When* we get out of this," she corrected. "Now shut up and let me concentrate. I've never shot an actual person before."

You can do this.

Focus.

Find your center.

No. Find his *center.*

One advantage Faith had was that if Drew continued straight toward her as he was doing, he presented the largest possible target.

The disadvantage was that with the huge tree behind her, she could become trapped, without anywhere to run. No way to escape.

She took a deep breath. Another. Narrowed her concentration, closing off the falling snow, the howl of the wind, the needle-like ice hitting her face.

Her sphere of vision narrowed. Until there were just the two of them. Faith and the man she'd foolishly, mistakenly considered a friend.

She stilled her mind.

Took a third, steadying breath.

Then pulled the trigger.

With every part of her being focused so intently on her attacker, Faith did not hear the crack of the limb overhead. Nor did she hear Josh's shout of warning.

She did hear the roar of the revolver. Felt the recoil force her arm up. The last thing she heard was Drew scream like a wounded animal.

"I got him," she murmured as the crashing limb dropped her to her knees.

51

Fuck, fuck, fuck!

What the hell did the bitch think she was doing?

Didn't she know who he was?

What he was?

He was the man who was once the boy raised by wolves. He was a predator.

You couldn't kill him! He was fucking invincible.

"Invincible!" he screeched, as a bolt of fire ripped through his upper arm.

As if validating his claim, a limb from the downed tree suddenly cracked off, falling through the shaggy branches. The hunter watched it strike the back of his adversary's head.

Felt a surge in his loins as she fell, face-down, into a deep drift of snow.

Invincible, he repeated as, clenching his teeth against the pain, he managed to slow his speed in a low skid.

Game on.

The snow was getting heavier. Wetter. The roads more and more treacherous. The good thing was that the sled could go where even the Cherokee, with snow tires and chains, couldn't get to.

Will had only been back in the valley six weeks. But some things a guy never forgot. Like all the forest-service and country, two-lane, dirt roads crisscrossing the landscape. When you were seventeen and looking for a place to make out with a girl, you pretty much kept a GPS in your head.

As he tore through the trees, he brought up a virtual map. Remembered that halcyon summer day when he'd been parked out in the woods with Vicki Dayton. It had been the first time a girl had ever touched his cock.

The road was close by and, if he remembered correctly — and please, God, let him be right — should be a shortcut to Faith's house.

Even better, Will thought, as he sawed the sled back and forth to avoid ancient ice-age boulders and fallen trees, the plows wouldn't have gotten out here yet to pack down the snow and risk it turning to ice.

The wind was howling, the snowmobile

engine was screeching, but Will had spent too many hours on the police range not to recognize the sound of a gun being fired.

It ricocheted over the snow, through the trees, slamming into his brain.

Will couldn't remember the last time he'd prayed. Even when he'd been lying on those cobblestones, a dead man a few feet away, sirens wailing, and Gray shouting into his face, it hadn't crossed his mind to request help from anyone.

But now, as he raced toward the sound of the gunfire, hitting the bumps at a speed that rattled his bones, one plea reverberated over and over in his desperate mind.

Please, God. Don't let Faith die.

He was bleeding. Blood was pouring down his sleeve, spilling over his hand, making the throttle slick and greasy. The damn bitch had winged him. And for that she was going to pay.

He hit the brake, intending to stop just long enough to stab his blade into her chest. A collapsed lung would keep her from running away. But she'd stay alive. For a long time. Long enough for him to do everything he'd been dreaming of doing to her. All the dark and perverse things she'd been asking men to do for the last twelve months.

Oh, she hadn't said the words out loud. To do so, especially in these post–Janet Jackson Super Bowl incident days, would have gotten her kicked off the airways. But you didn't have to be a psychological anthropologist to know that there wasn't a man in the high country who didn't listen to *Talking After Midnight* and know, deep in his gut, his groin, that Faith Prescott was just begging him to get down and dirty with her.

And this man was more than willing to oblige.

As he approached the tree, the sheriff's kid was down on his knees, trying to lift her out of the snowbank.

Change of plans. Actually, he'd go back to the original. Kill the kid, quick and sweet. Then deal with Faith.

He'd bought a hunting cabin from a math professor this past fall, not quite sure what he was going to do with it. But now he realized the real estate deal was serendipity.

The former owner was currently spending the holidays in Greece, which meant he wouldn't be around to tell the sheriff that he'd just happened to sell a remote one-room hideaway to the hunter the entire country would undoubtedly be looking for by dawn.

He'd have plenty of time to do everything he'd been fantasizing. After he was finished with her, as he'd promised back in that cozy kitchen, he'd let her go.

Then he'd hunt her down.

And this time, he would kill her.

52

Will was racing toward where he'd heard the gunshot, teeth chattering from the rough ride, the snowmobile bucking under him, swaying.

The snow was blowing against his face shield so hard it was beginning to stick, making visibility next to zero. He had two choices. He could keep wiping the damn snow off the shield, thus risking an accident by driving with one hand, or he could throw up the shield, even knowing that skin froze quickly in such temperatures, especially at such high speeds, and hope for the best.

Stuck between a rock and a hard place, Will threw up the shield, ducked his head, and flew over the top of a small hill.

And damned if they weren't all there. Faith, the killer, and . . . Josh?

He landed with a thud and, while struggling to keep the snowmobile upright, reached beneath his jacket, pulled out his

Glock, and got off a shot.

Which hit the damn tree.

"Police!" he shouted.

Last time he'd tried this, back in Savannah, it hadn't worked. He seriously doubted it would this time. But as long as there were bottom-feeder defense attorneys out there nit-picking every little detail of an arrest, Will was going to play by the rules.

"Turn off the engine. Get off the damn sled," he shouted into the wind. "And put your hands on top of your head."

He couldn't hear what the guy said, but it sounded a lot like "Fuck you." Which was a long way from "I surrender, Officer."

Gunning the black sled, the perp took off.

Will wanted to go after him, but there was no way he was going to leave the two people he cared about most in the world.

"How are you?" he asked them.

"I'm fine," Josh said. "But Faith got nailed with a tree limb. She was knocked out for a second —"

"Christ." Will glanced toward the sled, which was racing away at what had to be eighty-plus miles an hour. Faith's head was bleeding. "Let me see —"

"I'm fine," Faith assured him. "But Drew killed Sal."

"No, he didn't. The doctor said the guy's

got the hardest — actually, he said *thickest* — head he's ever seen. The bullet lodged in his skull without entering the brain. He's spending the night in the hospital with a Russian roommate."

"Thank God! Now go after Drew before he hurts anyone else."

"I'm not leaving you here alone, hurt —"

"She's not going to be alone, Dad," Josh argued. "Hell, I've gotten a lot harder hits from my board surfing. Go get Dr. Hayworth. He freaking tried to kill us. But Faith shot him."

Outside, Will was freezing. But as he looked down at Faith, something warm, something that felt like love mixed with an extra helping of pride, flowed through him. "With the cannon?"

"Yes."

"That is one big freakin' gun." Josh's lashes were so caked with snow he could barely open his eyes. But that didn't stop Will from seeing the reckless amusement in them. His kid, he realized, had inherited his own sick sense of humor. Hell, you'd almost think he were a cop.

"You called that one right." Will looked down at Faith again, clearly torn between love and duty.

"Go," she insisted. "I'll be fine. Josh and I

make one helluva team. You should have seen him driving that snowmobile. You'd never know he grew up in California."

"Go get the bastard, Dad," Josh seconded Faith. "And take him out."

Will's breath blew out on a ghost cloud of frosty air.

"Okay." There was one more thing he had to say. "I'm not sure what all went down tonight, Josh. But I do know I'm damn proud of you, Son."

The teen's cheeks were already so red, it was hard to tell, but Will thought he blushed. "Thanks, Dad."

Will tossed Josh the cell phone. "Call #HELP. Hopefully you'll be able to get through. Tell Earlene we're at the base of Elk Ridge."

"Yessir." Pride beamed on the ice-encrusted face, reminding Will of Honeycutt, making him wonder if just maybe his son might want to follow in his footsteps and become a cop.

As he kicked the sled into high gear again, taking after the psychological anthropologist, he thought about how much things had changed in just two days. His kid was actually talking to him, a sexy woman was in love with him, and here he was, driving a snowmobile hell-bent for leather through the night, during a blizzard, chasing a bad guy.

Life couldn't get any better than this.

Dammit! His arm was going numb. He could barely steer and the falling snow was piling up on his helmet shield so thick he could barely see. The helmet lantern was doing no good, the thin yellow light only allowing him to see an inch or two in front of the sled.

He no longer knew where he was. Only knew that he needed to keep going. To stop was to die. And he was not yet prepared for that to happen.

He swerved around a boulder the size of a Volkswagen, managed to dodge a pine tree that seemed to suddenly appear out of nowhere, then, unstable because he'd gone onto a single runner to avoid the tree, couldn't correct fast enough to avoid the huge snow-covered mound that came looming out of the flying snow.

He hit it straight on, went flying over the windshield, and landed with a thud on top of what turned out to be a pair of moose antlers. The moose had undoubtedly died of exposure; the hunter, vowing that it would not happen to him, clambered off the huge dead animal and tried to tilt the sled upright, but it had sunk too deep into the snow for him to pull out with one arm.

With no other choice, he took off, his left arm hanging uselessly at his side, lumbering toward the thick stand of trees at the top of the ridge.

If he remembered correctly, a numbered county road was on the other side of the ridge. Although it was unlikely that anyone would be foolish enough to be out driving in a Wyoming blizzard, you never knew. And if someone did happen by, up here in the Rocky Mountain high country, people watched out for their neighbors.

Any driver would stop for him. And he shouldn't have any trouble talking himself into a ride. He had, after all, always been able to fit in.

Well, not always. But that little experience with Snowball and her owner's mother had taught him that you could do a lot more damage by staying under the radar.

So. The new plan was to get to the road. Thumb a ride. Make up a story about having an accident while practicing for this weekend's ride.

Then kill the driver, take the truck, and move on. To a new town. A new state. A new hunting ground.

■ ■ ■ ■

Despite Hayworth's head start, Will had no trouble catching up with him. Especially since he had apparently suffered a close encounter with a bull moose.

He was staggering up the hill, the arm Faith had shot hanging loose at his side, throwing him off-balance. The trail of blood was as effective as Hansel and Gretel's bread crumbs.

The landscape going up the ridge was riddled with thick brush and boulders deposited by the last ice age. Ditching the sled, Will continued after Faith and Josh's attacker on foot.

"Give it up, Hayworth," he called out as he ripped off his gloves. He was about ten feet away now. "You're not going to get out of this one. It's over." Will was still wearing his rifle on his back, but didn't think he'd need it. Not when he had his faithful old Glock in his hand.

"That's what you think." Hayworth had reached the top of the ridgeline and was swaying like an aspen in gale-force winds. Just when Will thought he'd collapse on his face and fall over the edge, he spun around and came running back down, like some wild-eyed guy from a World War II movie, holding the knife out in front of him like a bayonet.

"I'm warning you," Will shouted. "Put. The. Knife. Down."

It could have ended there. Should have. But, of course, just like in Savannah, it didn't.

"You can't kill me," Hayworth screamed. "I'm invincible! I'm a hunter! The man raised by wolves!"

He lunged. Will's bull's-eye shot nailed him in midair and he dropped like a stone.

Snow swirled around him as Will stood looking down at the body sprawled on the snow. This man had been responsible for the deaths of at least two people he knew. He'd also intended to kill the two people Will loved, the son he'd recently found and the woman he intended to spend the rest of his life with.

And who knew how many others he'd murdered all over the world. Now that Dr. Drew Hayworth's secret was out, some of those past crimes would undoubtedly come out. Will suspected there'd be dozens, maybe even hundreds more victims who'd never find justice. At least in this life.

"Funny," he mused aloud. He heard the scream of sirens over the howling wind, suggesting Josh had gotten through to dispatch. "I always figured wolves were a lot smarter than that."

53

They were waiting for him, together, Faith's arm around Josh's waist, his around her shoulders.

Mine. It was what he'd thought when he'd made love to Faith, but now the idea included them both.

Damned if somehow, when he hadn't been looking, he'd landed himself a family.

Faith broke free from Josh and went running toward him, stumbling to her knees into a white snowdrift.

She pushed to her feet and continued plowing through the snow, and then he began running toward her, like some crazed guy from one of those TV shampoo commercials, and she launched herself into his arms.

"Put a big red *S* on this man's chest and give him a cape," she said as she began covering his snow-encrusted face with kisses.

Her lips were cold and frozen, but that was okay, because Will had every intention of spending the rest of the night warming them up.

It had been a while since Will had felt anything like a hero. He decided he liked the idea. Liked the idea of being Faith's hero even more.

"Guess what?" he said.

"You love me?"

"Well, yeah. Sure, I do. But it's my heart. It didn't glitch out while I was chasing Hayworth."

"Of course it didn't." She smiled up at him and placed a hand against his chest. "Everyone knows that love's the best cure for a broken heart."

Will wasn't about to argue with that.

He touched his fingertips to the lump at her temple. With her fair skin, she'd be black-and-blue for a month. But it could have been worse. Much, much worse.

"How's the head?"

"I'll be fine," she brushed off his concern. "There's nothing wrong with me that a little bed rest won't cure right up."

"I'm with that program."

He laced their fingers together, and together they walked back toward Josh, who'd been watching them and was grinning like a damn fool. Will figured he looked exactly the same way.

"By the way," he said, as what appeared to be the entire Sheriff's Department arrived on the scene, sirens screaming, lights flashing. Will figured Honeycutt was undoubtedly in hog heaven. "You really are spectacular."

Faith grinned up at him. "You're not so bad yourself, cowboy."

"So, what would you say to getting married as soon as the law allows?" He put his arms around her and held her close. If he had his way, he'd never let her go.

Her heart was shining in her eyes as she laughed. "I'd like to see anyone try to stop me."

ABOUT THE AUTHOR

JoAnn Ross, the author of more than ninety novels, has been published in twenty-six countries. She is a member of the Romance Writers of America's Honor Roll of bestselling authors and has won several writing awards, including being named Storyteller of the Year by *Romantic Times.* Her work has been excerpted in *Cosmopolitan* and featured by the Doubleday and Literary Guild book clubs.

With her husband and two fuzzy little dogs, she divides her time between the mountains of East Tennessee and the coastal lowlands of South Carolina.

Visit JoAnn on the web to subscribe to her electronic newsletter, at www.joannross.com.

The employees of Thorndike Press hope you have enjoyed this Large Print book. All our Thorndike and Wheeler Large Print titles are designed for easy reading, and all our books are made to last. Other Thorndike Press Large Print books are available at your library, through selected bookstores, or directly from us.

For information about titles, please call:

(800) 223-1244

or visit our Web site at:

www.gale.com/thorndike
www.gale.com/wheeler

To share your comments, please write:

Publisher
Thorndike Press
295 Kennedy Memorial Drive
Waterville, ME 04901